CHAPTER ONE

Smoke wafted from the broken treetops, their shattered branches smoldering from the devastating contact with the emergency landing jets and orange-hot underside of the Raxxian vessel as it plummeted through the atmosphere and smashed down into the dense woods.

Burgundy leaves had been stripped from the vegetation by the impact like an explosively shredded cloud, the remnants wafting slowly in the breeze as the dust settled on the wreckage. The Raxxians had designed the transport compartment to automatically home in on the nearest planet or moon, then, upon finding a landing solution, slowing its descent with emergency thrusters. With the main body of the ship in ruins, the segment had done its job.

Their living cargo was valuable, after all, and on the off chance some sort of emergency was to occur, the ideal scenario would be to salvage as many of the individually sealed compartments as possible.

Unfortunately, the attack that had broken the Raxxian capture and trading vessel into pieces had caused far more damage than the design specs had accounted for. As a result, the holding compartment was tossed about violently as its thrusters failed when it plummeted into the atmosphere. By the time they kicked back in, it had reached terminal velocity, the prisoners held within suffering the brunt of the descent.

The impact was ultimately slowed by the thrusters, but the force had been substantial nonetheless, throwing dirt and debris high into the air as the wildlife on the ground fled in a panicked rush. By the time the dust settled and the smoke began rising with the updraft, the area was utterly silent, devoid of the slightest hint of native life.

Across all worlds and galaxies, one thing held true. The instinct for survival was strong, and even the simplest of creatures knew full well this was the last place they wanted to be.

That gut-level drive to stay alive no matter what was also present in the tall alien male pushing aside a piece of battered wreckage, creating a relatively clear path out of the debris and into the fresh air.

He shoved the metal hard, looked around with a wary eye, then ducked back inside, emerging a moment later carrying a much smaller human woman in his muscular arms.

He barely knew her from their shared time on the Raxxian vessel, but he owed her a sizeable debt.

His life, in fact.

He held her carefully in his thick arms as he stepped cautiously over the upturned soil and smoking wreckage, walking with purpose until he reached the part of the tree line that was still intact. Safely under cover from observation from above, he turned back and scanned the crash site.

They'd hit hard when the thrusters failed for the final time, the impact forming a small crater in the soft ground. Tall trees surrounded them on all sides, the dense foliage blocking the

THE WARRIOR'S OATH

MARK OF THE INFALA 3

KIRA QUINN

view of the surrounding area. Mountains were visible in the distance, but up close, all he could see were trees.

He smelled the air. Fresh. Clear. The breeze blowing the smoke away from them, at least for the time being. The vegetation was lush, providing very little dry kindling for the embers to spread their blaze. They would not have to worry about being overcome by a forest fire. At least *that* was going their way.

He looked down at the woman in his arms. She seemed tiny, really. Much smaller than the women of his own race. And she lacked the intricate runes and markings on her skin that all who inhabited the Dotharian Conglomerate bore as the law demanded.

The tall alien gently set her down and jogged back toward the wreckage, scanning the ground for anything that might be of use to them. A few useful items were salvageable, but this was not an escape craft and it had not been outfitted for wilderness survival. Worse, the rough landing had destroyed most of the components that might have had value.

He moved fast. Time was of the essence. Not only was the area unstable and partially on fire, but there was no telling if the Raxxians might come looking for their lost cargo sooner than later. He hurried and gathered up his salvaged booty, wrapping the bits and bobs in a stained bit of fabric he dug from the debris. It wasn't a backpack by any stretch, but the makeshift sling would have to suffice.

He stepped out into the open and scanned the skies above once more. They were still clear. Holding his prize close, he ran for the trees, doing his best not to drop anything.

Safely out of sight beneath their cover he slowed his pace, stopping where the human female lay. He put down his salvage and hovered over the woman, looking at her with a mix of curiosity and frustration in his gold-rimmed, violet eyes.

The woman's lids slowly opened, her eyes struggling to focus on the golden-tan alien male looming over her. She seemed about to say something, but unconsciousness beckoned her once more and she succumbed to its siren song, sliding back into the darkness.

She would wake soon enough; her head injury was merely a nasty bump and the accompanying concussion. And when she did, she would discover just what sort of mess she was in, jumping from the frying pan into what could very well be the fire.

Time would tell.

CHAPTER TWO

Nyota felt the warmth of sunlight on her face, but also an unexpected coolness on her forehead. As she regained sensation throughout her body, it dawned on her that pretty much her entire body ached. She also realized her vision was dark because her eyes were crusty and stuck shut.

With painful effort, she tried to force them to open, her head pounding from the effort.

Slowly, her lids began to part, finally separating with a sticky pop. Her vision was blurry at first. Blurry, and particularly *odd*.

This can't be right, she thought as she tried to focus on her surroundings.

Strange trees with burgundy leaves filled her vision, the dappled light seeming far too bright for her aching orbs. Her pulse thudded steadily in her ears, her aching head throbbing in time.

"Oh, that hurts," she groaned. "What the hell?"

A deep voice nearby startled her. "Do not move. You suffered a blow to your head."

Nyota turned to find the source of the advice. It came from a very tall, very muscular man, standing perfectly still, leaning up against a partially shaded tree. He was standing so still you could almost miss him if you didn't know he was there. Alert, quiet, and silently watching her.

Her eyes cleared a bit and she saw he wasn't a particularly large human but rather an alien, though one humanoid in shape.

He wore a short-sleeved shirt, making visible his tattooed, deeply tanned skin that seemed to give off a subtle, almost golden glow where the sunlight hit it. He looked as though he had been pretty well banged up from the crash as well, his clothing torn in places and his body scraped.

The crash! she suddenly remembered. "Hey, we were on a ship. Something happened!"

"Yes."

"The big lizard-looking guys. The Raxxians. They were holding me prisoner. They were holding a lot of us."

"Livestock," he replied plainly. "*Not* prisoners."

"What?" Nyota said, confused, trying to prop herself up on her elbow and failing miserably. "Ow, my head."

"I told you, do not move. You are intact and nothing is broken, but you hit your head quite hard. You must move slowly."

Nyota slid back down, resting her head on the ground. It wasn't so much that she wanted to heed his advice, but more that with the way her body felt, there really wasn't any other option.

"Oh man, I must've taken a hell of a knock."

"That would be putting it mildly," he replied with only the slightest hint of amusement.

"But hang on. Back up. What did you mean, *livestock*?" she asked, trying to relax her neck to relieve some of the tension throbbing in her poor cranium.

He cocked his head slightly, as if sizing her up. "We were all taken by the Raxxians."

"Right. That's what I said."

"We were taken to be used as a food source. You should already know this."

"Food?"

"Yes. Most of us, anyway. A few they had other uses for. My general, for one. Rumor had it that when they captured us, they kept him alive. I fear most of our compatriots did not fare so well."

Nyota struggled to shake the fog from her mind. She was concussed, clearly, and that meant she was not thinking straight. But the fact that she was with it enough to realize she wasn't thinking straight meant perhaps it wasn't as bad as she'd first worried. And now that she thought about it, yes, there was something seriously wrong going on aboard the Raxxian ship.

"Oh, hell," she mumbled. "That's right. The Raxxians eat people."

"It is coming back to you. That is a good sign."

"But what happened? I-I was in a holding compartment."

"Yes, as were we all when the ship fell under attack."

"The attack. Right. *Right!* There were explosions. And then the compartment door locking system broke. Everyone took off running."

"In the course of the battle, many of the livestock compartments were unsealed. Several took flight down the corridors, including yourself. It was a chaotic time."

Nyota's head pounded miserably as she tried to recall more details. But thinking *hurt*. The additional blood flow was not doing her concussion any favors.

"We were attacked, and the ship broke apart," she said.

"You are correct. The individual compartments are designed

to preserve their cargo. It is how we survived the main body of the transport ship's destruction."

"But how are we *here*? We were in space."

"The automated systems locked onto the nearest planet and set us down here, albeit rather roughly."

"Then where are the others?"

"It was just you and I."

"What do you mean?" she asked. "There were other people. Humans."

"During the attack you—" He paused, a hint of annoyance in his voice.

"I what?"

"You saved me," he said with a sigh, his eyes flashing with irritation more than gratitude.

She looked up at the tall, muscular alien. Even banged up as he was, he nevertheless seemed as though he could most definitely take care of himself.

"*I* saved you."

"You did."

"Me."

"Perhaps you hit your head harder than I realized. The repetition—"

"Seriously? Look at you. How is it even possible?"

He sighed, a shadow falling over his mood. "I was freed from my bondage when the attack began. I had been separated from my general when we were captured. It was a long incarceration, and I had not seen him the entire time I had been held by the Raxxians."

"But you knew where he was?"

"No. But the opportunity presented itself and I set out to find him, or, if the gods did not smile upon me, at least learn his true fate."

"So what happened?"

"I was moving from compartment to compartment, unsealing the doors, hoping I might succeed in my task."

"*And*?" she asked, exasperated by his disjointed storytelling.

"I was attacked by a Raxxian, taken off-guard. Unarmed as I was, and with my hands bound, the odds were not in my favor, and I found myself struggling to avoid his weapons blasts. Then, just when I feared I might succumb to the assault, you stepped in and saved me."

Nyota chuckled. Her head pounded harder as a result.

Note to self. No laughing, she decided in an instant. "Look at you. You're massive. If you couldn't stop him, what could I possibly do?"

"You had somehow obtained a weapon," he said, pulling a blood-stained blade from his belt. "This dagger. You jumped on the Raxxian guard in a rage, stabbing him violently just at the moment he pushed away from our fight to create space in an attempt to line up to shoot me. I was a dead man, but your actions made him miss. You wounded him, but more importantly, you distracted him. And *that* gave me the opportunity to put an end to him."

"*I* did that? *Me*?" she asked, shocked.

"Admittedly, I was just as surprised as he was by the ferocity of your attack. You are so small and weak, after all."

"Gee, thanks."

"I mean no insult. It is simply the truth. But greatness sometimes lurks in the unlikeliest of packages. You, it seems, are one such example. You saved my life, and I now owe you a life debt."

Nyota struggled to process all she was hearing. It just seemed impossible. But the more he spoke, the more the events began to come back to her. She vaguely remembered jumping on someone. Was it a Raxxian? Did she have some kind of death wish? And where did she find a dagger?

"Someone killed a guard," she muttered.

"What was that?"

"I just remembered, there was a dead guard in the corridor. Someone had killed him. His rifle was gone, but he still had a knife. I took it."

"And put it to great use."

"But you still didn't tell me how we wound up here all alone."

The alien cocked his head once more, his gold-rimmed irises sparkling with curiosity. "You truly do not recall."

"I told you it's all fuzzy."

"The ship began breaking apart. It was clear the Raxxians had lost this fight, and we had no time to stop and plan. The hull was breached and we began to lose air pressure. We had to act immediately before the void claimed us. You and I dove into the nearest open compartment and I sealed the door behind us. We barely made it in time. The Raxxian craft broke apart moments later."

"And the others?"

"You and I were the only ones in that particular compartment."

"So the other humans?"

"I cannot say."

"And your general?"

He shrugged in stoic silence.

Nyota reached out and rested her hand on his ankle, the only part of him within reach. "I'm so sorry."

He nodded his appreciation and crouched down beside her. "Thank you. And I am sorry about your compatriots."

"There was nothing you could do."

"That *either* of us could do," he corrected, brushing her hair aside and examining the bruise on her temple. Nyota winced. "At least the skin was not broken."

"Be happy for the little things, right?"

"Indeed."

She looked up into his violet eyes, the gold rings around his irises glinting in the dappled light. "We haven't been properly introduced. I'm Nyota."

"I am called Korvin," he replied.

"Nice to meet you, Korvin. I wish it was in better circumstances."

The slightest hint of a smile creased his lips, but only for an instant. "Yes, this is not ideal," he said. "Now, you should rest. You need to recover from your injury."

"But what if the Raxxians—"

"I have ensured we are well hidden from sight. You are safe for the time being. Now rest."

Nyota considered protesting, but her pounding head and exhausted body had other ideas. She quickly began drifting off to sleep, Korvin keeping watch. But while his imposing presence was likely comforting to the injured woman, her guardian could not help but wonder just how safe they actually were.

CHAPTER THREE

Concussion protocol back on Earth was pretty straightforward. Basically, the main point was to keep anyone who suffered from a loss of consciousness from a head injury awake for a day or so. It sucked, but this was to ensure they didn't have a subdural hematoma slowly leaking into their brain, gradually applying pressure, ultimately causing them to go to sleep but never wake up.

The rationale was that one would be able to notice the change in their level of consciousness and overall mental capacity long before a slow leak developed into something major.

On Korvin's world, however, it seemed that system of rules did not exist, and as a result he let Nyota sleep as long as she needed. As it turned out, that was well into the night.

It wasn't a restful sleep, however. Nyota tossed and turned as fitful dreams danced around in her traumatized head. Memories of her life on Earth. Flashes of her abduction. Glimpses of faces she seemed to know. Faces from a variety of races, and not all of them human.

She had been going about her life. Nothing out of the

ordinary, just a day at work, followed by a quick stop at a nearby food stall to pick up her meal for the night. It had been a busy afternoon and she simply didn't have the energy to cook. It was an indulgence she had gotten over fretting about and now allowed herself without guilt.

Sometimes you just had to do a little self-care. And sometimes that meant taking it easy and letting someone else do the cooking.

It was funny, actually. She had discussed the idea of laziness with her cousin that very week. How so many cultures had the general concept of an overall "take it easy" attitude in their vernacular, but it was really the Puritans who seized on the idea as something to fight against and punish in others.

It seemed the Puritans had advanced a lot of distasteful beliefs in their time, and the damage they had done spread far beyond their own xenophobic circles.

Nyota, however, had been in therapy and done the work. If her body needed rest, she let it. If her mind required a break, she made sure to carve out time for mindfulness and unwinding. And if she was just too spent to put in the time and effort cooking, she allowed herself the occasional takeout meal. In warmer weather, she would sometimes even climb on the roof of her building to enjoy it, relishing the comfortable relaxation flowing through her limbs as she lay back and stared up at the sky.

That was precisely what she had been doing when her world abruptly went black, the stars and city lights gone in an instant. When she awoke, they had been replaced by a metal ceiling and the curious stares of a dozen or so unfamiliar faces.

They were a motley group from all over the globe, it seemed. Traditional garb made that much clear, but they all seemed to be speaking the same language. Nyota commented on it, curious how that could be.

"I have placed a translation rune on the skin behind your ear," a tall alien male with the same tan-gold skin as Korvin said. The same race, though the tattoos covering his body were more visible than his kinsman. "You still lack the other runes, and the Raxxians would not afford me the pigment to apply them, even if they did have it at their disposal."

"Translation rune?" Nyota had asked as her head cleared.

"Yes. As I have explained to the others, your planet is clearly not part of the Dotharian Conglomerate or you would have been given one in childhood."

"The Dotharian what?"

"Conglomerate. A union of planets far from your own. But none of that matters. What does is that you are aboard a Raxxian transport vessel. Try to stay alive. The others will explain."

"*Planets*? You say that like you're from some other planet."

"Is that not obvious?" he replied with a shrug. "I have had this discussion with those taken from your world too many times. Discuss with them. I have done my part."

With that, he turned and climbed into a bunk embedded within the smooth metal of the wall.

"Wait. What's your name?"

"I am Heydar," he replied as he slid into the shadow of the bunk.

Nyota looked around at the diverse faces watching her with interest. The others were all human, it seemed. Only Heydar was an alien among them. An alien. An *actual* alien.

"We're on some sort of ship?" she asked the group.

"Livestock transport," a woman replied. "And before you start asking, just sit and listen. It takes a little while for the stun effect to wear off anyway."

Nyota nodded silently.

"So, the Raxxians? You'll see them. Big bastards. Green with scaly skin. They are *not* friendly. You'll do well to keep quiet and not draw their attention. The smart ones survive. The foolish? Well, they get eaten."

"Eaten?"

"Like I said, we're livestock to them, though that one seems to be a favorite pet of theirs," she added, nodding toward the alien reclining on his bunk. "Point is, don't give them a reason to decide you're too much trouble to have aboard and hopefully you won't become their next meal."

Nyota felt her stomach flip.

"In that hole in the floor over there if you're going to be sick," the woman said, gesturing to the opening.

Nyota hurried over to it and emptied the contents of her stomach. There wasn't much, however. That meant she'd been here a while. Long enough for her dinner to have digested, at the minimum.

"How long have I been here?"

"I'd say ten hours or so. It's hard to tell without a clock on the wall. Some sleep longer, some less. You're about average."

"Yay, me."

The woman cracked a grin. "I'm Shalia, by the way."

"Nyota."

"I'd like to say it was nice to meet you, but given the circumstances..."

"Yeah, I'm with you on that," Nyota agreed. "So, what do we—"

The door slid open and a monster of a creature strode in. Tall, muscular, carrying what looked like a rifle of some sort, though with those sharp teeth that could easily rend flesh from bones, she doubted it would need to use it.

Nyota felt adrenaline flood her system as panic began to rise. Her vision blurred suddenly, and nothing made sense.

She cried out, snapping from her dream and jerking upright

in the dim moonlight of the alien world, her head pounding, albeit less than before. Korvin looked up from the pile of what appeared to be salvage from the wrecked ship he had been sorting through.

Nyota noted the fluid nature of his movements as he set back to work. Something about the way he was doing it seemed off. Different. She quickly realized it was the long fingers on his hands. They were not like a human's hands. These hands sported an extra joint on each finger, and it was that subtle difference that made them move in such an unusual way.

His kind must be pretty dexterous, she mused as she settled back down, watching him continue his work. There was the sound of water nearby, she noted, and perhaps the faintest whiff of moisture, but the pounding in her head put that thought on the back burner in a hurry.

Korvin glanced over at her, then back to his work, a look somewhat near contempt on his face, though he at least made an attempt to hide it. But she saw it, plain as anything. For whatever reason, the man who had crashed down with her seemed to resent her. She had no idea why. Hell, she'd barely spoken to him at all. And he'd carried her from the ship to safety. So what was the deal? Why was he upset?

As if he felt her still staring at him, Korvin looked up from his work once more, forcing his face to appear neutral at best. "You are still in need of rest. Sleep. We will have a long day ahead of us tomorrow."

Whatever his problem was, Nyota still felt he would protect and watch over her despite his ire. It was in the way he carried himself. How he spoke to her. She couldn't place exactly what his reasoning was, but with the state of her aching head she didn't exactly feel up to pondering the intricacies of interspecies diplomacy at the moment.

With a little sigh, she lay back down and closed her eyes.

Answers would be had soon enough. But he was right. She needed rest, and sweet slumber took her almost immediately. She tossed and turned at first in the cool night air, but when Korvin finally lay close to her, sharing his warmth, her dreams seemed to quiet, and she slept soundly through the night.

As for what the new day would bring, that would have to wait until sunrise.

CHAPTER FOUR

Once more a ray of warm sunlight roused Nyota as the burning orb overhead transcribed a lazy arc across the sky, its light drifting across her face until it reached her closed eyes. The orange glow of the inside of her lids pulled her from her slumber much more gradually and pleasantly than an alarm clock. At least she had that going for her.

She roused, rolling to her side and pushing up to one elbow, forcing her weary lids to open.

"How long have I been out?" she wondered.

It was morning, so clearly she'd slept straight through the night. And judging by the aches in her body, she hadn't moved much, if at all. Of course, a good many of those were also day-after bruises forming as a result of her violent arrival on this world.

Her eyes opened fully with a jolt of adrenaline flooding her system. "Oh shit," she gasped as the prior day's events flashed back through her mind. "We crashed. And I was... wait, how did I get here?"

Nyota looked around. *Korvin.* That was his name. The one who'd pulled her from the wreckage. She noted the pile of salvage he had been sifting through the night before, now separated into different groups of items, though she had no idea what any of them were for.

A pile of his clothing lay beside her, but her rescuer was nowhere to be seen.

The faint sound of running water made her roll over and look in the other direction. What she hadn't been able to see the prior night was the small stream she had sensed was in fact flowing just a little way down a gentle hill from where she lay.

She noted they had camped out high enough to not be impacted by the cool, damp air directly beside the water and was grateful Korvin was apparently an experienced enough outdoorsman to know better.

Movement caught her eye. What she had thought was merely a rock in the water abruptly rose. A head, it turned out to be, attached to a tall, muscular, and utterly naked male.

Korvin took a moment to scrub himself with his meaty hands, his long fingers sliding over the chiseled divots and bulges of his impressive physique. His golden-tan skin almost glowed in the morning sunlight, and the water only served to enhance the effect.

His skin was beautiful. She could also see, now that he was totally naked, that it was also decorated with flowing lines of tattoos connecting more detailed designs scattered across his body. A few of them seemed to be broken by thick scars, she noted. Whether it had been their Raxxian captors or some other conflict that had caused them, she hadn't a clue, but it only added to his powerful image.

In any case, she was more than content to study him from her vantage point, taking in the impressive sight with unexpected relish.

Korvin stood in the waist-deep water a moment, rolling his shoulders slowly, then rotating his head around a few times to loosen the muscles, his broad back flexing as he moved. Nyota's breathing sped up at the sight.

He stood still, glistening, breathing the clean air deep into his lungs, then dropped below the surface for a moment, rising again with a splash.

He turned and began sloshing toward the shore, the water washing over his body, flowing down his magnificent physique as he did. Nyota may have been concussed, but her head didn't need any help processing what she was seeing, and her body reacted of its own accord.

A glowing warmth blossomed in her belly, radiating down between her legs in the most delightful tingle of sensation as she watched him walk. The way his muscles moved under his skin was enough to drive anyone to at least a little distraction, but the sight of the impressive, thick cock that dangled between his legs made Nyota's pulse quicken more than a little and made her mouth involuntarily water. She stared, transfixed.

Rivulets dripped from its length, catching the light and accentuating the raised flesh that ringed his sizable manhood. She found herself wondering if the rings were purely decorative to his kind or if they served some other, more *interesting* purpose.

The tattooed lines covering his body thinned and crossed his lower abdomen, dipping down and intersecting a small design inked just above his cock, right at the base of his pelvis. It was eye-catching, and with the heat between her legs most definitely growing, she suddenly found herself very much wanting to get a better, up-close look at it.

What are you doing? He's an alien, she chided herself as her impulses registered. *"You've got a head injury, that's all. You are not getting worked up over an alien."*

The spreading glow in her belly knew that was a lie, even if her conscious mind wouldn't admit it.

Korvin stepped ashore and shook the water from his body, his attention-grabbing length swinging from the motion, gently striking his thigh. He was close enough that she could just make out the wet smacking sound.

Nyota involuntarily let out a little groan as she shifted her thighs.

Korvin's gaze darted up, his gold-rimmed violet eyes meeting hers. Calm, unabashed, he made no effort to cover himself, but rather began walking up the slope right toward her, his cock swaying in the breeze, his powerful thighs flexing with every step.

"You are awake," he said, standing over her, on full display and even more impressive up close and personal.

"Uh, yeah. What time is it?"

"Morning. Late morning, actually. I did not wish to rouse you earlier. You needed the rest."

"Yeah, I guess I did."

"But now you are awake. Come, bathe. You will feel refreshed," he said, reaching down and grasping her arm.

"Hang on. I don't know about that."

"Nonsense. You must be ready for our trek, and this will prepare you," he said, pulling her clothes off with clinical efficiency.

Nyota thought to try to stop him, but he was huge, and if he wanted her nude, there was little she could do about it. But his motions were not of *that* nature. He was being calculating and precise, speeding their progress now that she was awake, nothing more.

She didn't know whether she should feel relieved or annoyed.

"Ow!" she blurted as a rock dug into her foot.

Without hesitation, Korvin scooped her up in his arms and carried her down the slope as easily as if she weighed nothing.

He was strong. *Really* strong. And his skin was so warm even while still damp from the stream. And on top of that, this close she could smell the faintest whiff of his manly musk. Not body odor, not sweat, but some unknown scent that was just a part of him, the aroma nestling pleasantly in her nostrils.

The cold water splashing up on her skin snapped her out of her daze as he waded into the stream. He stopped in the shallows, politely setting her down rather than tossing her in the deep end. Nyota wobbled a little, the cool water and upright position shifting her blood pressure enough to make her a bit lightheaded.

"I will help," he said plainly, scooping up water in his enormous hands and pouring it over her body.

"I-I think I can manage."

"Nonsense. You move slowly. I will speed the process."

Without further ado, he began applying water to her body, rubbing it with his warm hands, his long fingers running over her, washing away the sweat and grime from their hasty arrival on this world.

The strangeness of having an alien scrubbing her down in a stream in the middle of nowhere aside, the cool water actually *was* beginning to make her feel a bit more like herself. Korvin wasted no time, running his hands down each of her arms, splashing them with water before rubbing her back, easing the knots while being careful not to agitate the bruises settling in.

"Oh, that's good," she muttered as a million pounds of stress flowed out of her tight muscles. "Yeah, like that."

Korvin worked in long strokes, pulling and rubbing, bringing warming blood flow to her body. His own natural heat was also radiating against her from behind in a most distracting way.

Nyota gasped as his hands slid forward around her hips, dipping low down her thighs, then sliding up her torso toward her shoulders, his fingertips grazing her rock-hard nipples as he did.

A jolt of sensation shot to her clit, her knees weakening for a moment as hot wetness pooled between her legs even as she was standing in a cool stream. His grip firmed, hands on her waist and breast, pulling her close and keeping her on her feet. She felt his flaccid hot length pressed up against her ass and turned in his arms, her hand grazing his cock as she did.

The slumbering beast between his legs twitched to life for a brief moment, but the look on his face made her wonder if it had simply been a physical reaction to contact rather than one of arousal.

"We should dress and move," he said, releasing his grip and heading for the shore.

That answers that question.

Nyota followed him to the shallows but paused just shy of the rocks.

"Uh, would you mind?"

He looked at her feet, then the ground, and sighed. "Very well."

Without fanfare, he picked her up once more and carried her to their impromptu campsite, and deposited her beside her clothing.

"Be quick. There is a risk the Raxxians will soon have a search craft out looking for lost cargo."

"I thought you said we were alone down here."

"Our compartment contained only you and I, but there will be others that separated during the attack and crashed down elsewhere. And the Raxxians are not ones to readily give up on their cargo. In all likelihood, we should have at least a few days, if not longer, before a retrieval unit arrives, but one cannot be sure."

"And it's better to be safe than sorry, right?"

Korvin actually smiled, albeit a tiny one.

"Exactly. Clever woman. Perhaps more than I initially gave you credit for."

Nyota took the praise, backhanded as it was. Seeing the stoic alien show *any* emotion was a win, but to see a hint of mirth? It went a long way toward putting her mind at ease.

"What are you doing? We do not have time to stare off in the distance. We must be on our way," he said, hastily donning his clothes then turning his attention to the piles of wreckage at his feet. "Hurry. I will gather the best of what little salvage might be of value while you dress."

"But why?" she asked. "Why carry the extra weight?"

"Because it holds value in trade, which we will most certainly need," he replied.

"Need?"

"We may not be alone on this world."

CHAPTER FIVE

The pair moved fast once they finally got underway, and they made good time exiting the immediate area of their unfortunate crash-down. Say what you would about his process, the alien had been correct in his assertion that a refreshing dip in the stream would revitalize them and aid in their trek.

In fact, in relatively short order they had covered enough ground to slow their pace a bit and properly take in the scenery and even forage for edible plants as they walked.

Nyota stared in wonder at the trees. The unusual coloring of the bark and the strange shape and shade of the leaves. Even the shrubbery below was just so alien, and the undulating canopy above was letting enough light through to give it all an otherworldly feel with its shifting illumination.

But then, it *was* another world.

She walked on, studying the tall male silently leading the way. His tan skin that seemed almost golden when exposed to sunlight. That, and the unusual lines covering it.

"Korvin?"

The tall alien slowed his pace and glanced back over his shoulder with an annoyed look. "What?"

Nyota hesitated. He had taken her under his wing, but he didn't seem too thrilled about it.

Okay, he's in a mood. Maybe it's not worth asking, she thought.

"Well? What is it?" he persisted, seemingly more annoyed now that he had responded to her only to meet silence.

"I-it's just your skin."

"My skin?"

"Yeah. I was just wondering. All of those tattoos. Is it some sort of cultural thing?"

He looked down at the lines decorating his body as if really seeing them for the first time in ages. And if he'd had them for a truly long time, he might very well have almost forgotten they were there. That is until the human woman pointed them out.

"My runes, yes," he replied. "Not merely cultural, but specifically required by all who live under the Dotharian Conglomerate."

"The what?"

"*Who*. The Dotharian Conglomerate is the ruling body that oversees a vast number of worlds, mine included."

"So those are some kind of Dotharian decoration?"

"Not decoration. A specific set of runes. They will vary slightly depending on the race they are applied to, and some possess enhanced versions, but they are roughly the same. You see this?" He pointed to a complex twist of ink on his arm connected to the rest of his art via a pair of thin lines. "This is a strength rune. The pigment used for this type specifically channels power to a limb, giving it more strength."

"Hang on. You're saying you've got magical space tattoos?"

"Magic? Hardly. This is merely galactic power absorbed by the plants the pigment is extracted from. The same energy from the many suns throughout the galaxy flowing through us all. Condensed and implanted in one's skin, the pigment symbiotically bonds to its host, providing life for itself and a power benefit for the recipient."

"Sounds like magic to me."

"Trust me, it is not."

"Well, I guess magic is just science we don't understand yet."

Korvin's brow raised slightly. "An astute observation. Did you just come up with that?"

Nyota stifled an amused chuckle. They were a bazillion miles from Earth. Of course, he'd never heard the saying.

"Uh, yeah, I did."

"You are wiser than you appear."

"Gee, thanks?"

Her sarcastic tone went right over his head.

"So, what now? Do we just trek all day? I'm feeling wiped out."

Korvin studied her a moment. "Wait here," he said, then stepped off the trail into the brush.

A moment later he emerged with a small lumpy fruit the size of a tennis ball. It was oddly shaped, as though someone had taken a handful of berries and squeezed them together into a single unit. He held it out to her.

"Boodzin pods. A bit tart, but nutritious. You look a bit pale. This should provide your body with necessary compounds to revitalize your energy levels."

Nyota took it from him, her head a bit cocked to the side. "You're saying I need to boost my blood sugar? I had an ex who called me grumpy once. *Once*."

Korvin seemed unfazed by her snark. "What is blood sugar? I have tasted blood. It is not sweet."

"Okay, I'm not even going to ask why you've been drinking blood."

"I said *tasted*. Not imbibed."

"Well, that's a *whole* lot better," she joked.

Korvin shook his head. This human woman was far more trouble than he'd first assumed. "Your skin."

"What of it?"

"I could not help but notice that you lack any runes at all."

"I've never really had any interest in getting inked."

"But it is Dotharian Conglomerate law."

"Well, I'm from Earth, and I've never heard of your Dotharian Conglomerate."

Korvin seemed perplexed by this admission. "All living under Dotharian rule receive their first markings as children, with more added as they grow older. The Infala rune is absolutely required on all who have come of age."

"Like I said, we humans aren't part of your little club. And the *what* rune is required?"

"The Infala," he said, pulling his shirt open and showing the rune on his chest. It was more complex than the others, featuring many smaller lines folded into the larger design.

"Pretty," she remarked.

"It is the bonding rune. The one that determines our mate."

Nyota pulled back. "Determines your mate? You don't have any say? What kind of society is this?"

"No, you do not understand. It is not like that. We may choose our own mates if our Infala has not found its match. And this happens often. To encounter your bonded Infala mate is something we hope for, but it is not a simple affair."

"Why not? And I still don't get how a tattoo determines who you're with."

"The pigment in the rune is alive, always growing. Shifting. And when it comes in proximity of the one it is destined to bond with the designs will connect with each other and begin to change in both parties until eventually they share the same rune."

"Matching tattoos. How quaint."

"It is not a thing to be mocked," Korvin snapped. "If you weren't from some uncivilized world, you would know this."

Nyota bristled. "I'm sorry, did you just call me a *savage*?"

"I did not say that."

"It sure sounded like it."

"You know full well..." he groaned. "Frustrating woman. I simply mean you should mind your words on subjects you do not understand, which is surprising as you clearly possess a translation rune."

Nyota's fingers moved subconsciously to the newly applied patch of ink behind her ear. "That was involuntary. They did it to me when I arrived. While I was asleep. I didn't consent to it."

"The Raxxians do not ask for consent from their livestock," he replied. "I must admit, however, for so brutal a race they actually did a surprisingly good job. Especially for a Raxxian."

"Oh, it wasn't one of those bastards who did this. There was a man who did it. A prisoner. Actually, he looks kind of like you."

His jaw twitched. "Like me, you say? Then others of my kind still live."

"At least one does, yeah. He was being kept in our holding compartment. Really big guy. Bigger than you, even. Had a few more markings on him from what I could see."

Korvin's interest piqued. "*More* markings, you say? And skilled with applying the pigments? Did you happen to learn his name?"

Nyota thought back to her time in the shared compartment. "Uh, it was Hobar. Or Heyfar. Something like that."

"Heydar?"

"Yeah! Heydar. That was it."

Korvin's back straightened and a new fire burned in his eyes. "My general. He lives!"

"Last I saw. But with the ship blowing up and all, I don't think we can really say for sure."

Korvin ignored that last part, focusing on the news that his leader had survived their Raxxian capture. "I must find him," he said, picking up his pace.

"Hey, wait up!"

"He is out there somewhere. It is imperative I reunite with my general."

"I get that you're all gung-ho to find him, but we have no idea where he might be, even if he did survive the crash."

"That is no excuse for not trying."

"No, it's not. But your legs are like twice as long as mine, and there's no way I can keep up with you if you just take off like that."

Korvin's face contorted. Just for an instant, but she saw it. He was upset. Torn. He had pledged to guarantee her safety, and she could already tell that for a man like him his word was an unbreakable bond. And now she'd just put him in the uncomfortable position of having to make a choice.

"I will slow my pace," he said after taking a few deep breaths, calming himself. "You remain under my protection. But we now have a course to follow."

"We do?"

"Yes," he said, a look of satisfied resolve in his eyes. "We will trek to the other crash-down sites until we find him."

"And if he didn't survive? Sorry to be a downer, but you've got to be ready for that possibility."

Korvin nodded, his jaw flexing. "I am aware of that," he said. "And if that is the case, we will adjust from that point. But for now, at least, we have a purpose. Come, we need to make the most of the daylight."

Without another word he turned and walked off. Fast, but

not so fast that Nyota couldn't keep up. She popped the last bite of the Boodzin pod into her mouth and set off after him. He was excited and eager to go, and that meant it was going to be a long, long day.

CHAPTER SIX

Korvin had pushed the pace, as expected, eventually altering course, guiding them to the top of a small rocky hill to use as a vantage point. From there he said he was hopeful to spot the location of at least some of the other crashed containers from the Raxxian ship.

Of course, the craft had broken up in orbit and the constituent surviving pieces had scattered upon entering the atmosphere. If any others had survived—and that was a big *if*—there was no telling how closely or spread out they would have come down.

If they were lucky, the gravitational pull on the compartments would have brought them to roughly the same area, seeing as they came from the same place. But from ground level, and below tree cover no less, there was just no way to be sure. Hence the need to climb.

Nyota's legs were most definitely feeling the exertion.

They crested the small hill and Korvin dropped their supplies, quickly scaling a tree with impressive agility. Nyota watched as his powerful arms hauled him up, up, and up until he was atop the canopy.

"See anything?" she called up to him.

"I see many things," he replied. "Among them is what appears to be an impact area not far from here."

"You sure?"

"Sure?" he scoffed. "Not in the slightest. This hill, while somewhat elevated, is still far too low for a proper view. I would much prefer to be atop that small mountaintop you can see peaking over the treetops. However, I would wager that there is a fifty-fifty likelihood of my impression being correct. That is, unless this world naturally has large gaps in the growth of its trees."

"Meaning?"

"Meaning it looks as though something quite sizable crashed down through them, and recently. I can make out what seems to be a gap in the foliage. It is a fair distance from here, and the trek will take much of the day, provided we do not encounter any unforeseen difficulties with the terrain."

Korvin began climbing down from his perch, his long limbs making quick work of the descent, the additional joint in his fingers giving him a more secure grip than a human could ever hope for.

"We will set out at once," he said as his feet landed beside her with barely a sound, which was impressive for a man his size. "I am not yet sure of the length of a day on this world. We should assume it is short until proven otherwise. It is not a journey we would wish to undertake in the dark. At least, not until we know what sort of predators may lurk here."

Nyota didn't like the sound of that. "Well, that's not reassuring at all. And did you say you want us to hike all day on a hunch? How can you possibly know that you're right about that being a crash site?"

"I cannot be certain, obviously. But given the change in coloration from what looks like broken limbs among the leaves, it is a logical assumption the damage was caused by something large coming down through the treetops."

"How can you even see that? You said it's almost a day's hike away."

"Because, unlike your kind, I possess the markings of all who live within the Dotharian Conglomerate. And as a soldier, I have received certain specialized runes that enhance other abilities. Sight, for one."

"You're saying you've got bionic eyes?"

"What is *bionic*?"

"You've got *super* vision?" she clarified.

"Compared to a basic such as yourself, yes, I suppose you could say that. *I* would not phrase it as such, but one coming from your primitive culture might."

"I'm sorry, what was that? *Primitive*? And did you just call me *basic*?"

"I mean no disrespect. It is just a statement of fact. The runes are not part of your world, and as a result you are simply not as advanced as those in the Dotharian Conglomerate."

"You are such a dick," Nyota snarked with an agitated glare.

Korvin ignored her comment and picked up his sling pack of salvage. "Come. This way."

Nyota was angry but bit her tongue. Much as this man was an antagonizing prick, he was also the reason she would survive on a potentially hostile alien world. The simple fact was, he remained her best chance at maybe, just maybe, finding a way home. With no other options before her, she fell in behind him as he headed off down the hillside.

It was a long walk, as he had said it would likely be, but at least the terrain was working in their favor for the time being. Relatively flat and with the trees and shrubbery spread out far enough to make their trek fairly straightforward, Nyota found she was able to keep up with her alien guide with ease.

The trees in this area were leaner than before. Their trunks were tall and slender, with a thin white bark that peeled off like paper when she brushed against it. The inside was faintly violet colored, and she found that if she pressed her nail on the outer part, the indentation would show as violet on the white surface. Almost like a natural writing surface.

She thought about a message in a bottle, so common on her own planet. But she had no bottle in which to put one, and even if she did, she would have to launch it into space rather than set it adrift on the tide.

A flare of panic rushed through her body. *I'm alone. Like really alone, stuck on another world.* Her adrenaline pumped through her body, the realization that there would be no rescue clear in her mind. Her own kind couldn't even get to the moon reliably. Finding her in another solar system was not even remotely an option.

Keep it together, Nyota. Freaking out isn't going to help.

She took a deep breath and forced her pulse to slow, at least a little bit. She would just have to make the most of the situation day by day and leave it at that. Panic was not going to do her any favors.

Korvin, on the other hand, seemed utterly calm as he walked in silence, focused on their path and keeping them roughly on course as they made their way around the few obstacles that lay in their path. Craggy outcroppings and wider streams were easy enough to circumnavigate so long as one was able to remain oriented to their original course.

They didn't speak so much as a word for six hours, pausing only to drink from a clear spring then get moving once more as soon as their thirst was sated.

It wasn't until the late afternoon that they came upon the first pieces of debris scattered around the woods. Small, burned patches surrounded the most damaged of them, their orange-hot metal igniting the undergrowth where they struck down.

But the woods were lush and there was little dry fuel, preventing the small fires from growing into a full-fledged blaze.

Korvin stopped and squatted down, prodding a piece of twisted metal. He lifted it, turning it over in his hands.

"Do you still have doubts?" he asked rhetorically.

"Fine, you were right."

"Of course I was. The compartment should not be much farther. We can easily make it there while it is still light out."

With that he stood tall and set off with long strides.

"Hey, wait up!" Nyota called after him, hurrying to keep pace.

Korvin's body had a different posture now. More tense, but also fluid, if that was possible. As if he was on alert and ready for a fight but somehow making his muscles stay loose while being primed for action.

Nyota, on the other hand, was feeling the wear on all her body from her head to her feet. It had been a long day, she was still concussed, and picking up the pace when she was already this tired was putting a fair bit of strain on her already taxed limbs.

The alien turned and looked at her, letting out a frustrated sigh. He was annoyed, but he slowed his pace despite his clear desire to move faster. Even so, they still reached the edge of a flattened section of forest in less than an hour. Korvin held up his hand, signaling Nyota to stop and stand quietly.

Crouching low, he crept forward, carefully parting the foliage and peering out upon the landing site. He turned his head, scanning the area for a solid minute before pushing ahead into the clearing.

The compartment's emergency landing jets had functioned as designed, bringing the unit to a safe landing, though it had smashed a large number of trees in the process. The ground was cold now, but it had been scorched from the touchdown, burning off the undergrowth in an instant, leaving no further fuel to feed any small fires.

Nyota made her way to the edge of the clearing and watched as Korvin stealthily ran to the downed compartment. She couldn't help but admire the way he moved, so fast and fluid despite his size. In a flash he had crossed the exposed area and was pressed up against the side of the vessel.

Korvin activated a keypad, opening an airlock door she hadn't even noticed seated seamlessly into the hull. Impressive alien tech, she marveled as he vanished inside in a flash, leaving her all alone.

She studied the ship's exterior with a more critical eye. It wasn't really a proper hull, she realized. It was just another part of the larger ship that had been torn apart and thrown toward the surface. An impromptu vessel of sorts. A life raft.

Much as she hated the Raxxians, Nyota had to appreciate the design. The craft had been intended to salvage the Raxxians' living cargo, but whatever its original purpose was, the long and short was it had saved her and Korvin's lives.

And now he was inside of this other segment, facing lord knew what dangers while all Nyota could do was watch and wait. The feeling of useless helplessness was maddening.

Minutes stretched on painfully slow as her eyes sat fixed on the gaping airlock door. What might come out, she wondered. There was no way to tell.

Movement caught her attention. Korvin stepped out into the light, a grim look on his face. His posture was relaxed, his limbs hanging loose. There were no threats here.

Nyota didn't wait for him to signal her. She hurried from the brush, quickly joining him at the ship.

"You do not want to go in there," he said quietly but firmly.

"What is it? Are there any survivors?"

"Just death and ruin."

Nyota looked at the craft. It seemed perfectly intact so far as she could tell. "What do you mean? It all looks okay?"

"The compartment was not designed to withstand extreme stresses of attack like a normal ship. They lost pressure at some point," he replied. "Those inside perished, the craft's systems melted to slag. Whether it was the cold of space, heat of reentry, or loss of oxygen that killed them is anyone's guess. None will be telling their tale."

Nyota didn't want to ask, but she had to know. "Were there humans?"

"Yes."

"Oh." She felt a knot form in her stomach. "And your general?"

"Not present, though one of my kind was. Fortunately, it would have been a quick death."

He took a deep breath, held it, then let it out. Rolling his shoulders and standing up straight he turned and quickly scrambled atop the compartment, scanning the area, using the elevated position in the clearing as a means to get a better look at their position. A moment later he climbed down to the charred ground.

"There is a small ridge in that direction. A steep climb but ample elevation. From that vantage point I will be able to determine if other compartments came down in the area."

Nyota sank down to the ground, exhausted. "I need to rest."

"My general is still out there somewhere. We can rest once he has been found."

"You don't get it. I'm not a machine. And I'm obviously not in the same shape you are. I can't keep up this pace. Not for much longer, anyway. I need to recharge."

Korvin's jaw twitched, but he remained silent, his violet eyes fixed on the human woman sitting at his feet, forcing him to proceed so infuriatingly slowly. He took a breath and held it a moment, calming his mind. "Very well," he said, the tension still clear in his voice. "We will trek clear of this place and make camp."

"Why not just camp here?"

"The same reason we departed our own landing site. The Raxxians could come at any time. Unarmed and alone as we are? We do not want to be anywhere near if they do."

She hated to admit it, but she knew he was right. The Raxxians were evil bastards, and she had no intention of ever letting them capture her again. She would have to push on for a little while longer.

"Okay," she said, struggling to her feet. "Your point is well taken. Lead the way."

CHAPTER SEVEN

Korvin walked in annoyed silence as he led them from the downed Raxxian transport ship compartment. His body was not as relaxed as before and his eyes were moving constantly, scanning their surroundings for any sign of a threat. Fortunately, none was apparent. Nevertheless, the tension in the air was palpable.

Nyota picked up on his mood and opted to stay quiet as they walked, letting him stew in his own juices rather than try to understand his strange, alien psychology. Korvin was stoic and a man of few words, but he had also showed moments of fire in him.

She did not want to be the cause of another flare up if she could help it.

At least he was walking at a slower pace, though she had to wonder if it was more because he was searching for any signs of survivors. The way he had reacted when he'd learned she had known his general had taken her a bit by surprise. Whoever he was, this general was clearly more than just a leader to him. And now he had a singular purpose driving him, and her tired legs had no choice but to follow.

As the day slid into dusk Korvin led them over a small rise and down toward a thicket of dense trees with deeply creased brick-red bark and bulging roots that spread like tentacles of some old-world octopus of lore. He paused, surveying the area. There was a small creek nearby, but they were far enough away from it to avoid the chill and possible influx of insects that would accompany nightfall.

"There," he said, pointing to an outcropping of tall rocks nearby. "That is where we will make our camp for the night. Clear the area against those rocks of debris and smaller stones. I will return shortly."

"Where are you going?"

"To see what game might be drinking at water's edge. We have limited food supplies. I would add to them."

Without another word he turned and strode away, leaving her to her task.

He would not be gone long.

Korvin appeared out of nowhere, his stealth, especially considering his size, surprising her. He was carrying a small animal of some sort, already cleaned and skinned, impaled on a skewer and ready for roasting.

An unusual bit of color caught her eye as well. A pair of small alien fish of some sort, mostly dark but with vibrant orange spots, hung cleaned and gutted, dangling from a cord made of braided plant of some kind.

He stood quietly a moment and surveyed the area she had prepared, nodding his approval.

"This will do well," he said, then rested the cooking stick against the stone face and crouched down, quickly arranging a small pile of stones in a circle, two taller stones on opposite sides from which he would set the skewer to roast their meal. He then placed a thick piece of fallen wood in the stone ring.

"Don't you need kindling for that?" she asked.

"No."

"But that's a really thick branch. And we don't even have any matches. How are we supposed to—"

"Please be silent," he said, keeping his annoyance in check as best he could. "I have much experience surviving in the wild. Allow me to work in peace."

Nyota was about to fire back but remembered this man was an alien, and a soldier at that. Who could say what techniques for fire starting he knew? She watched with fascination as he placed his hands just above the wood and squinted, as if focusing his internal energy on the log.

She almost laughed at the display, but a faint glow grew between his hands and a moment later the log caught fire, its entire length crackling in a slow, steady blaze.

"How the hell did you do that?" she gasped. "You just waved your hands and it caught fire!"

"I did not just wave my hands. I drew power from this rune here," he replied, tapping his finger on a small, intricate design inked on each of his wrists. "The pigment in these runes is of a special variety, and the rune shape channels it to my will, granting me greater strength, as well as several other abilities."

"Yeah, like making fireballs!"

"It was not a fireball, do not be ridiculous. No one can do that. This is merely an exchange of the power contained in the pigment between both hands. The transfer can be focused to heat items between them. In this case, a piece of wood."

Korvin laid the meat over the fire and dug through the nearby growth until he found a suitable stick to cook the fish with. He then placed those above the flames as well, but at a greater distance to keep them from overcooking.

Nyota watched in rapt silence, staring hard at the markings she could see on his exposed bits of skin. Designs. Runes, he called them. And apparently, they really did give him special abilities.

She was able to understand an alien's speech thanks to a similar pattern marked behind her ear, so she guessed the impossible wasn't so impossible after all. She knew firsthand it actually worked, and in a few ways now, though the precise mechanism behind it was still beyond her comprehension.

She hoped to change that.

Nyota scooted closer to her alien protector. "Can you teach me that?" she asked.

Korvin's near constant annoyance seemed to dissipate for a moment as he sized her up in a glance. "If you were properly marked? Yes. It is rather straightforward, but it requires practice."

"What do I do?"

"Do? You do nothing. You do not possess the needed runes."

"But if I did? Help me understand, please. I want to learn."

He stared at her a moment, the gold rings encircling his violet irises gleaming in the firelight. "It is the focus of internal energy," he finally said, holding up his left hand so she could see the rune on his wrist better. "The power is within the pigment forming the rune, but without direction it is just a design and nothing more."

"Direction?"

"Intention. Will. Call it what you like, one must guide the energy to do one's bidding. It takes practice, but the runes will guide you once you understand the basic principles. In this case, I am now picturing heat traveling from my core, flowing through me to my palm."

A faint glow formed around his hand. Nyota reached towards him. She could feel the heat radiating from his skin, and more than just his normal alien warmth.

"Go ahead. It is safe," he said, the glow diminishing as her fingertips drew near.

A little shock tingled her fingers as she touched his skin, the sensation of heat but something else as well dazzling her senses. Korvin let her rest her hand on his a moment longer then abruptly drew away, the rune going dark in an instant.

"And now you understand."

"But how can ink do that? It still makes no sense."

"*Pigment.* I told you this."

"I know. But it's just all so strange. Ink–*pigment* made from plants that absorb power? It's unheard of."

"On your world, perhaps. But here it is the law. And one which could be of some concern if we encounter others."

"How so?"

"Look at you," he said, gesturing to her unmarked body. "If you were to be seen like this, you would cause problems."

"Problems? Like what? It's not like I'm from around here."

"None will care. You break the law, plain and simple, and ignorance of it is no excuse. For that reason, if we come across others, you must stay covered."

"You mean *when* we find other people. We're looking for your general, right?"

"Yes."

"And he's other people."

"He is. But he is more than that."

"Obviously. He's a general."

"General, yes. And heir to the Nimenni throne. And more importantly, he is my friend. We have known one another since we were boys, and I have been at his side as we both rose in the ranks."

"But he's a prince, right? So the general thing is what? An honorary title?"

"Nimenni must earn their place, even the royals. And Heydar excelled independent of his provenance."

"Until the Raxxians came."

"We have fought them before, but our small group was cut off from the main body of our forces and captured. We were separated when we were taken prisoner. There were six of us at the time. Thanks to your information, aside from poor Rillax whose body I discovered in the crash site, I now know at least one other of our group managed to survive."

"Your friend."

"Yes. And it is my duty to find him."

"Duty is important. I get it."

"Do you, though?"

"I do. We have similar things back on Earth. I've heard our military people say it before. Leave no man behind."

Korvin nodded his approval. "Then it seems your kind are more advanced than I gave credit. Here, be careful not to burn yourself."

He removed the pair of fish from the fire and passed one to Nyota while the rest of their meal cooked. She carefully pulled hot pieces from the bones and slid them into her mouth with relish.

"Oh my God, this is amazing."

"I apologize for the lack of seasoning."

"You cook?"

"Of course. Preparation of food for yourself and others is a skill all should possess, though, admittedly, some are better than others."

"And you?" she asked, her eyebrow arching slightly upward.

"Some have said I possess a talent for it," he replied without ego.

The two devoured the fish in short order then moved on to

the roasting animal. Korvin pulled off several pieces and placed them atop a hot rock to dehydrate into jerky for the next day's trek, then gathered the bones and scraps and bundled them in a large leaf.

"Where are you going?" Nyota asked as he rose and headed off into the woods.

"I am burying these far from here. We do not know what larger wildlife is present and it would not do us well to have temptation nearby."

"But the jerky strips?"

"Wrap them in a leaf and bury them near the fire. We will retrieve them in the morning when we depart."

Korvin vanished into the foliage, not so much as a twig cracking at his feet.

"Well, that was interesting," Nyota mused, then gathered up the dried meat and wrapped it up and buried it as she'd been told.

It was getting dark out and the temperature was dipping but the fire felt good and the rocks surrounding it had absorbed a lot of heat. She was just tossing another log on the fire when Korvin returned.

He looked up at the darkening sky then kicked dirt on the flames, extinguishing them.

"Hey! What are you doing?"

"The canopy above dissipated smoke and light during the day, but at night, exposed as we are, a fire would draw attention. And if the Raxxians are out there, that is the last thing we want. Recapture is not an option."

Nyota's objections died on her tongue at the thought of being back in a Raxxian holding pen, nothing more than a meal waiting to be eaten. At least the rocks would continue to radiate their stored heat for a while. The fire might be gone but that one bit of comfort would remain. The question was, for how long.

In the dark of night Nyota got her answer.

She woke from her sleep with a chill running through her body. She had bedded down closest to the fire circle stones, but now that they were well and truly cold her instincts kicked in, searching for any sign of warmth.

A low heat radiated toward her from behind. Korvin's kind ran hot. *Very* hot, it seemed. What was a cold night for her was likely merely a temperate one for him. Nyota scooted backwards up against him, her body almost vibrating in joy at the warmth. She wiggled closer still, the little spoon to his big one, nestling as close as she could, drawing his heat into her with every inch of contact.

Korvin shifted slightly, his arm sliding over her body, his warm hand instinctively cupping her breast as his arm flexed, pulling her closer. Nyota's nipples went rock hard, sending confusing waves of pleasure shooting between her legs.

Without knowing what she was doing her body took over, her ass grinding back against him. She let out a gasp when she felt the heat from his thick cock press up against her, his length stirring within his trousers, the material barely containing his impressive member.

She shifted again, sliding against him, moving on auto-pilot before she even realized what she was doing. Her breathing grew faster as the heat between her legs spread through her belly. Korvin, however, remained still, his breath slow and steady.

He was still asleep. Asleep, but his body knew what to do, regardless.

Nyota was torn. Filled with wanting but not daring to wake him for fear he would push her away in annoyance.

What are you doing? she asked herself. *What would your family think? Your friends? Getting frisky with an alien? Just go back to sleep, Nyota. Don't go making bad choices.*

Torn, she forced her body to lie still, aching to be taken but not giving in to the desire. She wondered how long she would lie like this, tormented and horny, but the day's exhaustion soon caught up with her as the alien's warm embrace lulled her back to sleep.

CHAPTER EIGHT

Nyota roused as the morning light shifted, her eyes, while closed, still recognizing the change of color, the increasing ambient glow of the sun's rays turning her lids a warmer shade over her groggy orbs.

Her body was already getting used to rising with the sun and instinctively shifted to a semi-waking state, pulling her from her slumber at the warm confirmation that day was upon them. It was light out. Time to wake up.

No matter the planet, basic biology ruled the day, it seemed.

Nyota stretched and yawned, forcing blood into her muscles, and working out the kinks from the prior day's efforts. The sunlight felt good, but the wonderful furnace of a man who had been sleeping behind her was not there. Strangely, she found herself a little saddened at the realization.

But he was a soldier, and the whole up at dawn or earlier thing must have been drilled into him ages ago. Anxious as he seemed to find his general, she was still confident he wouldn't leave her alone. He owed her his life, and it seemed he took that debt of honor *very* seriously. Being stranded on an alien planet who knew how many bazillions of miles from home, she was glad for it.

"Enough lounging, lazy bones," she quietly chided herself. "Rise and shine. A new day is upon us."

She opened her eyes, amazed at how beautiful this strange world was as she looked around at her surroundings in proper daylight, and with her pounding concussion headache finally gone.

"What's this?" she wondered of the large leaf covering something in front of her.

It hadn't been there the night before; she was sure of it. And she'd buried the dried jerky as instructed. Cautiously, she reached out, sliding the thick, waxy leaf aside.

A smile crept onto her lips.

"Breakfast in bed? Really?"

A small gourd had been cut open, cleaned, and filled with fresh water. Beside it a small assortment of fruit and even what looked like this world's version of some kind of nut were laid out for her to choose from. She had to hand it to him, even roughing it in the wilderness, and without the benefit of a proper kitchen to plate his offering, nevertheless, his presentation skills were on point.

"He even picked flowers," she nearly gushed as she admired the splash of color added to the offering.

Rough and tough soldier or not, it seemed Korvin had a more refined side as well. It made her wonder what other secrets he contained.

Nyota's belly grumbled, snapping her from her pondering. She picked up what kind of looked like a slice of mango, but when she took a bite, she found the flesh was firm at first, almost like an apple, but as it warmed in her mouth, it quickly dissolved into hundreds of tiny pods, sort of reminding her of how each segment of an orange contains myriad individual juice sacs.

She chewed them, bursting them and releasing a mouthful of incredible flavor. It was unlike anything she'd ever tasted. Tropical, sweet, but one she couldn't really compare to anything back home.

Whatever it was, it was amazing. She popped another piece in her mouth and bit down, reveling in the new flavor. She forced herself to slow her roll, careful not to bite her cheek in enthusiastic haste. After a few more bites she washed it down with a swig of water and moved on to something else.

The next thing she selected was a large berry that looked a bit like a blackberry but rather than possessing a great many small parts, this one appeared to only be formed of a dozen or so. Tentatively, she popped one in her mouth and waited.

It didn't melt apart like the other fruit had, so she gently bit down until her tongue was coated with a tart yet sweet rush of juice. There was a hint of something else in there. Salinity, but it paired perfectly with the flavor, which, again, was unlike any she'd ever had. A happy smile creased her cheeks as she chewed.

"It is called a bolalla berry," a deep voice said from behind her.

She turned to see Korvin walking out of the woods. Silently, even in his boots, he moved like a big cat. A predator always on guard.

"It's amazing," she replied with a grateful grin. "Thank you so much for all of this. You really didn't have to."

"You are small and weak. You will require sustenance if you are to keep pace."

"Well, yeah, sure. But I meant the whole breakfast in bed thing. It's really sweet of you."

Korvin cocked his head slightly. "Are you feeling all right? Are you experiencing dizziness?"

"No. Is there—"

He crouched and put his hand to her forehead. "No fever."

"You're too hot to be able to tell."

"I can tell. Nimenni are a warm people, but our skin is very sensitive. Far more than most races."

Nyota almost blushed at the hint of a filthy thought that flashed through her mind.

"I don't understand. What are you worried about?" she asked, calming the heat that had stirred in her belly.

"You appear to be in perfect health, yet you talk of eating in bed. It is plain to see that you are lying in the dirt. I worry there may yet be lingering effects of your head trauma."

Nyota's laugh, bright and clear, took him by surprise.

"You think it's a head injury?" she asked, eyes glistening with amusement. "Korvin, I know I'm not in a bed. It's just an expression. You know, like when you bring your wife a surprise meal in bed."

"I am unbonded. I have not yet encountered my Infala mate."

"Okay, sure. Your tattoo mating thing, right. But what I mean is it's like that sweet thing you do for the woman you love."

He looked at her a long moment. "We do not eat in bed on my world."

"No?"

"No. It is frowned upon."

"Jeez, that's no fun. But I'm sure you still get the idea."

He looked at her with an odd expression. "Where I am from, the bed is for only two things, and dining is *not* one of them."

Again that flare in her belly threatened to distract her. Korvin's people ate in bed, she was certain, it just wasn't food they'd be using their mouths on. The heat between her legs returned as she looked into his sparkling violet eyes, the gold circling his irises picking up the morning sunlight. Nyota bit down on her cheek just hard enough to distract herself.

Don't go thinking those thoughts, she chided herself. *That's not what this is about. Besides, he's not into you, he's made that perfectly clear.*

But looking at his well-muscled frame moving easily within his clothing, she found herself staring with a more than purely clinical interest. Alien or not, he was an impressive specimen, as she had seen quite clearly back at the stream.

"So, trekking," she said, shifting her mind to the day's task at hand. "You have a plan for today?"

"I always have a plan."

"Ooookay. Do you plan on *sharing* said plan?"

He looked down at the little human woman and sighed. "As I have stated, my general yet lives, and if the compartment of the Raxxian ship in which he was being held survived its entry into this world's atmosphere, he will be out there, somewhere."

"Key word being somewhere," she added. "I mean, it's kind of a walk in the dark here. We have no idea which direction we should even be looking in."

"True, but in time we shall cover *all* directions if so required."

"You want to go wandering all over this place, not knowing where we are or where we're going, and then you just *hope* to stumble upon him?"

"It is, admittedly, not the best plan, but our options are few."

"Okay, but what if we find *other* survivors? Humans, like me? What then?"

Korvin quietly mulled over the possibility for a moment. Clearly, he had been fixated on the task of finding his friend and general, but Nyota made a valid point.

"We will take them with us as well," he finally said. "Provided they are in condition to join the search."

It wasn't what she'd expected him to say, but hearing his willingness to help other survivors even if they weren't his people served to put her mind a bit more at ease. Korvin could be a bit stubborn in his quest for his friend, but he still seemed to be a decent person, regardless.

As if he could read her thoughts, he turned a slightly less judgmental eye to his Earthling counterpart. "Eat well," he said with a sympathetic look. "You will need the energy. I was quite serious when I said you will need your strength."

CHAPTER NINE

"A day's trek, no more than that," Korvin called down from the tree he had scaled when they finally reached the peak of a rocky hill.

It had already been a pretty serious hike since morning, ascending and descending numerous smaller hills to scan for signs of wreckage from the crash, as well as crossing multiple streams and one actual river. Fortunately, Korvin was well-versed in all manner of outdoorsmanship and easily guided her on the lesser traverses.

For the river, however, he needed to do more than give direction. As a result, Nyota had found herself riding on his shoulders as he waded deep in the flowing water, a long pole he had fashioned from a fallen branch acting as an anchor point in the sandy bottom for leverage.

Korvin would swim a bit, then pull the pole free and jam it in further ahead, giving him a pivot point to push off from against the current, keeping them from being swept downstream.

The water was fresh and only a little cold at first, but with his exertion the muscular alien was positively exuding heat. Heat that Nyota felt radiating between her legs, clamped around his shoulders, spreading into her body as she rode him to the other side.

Once they finally reached the shore and resumed their trek, the pleasantly warm air dried them in short order, though after the heat and rubbing from Korvin's neck and shoulders as he carried her across, Nyota remained wet in one place the sunlight would not dry.

Korvin, however, remained focused. Stoic. A single-minded man with one task. Namely, find his general. That he was also honor-bound to protect this human woman was simply an inconvenient factor he now had to factor into his plans.

By the time they reached the highest hilltop in the immediate area, it was closing in on midday. And from high up in the tree, Korvin had finally spotted what he'd been searching for.

"Are you sure?" Nyota called up to him.

"I am." He descended from his perch with speed and agility, landing softly on the loamy soil beside her. "Just that way." He pointed in the distance. "You can make out the indentation where a section of Raxxian ship came to rest. The trees are snapped in a very telltale manner."

Nyota squinted, scanning in the direction he pointed. "I don't see anything."

Korvin shook his head. "Of course. I forget you lack the runes."

"How do tattoos make a difference? My eyes are my eyes."

"True, but as I have explained, the pigment used possesses qualities far beyond simple ink. This rune, for example," he said, tapping a small marking on his temple just inside his hairline, "is to enhance one's vision. The basic pattern channels the power contained in the pigment, directing it to sharpen one's eyesight. If you possessed this, you would see."

"All the way out there? It's too far."

"But not with the proper rune. Admittedly, my rune is a bit more robust than most possess."

"Because you're a soldier?"

"Something like that."

Nyota looked up at him, her eyes tracing the fine lines of the pattern that gave him superhuman—or super*alien* vision. Korvin bent down so she could better see the design.

"May I?" she asked, reaching out toward him. She hesitated a moment, her fingers hovering.

"You may."

She didn't know what she expected of the ink. Some magical zap, or at least a sensation of some sort, but as her fingertip grazed across the design, she felt no such effect. Whatever it was he had going on in there, it was entirely self-contained.

"Did it hurt? Getting it, I mean."

"No. There is a slight pinching sensation, but most of the pigments used also prevent pain. At least, mostly. It is part of the symbiotic relationship between the living organisms. As I have explained, we host the pigment and keep it vital, while it in turn absorbs energy from the stars and provides us its own benefits."

"Like super vision."

"Among other things, yes," he replied, standing up tall once more. "Now, follow close. We have a long trek ahead of us if we are to reach the landing site before nightfall."

With that, he set off, clearing the way for the much smaller woman following in his path simply by allowing his size to push aside the brush rather than using his hands to break it. A few moments after they passed, the foliage slowly settled back into place, leaving almost no sign anyone had passed.

They walked in silence much of the day. Idle chit chat may have been acceptable on a leisure hike, but on a strange and possibly hostile world, remaining quiet and alert could mean the difference between freedom, recapture, or worse. They had already encountered smaller animals, and as Korvin pointed out, where there was small game, larger predators typically followed.

So on they moved, a stealthy duo on an alien world. Nyota found herself able to keep pace now that she was better rested and well fed, though she had to wonder if perhaps he was slowing his pace just a little in deference to her shorter strides. Annoyed as he seemed at having a somewhat helpless tag-along, Korvin was, nevertheless, keeping her safe. And that meant keeping her close.

The sun was beginning to lower in the sky when they drew near their destination. Even without the benefit of vision runes, Nyota could clearly see glimpses of broken treetops as they approached. The days seemed longer here than on Earth, so odds were they had a fair bit of daylight to work with before night fell upon them, and as they quietly wove through the trees, Nyota was grateful for it.

The container section was visible up ahead, and it was intact. Scorched ground where the superheated hull had burned the vegetation was the only fire damage she could see. This ship hadn't crashed. It had landed.

Korvin motioned for her to crouch low. Nyota quickly did as she was directed. He held up one hand for her to stay put, then silently moved forward, vanishing among the trees and foliage before her eyes even though she knew where he was going.

She squatted there motionless for several minutes, her eyes and ears straining for any sight or sound that might tell her what was going on. She received neither.

"It is safe to stand."

She jumped.

Korvin's voice came from right behind her, and she hadn't even heard him approach. She spun around and smacked him in her surprise, noting the slight amusement in his gold-rimmed eyes.

"You son of a bitch, you scared the shit out of me!"

"Apologies. If you require privacy to relieve yourself, I will leave you—"

"No, not like that. It's a figure of speech. Jeez. Just don't do that again, okay? My heart nearly exploded out of my chest—Again, a figure of speech, Mister Literal."

Amazingly, a little grin creased the corners of the dour man's lips.

"Understood," he replied. His expression turned serious once more. "You may accompany me to the craft, but I warn you, it is not a pretty sight. There is death here. You may remain here if you prefer."

Death.

People had made it to the surface only to lose their lives as they were so close to freedom. And some of those might have been her friends. Or cellmates, as the case may be. They'd not really known each other long enough to form real friendships, though surviving together under Raxxian captivity was stress enough for a mutual bond to be forged, regardless.

Nyota steeled herself as best she could. "No, I'm coming with."

Korvin nodded, satisfied with her response. "Very well."

They pushed through the underbrush, stepping clear of a few fallen trees before entering the small clearing formed by the out-of-place craft plopped down smack in the middle of the forest.

The ship was intact, she noted. A bit scorched from the ordeal, but otherwise whole and sound, making her wonder what happened to the people inside. Had they lost pressure? What took their lives?

The answer became clear as they rounded the side toward the open airlock hatch.

"Is that..." Nyota gasped, staring at the bloody, green-scaled limb on the ground before her.

"Yes. An arm. Raxxian."

Despite his assurances they were safe, she nevertheless felt a rush of panicked adrenaline fill her body. As they moved closer, she saw other, far worse sights. Bodies, a few alien species she didn't recognize as well as several she did. Humans.

"The Raxxians found the ship and killed them," she said quietly.

"No."

"What do you mean, no? Look at the bodies."

"I mean, there were Raxxians already aboard this section when it separated from the main vessel, and they attempted to recapture the livestock when it crashed down in this place."

"That's what I said."

"You said the Raxxians found them and killed them. While they did kill several who had been attempting escape," he said, pointing to the charred blast marks in the backs of several fallen would-be escapees, "they did not find them so much as arrive with them. This clearly occurred immediately upon arrival. The bodies are cold and stiff. This was not a Raxxian recovery team. These were ship's guards."

"Same difference. They killed people, Korvin. Shot them in the back in cold blood."

"Yes. Raxxians are a cold-blooded race."

"That's not what I mean."

"You often say what you do not mean. It is most perplexing."

Nyota groaned with frustration. "*You...*"

"Me?"

"Yes. You—Ugh!" she grumbled as she fought to suppress her annoyance. She took a deep breath but as the stench of burning flesh filled her nostrils, she opted against another. It would only make things worse. "What I'm trying to say is the Raxxians brutally murdered these people."

"Clearly. Why did you not simply say that?"

Nyota wanted to slap his chiseled face but held back—barely. "Look, we're saying the same thing. The Raxxians did all of this."

Korvin gave her a look as one might to an ill-informed child. "Are you certain of that?"

"Yes, duh!"

"Then tell me, what do you see here?"

"Bodies, obviously."

"And what kind of bodies?"

"Humans. Humans and aliens."

"And what sort of alien bodies?"

"I saw one of those before on the ship but don't know what they're called," she said, pointing to a pale blue woman with a large hole in her back.

"Balvinians."

"Okay, I saw a Balvinian before."

"And?"

"And Raxxians, of course."

He nodded. "Ah, yes. And what does that tell you?"

"We were captured by Raxxians, what is it supposed to tell me?"

"Look at the scene. Envision what happened here."

"The ship crash landed, and the prisoners were escaping."

"And?"

"And the Raxxians killed them."

"Very good. But what else?"

Nyota felt her blood pressure rising with frustration. Nevertheless, she looked around the area once more, wondering what she was missing. Suddenly, it hit her.

"*Oh.*"

"Oh?"

"Oh, shit."

"Ah. You see it now?"

Her heart was beating faster but for a different reason now. "The Raxxians. Who killed *them*?"

Korvin nodded. "Good."

"No, I mean it. Who killed them? The blast markings are different. One had his freaking arm blown off. This wasn't a prisoner with a Raxxian weapon. And there are no guns laying around. Not a single one."

An actual smile spread across her alien companion's lips. "*Very* good. Many would not have noticed that detail."

"It's hard to miss once you know what you're looking at."

"To a trained eye, perhaps. You are not a soldier, which makes your observation all the more impressive," he said, moving away from her as he searched the Raxxian bodies.

"But what does it mean?"

"It means we are not alone on this world. And whoever is out there, they are well armed."

"Then shouldn't we be hiding?"

He shook his head, flipping over a Raxxian guard and digging through its pockets. "They have already been here. We are safe, at least for the moment. Others may also be present, but we will deal with that eventuality as it arises."

She took in the information with grim clarity. Their situation was complicated to begin with, and it had just become more so.

"What are you doing?" she asked.

"Seeking any items of value. I have already salvaged what I could from our own vessel, but we are on a planet I do not know, without any currency. In our situation, we may require every last item worthy of trade that we can salvage. Our very lives may depend on it."

CHAPTER TEN

Korvin was an impressive sight to watch as he made quick work dismantling sections of the Raxxian craft despite the lack of proper tools, scavenging pieces that seemed inconsequential to Nyota, but were, according to him, extremely valuable.

Whoever had the run-in with the Raxxians before they arrived had apparently only made the briefest of searches. They had either been in a big hurry, or they had been incredibly careless. Either way, it suited Korvin just fine.

"We are fortunate," he said. "The most hard to come by and valuable components are, in the case of the Raxxian vessel, also among the smallest."

"Which means less to carry," Nyota realized.

Korvin shoved another small tidbit into the pouch he had recovered from the craft. "Precisely. We need to be able to move quickly. Heavier salvage would slow us considerably. Perhaps the gods smile upon us after all."

"Perhaps."

"Whatever the case, we should not look a gift hatsukah in the mouth."

Nyota flashed an amused grin.

"What?" he asked.

"Nothing," she replied, keeping the joke to herself.

Korvin shrugged and set back to his task, gathering as much as they could reasonably carry before heading out. He had made it quite clear that the longer they stayed near this ship the greater the chance of a Raxxian retrieval vessel arriving would be, and neither of them had any desire to face that sort of trouble.

He also secured some material from which he fashioned a cape of sorts. It wasn't terribly fashionable, but it would serve its purpose.

"Put this on," he said, handing her the material.

"But it's warm out."

"It is. However, you are unmarked, and to not bear the pigments at your age is a dire violation of Dotharian law. If we should be noticed while you are uncovered, it could lead to a very difficult situation."

Nyota tried to read his face for any sign of humor.

There was none. He was as serious as a heart attack.

"Okay, but if it gets much hotter out, I'll take the risk of being spotted," she said, sliding it over her shoulders.

"Very well. All I ask is that you be careful."

Nyota had a few snarky comments on the tip of her tongue but the earnest way he was looking out for her wellbeing made her think twice about using them.

"I will," she finally said. "Thank you for your concern, Korvin."

He nodded once, then returned to his work. In just a few minutes he completed his last pass of the downed ship. Satisfied he had gathered as much of value as they could reasonably carry, he slung the pack over his shoulder and turned to Nyota.

"We go this way. Judging by the angle of the impact, gravity would have naturally pulled the other sections in that direction."

"What about the bodies?" she asked.

"We leave them for the animals."

"That's not right. They deserve a decent burial."

"What they deserve and what is prudent are not the same thing. If we disturb them after a conflict such as this, signs will remain, and any who pass by will know of our presence. As it stands, it looks as though a raiding party came upon them and a fight ensued, nothing more. This, in turn, covers our tracks."

She couldn't argue with his logic, but it didn't sit well, regardless.

"Yeah, but it feels wrong."

"I understand your empathy toward the dead, truly I do. But these victims were not your friends. Not your family. And their deaths now contribute to the circle of life. Animals will live because of them. Plants will gain nourishment. It is not ideal, I know, but I hope this perspective helps soften the blow. Now, we need to leave. There are still several hours before nightfall, and we should be far from this place by that time. Come."

He started walking, his pace even slower than before, giving his human companion an easier time of it. Nyota fell in behind him quietly, surprised by his words and mulling over this new, compassionate facet she had just discovered in his personality.

Sure, he was still leaving the bodies to the wild, but there was real consideration behind his actions, and a respect for the natural order that she found downright refreshing—from *anyone*, let alone an alien soldier.

Mom always said you could find bright spots in the damndest of places, she mused as she followed her alien protector. *I doubt she would have expected this.*

She followed close as Korvin carefully selected their path away from the area. He was choosing a more circuitous, rocky trail. One that would not leave footprints to give away their presence.

They walked in silence for a solid hour, not once stopping, but also not pressing the pace to one that would unduly strain the human woman's lesser body. She was starting to feel the wear and tear of the exercise and it showed. Korvin, however, looked as fresh as he had that morning. Whether it was his runes helping him or just his natural fitness she didn't know, but Nyota was grateful he was taking her physical condition into consideration.

A break in the forest came upon them abruptly. Trees towered around them, the burgundy and deep green foliage utterly alien but nevertheless beautiful in the fading light, but a wide gap now spanned between them.

A road.

Or something like a road, though there were no tire tracks that she could see. Korvin crouched down and cocked his head to the side, listening. Nyota moved next to him and did the same.

"Transport is moving closer," he said after a moment. "Several of them."

"I don't hear anything."

He tapped the rune behind his ear. It was like her translation rune, but it was more ornate, the additional markings apparently giving him enhanced hearing. She marveled at the way this organic pigment could alter a person's natural abilities like that and couldn't help but wonder what the living ink could do to a human body rather than an alien one.

"There aren't any tire tracks," she noted, looking at the untouched foliage.

"Tire?"

"You know, to roll on. On the ground."

Korvin looked confused. "Our transports operate with a

basic hover field and impulse drive. They do not touch the ground."

Nyota sighed, shaking her head. "Of course. Just one more alien twist to this whole situation. So, what do we do? Do we run? Hide?"

"We wait here."

"And then?"

"We see who is coming. Not all races are hostile. In fact, in the Dotharian Conglomerate, the majority are not. But prudence dictates we remain hidden until that determination can be made."

"Okay, that makes sense. How long do you think?"

He squinted as he strained his senses. "They should be upon us very shortly."

Nyota felt her heart speed up as a trickle of adrenaline entered her bloodstream. Korvin was confident, but this was all still utterly new to her. Without him leading the way she would be totally at the mercy of whoever—or whatever—stumbled upon her.

Sure enough, only a few minutes had passed before even her unaugmented human ears could hear the sound of *something* growing closer. A hum that she assumed was the drive system pushing the vehicle along. There were also voices, chattering away in what sounded like good spirits.

At least, she hoped they were.

Korvin stood up and strode out into the open roadway.

"What are you doing?" she hissed.

"It is safe to come out, but do keep your body covered."

"You sure?" she asked, cautiously joining him.

"I am. These are Pahvlin traders. I recognize the vehicles as well as the sound of their chatter. They will give us passage to the nearest trading hub for a reasonable price. Once we are in a proper city, we can fully assess our situation and determine how best to continue our search for my general."

"Okay, but just to be clear, these Pahvlin guys aren't going to try to rob us, right?"

"They are traders, and that would give them a bad reputation, and reputation is crucial in their work. They are a very talkative race, and they strike a hard bargain, but they are good people. We will be perfectly safe in transit."

"Sure, they're all right. But what about once we reach this trading city you're talking about?"

Korvin fell silent for a long moment before locking eyes with her. "On this world, I cannot guarantee that. But I am honor bound to protect you, Nyota of Earth. You have my oath. No harm will befall you under my watch."

Here he was, filthy, bruised, wearing prisoner's clothes, carrying a sack of scraps and salvage as their only currency, and pretty much unarmed, and yet Korvin was entirely confident in his ability to keep her safe. Cocky, and likely overconfident, but she at least admired his sense of honor.

"Thanks. Let's hope it doesn't come to that."

"Indeed. I firmly believe the best fighting technique is to simply not engage in one in the first place," he said as he waved his arms, drawing the attention of the approaching vehicles. The lead vessel slowed and came to a stop, the others behind it following suit.

It was a small convoy. Five mid-sized craft about fifteen meters wide by thirty long. They were open-top, loaded high with crates of their wares strapped in place by large cargo nets. And, as Korvin had said, they were floating on air about a meter above the ground.

The Pahvlin crew peered over the side at the tall Nimenni soldier. A trio quickly scrambled over the side and walked up to him, showing no trace of fear. They were bipedal, a bit round in the middle, with thick fingers and slightly elongated ears. They were much shorter than Korvin and had shockingly pink skin. To Nyota they looked almost as if they were made of bubblegum.

"Nimenni," the leader of the group said to Korvin. "What are you doing out in these woods?"

"We have escaped Raxxian captivity," he replied. "Perhaps you saw some of the sections of their ship come down in this area."

"Oh, we saw them. Even got a few bits from one that blew apart on impact some ways from here."

"You found salvage, then?"

"Hardly anything worthwhile."

"There are certainly more craft. What of them?"

"Oh, not all the way out here. This region is not a good place for salvage."

"Why is that?"

"Dohrags have been operating in this area lately," the Pahvlin said, spitting on the ground with disgust. "Not as bad as the Raxxians, but still a generally abhorrent race."

"And that is why you travel in a convoy."

"Safety in numbers, friend. I know you Nimenni have dealt with them in the past, so you know full well what they are capable of."

"Indeed, I do."

"I don't," Nyota said, her sense of security bolstered by the alien's friendly demeanor.

"I don't recognize your kind. You look almost Vallish, but you have too few legs."

"She is a human. Captured by the Raxxians from a planet called Earth."

"Human? Never heard of 'em."

Korvin chuckled warmly, pouring on charm she didn't know

69

he possessed. "Nor had I until recently. But she is in my care, and we require passage to the nearest trading outpost or town."

"You're in luck, we are heading to Molok. It's a large city with a robust trading center. Quite advanced for this world."

"Then tell me, friend. What would passage cost? We are sadly short of currency, but we do have items for trade."

The Pahvlin sized them up and gestured to the lead craft. "You are Nimenni. I trust you will pay with a reasonable trade. And we're reasonably close to Molok. With Dohrags around I couldn't in good conscience leave you out here. Not with a female. "

Nyota felt the hair on her neck stiffen as her ire rose. "What's that supposed to mean?"

The Pahvlin's hands went up defensively. "No offense intended, I assure you. It's just the Dohrags, they have a propensity for taking females."

Korvin turned and rested his hand on her shoulder with a sympathetic look in his eyes. "The Dohrag ships are crewed only by males, and their deployments are long. As a result, they are known to sometimes treat female captives *poorly*."

Nyota caught the gist, a small knot forming in her stomach. "Oh, I see."

"They will not bother a convoy this size," Korvin added. "And they know better than to attempt any such thing in a trading city, especially not a large one that likely has robust defenses."

"Speaking of which," the Pahvlin trader said, "hop on. We should be moving. Never fear, we'll have you in Molok in no time."

Soft but strong hands helped hoist Nyota to the deck while Korvin simply vaulted aboard in a single leap.

"Okay," the Pahvlin said with a friendly grin. "Next stop, Molok."

CHAPTER ELEVEN

Nyota had no idea what an alien city should look like. She had high hopes—it would be alien, after all—but beyond that she hadn't a clue. Even as night fell upon them, she couldn't help but wonder if their destination would live up to her expectation.

When they pulled into Molok, the small convoy flew a bit slower, winding through its roadways on the way to the trading center of the city. It was alien, all right, and she felt more than adequately satisfied on that count.

All around, the architecture was fluid in shape. No harsh, right-angle edges and corners. These buildings were softer in design, and though they were clearly made of some sort of high-strength material, they looked almost supple, as if carved by a master sculptor rather than manufactured.

The city was clean and rather compact, opting for mostly low-rise structures that blended well with the looming forests around them. There were, however, more than a few taller buildings that stood proudly towering over the others. Gleaming spires of technology jutting up above the vast wilderness. A guidepost for traders coming from far and wide to hawk their wares.

Eyes wide, Nyota gawked at all the different alien races milling about. Some were humanoid, walking on two legs, but others ambulated with undulating tentacles, while others simply had far more limbs than she'd ever seen on a person.

While some were grotesque, a few of the aliens were utterly stunning in their appearance, standing out to her human eyes for both the exotic look of their bone structure as well as the beautiful variety of coloring they possessed of both flesh, hair, and eyes. Whether the people of Molok considered them an ideal of beauty she had no idea, but to her they were almost too pretty to look at.

"Here we are," the Pahvlin said as the convoy pulled to a stop at the edge of the busy trading district. "I wish you the best of luck."

Korvin reached in his pocket and drew out a small orange crystal set in what looked like a gyroscopic bezel of some sort. It was no bigger than a cherry, but the Pahvlin's reaction made its worth clear.

"I couldn't. This is too much."

"No, friend, I wish for you to accept this," Korvin gently countered. "Your help is more appreciated than you know. And the Pahvlin and Nimenni have a long history, so please, accept this with my deepest gratitude."

The Pahvlin, though flustered, nodded once, quickly pocketing the small item. "You are a good man, my Nimenni friend. May fortune smile upon you all of your days."

"And upon you all of your nights," he replied. Korvin turned to Nyota. "Come, we disembark here."

He hopped gracefully to the ground, landing silently, his powerful legs absorbing his weight with ease. Nyota climbed over the side and slid into his waiting arms, the heat of which was almost as distracting as the sensation of her nipples grazing across his chest as he lowered her to the ground.

"Now what?" she asked, suppressing the warm tingle twitching in her belly.

"Now we exchange our salvage for currency."

"Will that be a problem?"

"This world is part of the Dotharian Conglomerate. All use the same currency."

"Must make travel easier. No getting screwed with the exchange rate."

"Exchange rate?"

"When you—oh, nevermind."

He shrugged and led the way, following the main roadway heading toward the smaller trade posts where he would get the best value for their wares. He walked with poise and confidence, his muscled body's outline clearly visible as he moved within the confines of his clothing. Nyota couldn't help but marvel at his amazing physique. She also couldn't help but notice that despite the hunk of a male in their midst, the women of this city were ignoring him. Wearing ratty clothing and dirty from their trek, it seemed they found him unworthy of their attention.

Nyota found herself oddly relieved.

Korvin veered off the main roadway onto a smaller side street, heading straight for an illuminated storefront.

"Are you sure about this?" she asked, eyeing the burly men gathered outside a nearby tavern.

"Yes. The sigil in the corner of the window, do you see it? This establishment is part of the Orvin guild. They would not risk losing their affiliation. We will receive a fair-trade amount here," he said, opening the door, letting out a warm gust of fragrant air. "Please, after you."

"Thank you."

He shut the door behind them and proceeded to the small creature sitting behind a small table. It was deep brown and hairless, its skin wrinkled even where there were no joints. From its elongated, thin torso protruded six spindly arms with equally delicate looking hands. Nyota thought it seemed totally vulnerable like that, especially for one handling large currency transactions, but the faintest of glow from the ceiling above made her almost certain there were security systems in place. They were just unlike any she'd ever seen.

"Greetings, quaestor," Korvin said. "May I place my wares upon the table?

"You may," the creature replied.

Korvin put the bag down and stepped back. Sure enough, the light from above shifted, drawing across the bag slowly before coming to a stop with the goods now on the other side of the light. A scanner of some sort, clearly, as well as a likely barrier or alarm.

The alien opened the bag and went to work, all six arms quickly sorting the items into a multitude of piles. It then clacked its fingers on a rippling device to its side, a fluid-like calculator or abacus of some sort.

It turned the display to face the potential customer. "This much."

Korvin nodded. "A fair price."

"More than fair. You bring valuable trade. Unusual, as well. Many items the average scavenger would overlook."

"I have a good eye."

The quaestor gave him a curious look. "Apparently. Might I inquire where you obtained this?"

"You may, but you will not find a reply forthcoming."

The alien chuckled. "Very well. Hard currency or credits?"

"Currency. We may not always have access to the network."

"Very well."

The items were cleared from the table, replaced by a stack of currency chits of some sort. Nyota didn't know how the

Dotharian conglomerate money worked, but she had the sneaking suspicion this was a *lot* of money.

Korvin watched as the pile was counted out. "Do you have a pouch? I am without my usual attire."

"Of course," the alien replied, sliding the stack into a small pouch that seemed to shift in shape to accommodate the amount. The quaestor then slid it forward. A moment later the light shifted back across it, leaving it on the customer side.

"Thank you," Korvin said, pocketing the money.

"Is that it?" Nyota asked.

"That is it. Come," he said, heading to the door.

"Where now?"

"First, we acquire clean attire. Then food and accommodation."

"Works for me. I'd kill for a hot bath."

He shot her a concerned look.

"Figure of speech, big guy."

An exasperated glare and accompanying sigh were all she got in reply.

They walked out into the street and made their way to another shop conveniently nearby. The clothing there was expensive, apparently, but with nothing to base her spending on, Nyota had no clue just how much her attire really was. Korvin didn't seem to care one way or another, casually pulling currency from his pouch and paying for the few outfits each had chosen.

Hers were all long-sleeved and had been tried on in the privacy of a changing area away from prying eyes. Sans tattoos and runes she would stand out like a sore thumb had she opted for anything even remotely revealing. At least with most people's runes ending at their wrists rather than their hands, she did not require gloves.

Korvin had selected plain but well-fitting clothing that hung perfectly on his rugged frame. Each only had a few changes of clothes, but it was enough to start.

"Now lodging and food," he said as they stepped out onto the street. "It has been a long day."

"About to get longer," a gruff voice said from the shadows.

Korvin put his arm across Nyota's chest and physically pushed her behind him, placing his mass between her and the owner of that threat. Or owners, as she soon saw.

A dozen men, all rough and large, spread out from where they had been lying in wait. A few looked familiar. The men from the tavern, she thought. They had followed them from the currency exchange, waiting for an opportunity. And on this smaller street, one had just presented itself.

"Your currency. Give it to us," the apparent leader of the group said.

Korvin made no move to comply. "I must decline."

"What did you say?"

"I mean you no disrespect, but we have need of it ourselves. Clearly, you gentlemen have coin of your own," Korvin said, gesturing to the man's healthy belly. "You do not lack food, and you are clothed. So, I beg you, please step aside and we will be on our way."

"You *beg* me?" the man growled. "Oh, you'll be begging me, all right."

Korvin raised his empty hands in front of him "Please, I do not wish for any trouble."

"Too late for that," the man said, lunging for him.

Nyota had no idea what happened, it was all over so quickly. One minute the burly man was charging at Korvin, the next he lay unconscious on the ground at his feet. If not for the slight flapping of his clothing, it almost appeared as if Korvin had not moved an inch.

The other men let out exclamations of confusion. Confusion and growing anger.

Korvin sighed, shaking his head slightly. "Please, just walk away."

In response five of the men ran at him at once. This was no Hollywood fight where each attacker waited their turn. It was an all-out brawl with the intent to cause serious hurt on the man who had just humiliated their leader.

Nyota's eyes widened with amazement as she watched her protector flash into action. His body moved with the speed and grace of a dancer, but while also dealing with the attackers with the skill and power of motion of a master martial artist.

Elbows blocked punches while feet snapped out, kicking the legs, stomachs, and faces of the attacking group. The elbows that had been defensive shifted to offensive in an instant, cracking hard across the jaws of two of the men, sending them to the ground for an impromptu nap beside their comrade.

"Fight!" a voice down the way called out, drawing a gaggle of onlookers rushing to witness the spectacle.

Korvin ignored it all, singular in his focus on the swarming mass of men greatly outnumbering him. Three were down, but nine remained standing.

"You're a dead man," a blue-skinned alien with a scraggly beard and enormous arms shouted as he pulled a wicked blade from his clothing.

The others gave him a little room, not wanting to inadvertently taste his weapon's edge in his rage. They needn't have bothered.

Korvin's hands flowed in a blur, deflecting the attack while trapping the man's wrist and taking the knife from him as if he were a child. The attacker's eyes went wide with fear, but Korvin merely threw the knife aside before delivering a brutal punch to his temple, dropping him in a heap at his feet.

The others all attacked at once, eight on one. Korvin spun and parried, blocking and striking, keeping them from landing any blows of consequence. But he was facing dangerous odds, and the likelihood of coming out of this unscathed diminished with every second.

"Break that up!" voices shouted from down the street.

Nyota saw four men in uniform running toward them.

"Shit! The cops!" she shouted.

Korvin turned at her exclamation, a questioning look in his eye. The distraction was enough for two of the men to land solid blows to his chest and jaw. He staggered back, the first flash of actual anger she'd ever seen from him clear in his eyes.

"Enough!" he bellowed, the runes on his arms visibly glowing through the tears in his new shirt.

Korvin punched out in a flurry, his fists impacting each of his attackers with impossible speed and equally impossible power, sending them all flying off their feet into the opposite wall with a massive crash.

The police came to a skidding halt, the sight of the defeated men slumping to the ground leaving them at a loss. They stared at the newcomer with shock and a healthy sense of awe, their weapons raised, but not firing.

He glanced at them, registering who they were through the red haze of battle. Police. And in this case, not a threat.

His chest heaving, Korvin forced himself to relax his fists, taking deep gulps of air, slowing his breath with every inhalation. Slowly, his pulse dropped back to normal and the runes on his arms dimmed their disconcerting glow. Nyota thought it was the first time she had seen him actually look a little tired.

The police captain took a hesitant step forward. "You did *all* of this alone," he stated in awe. It was not a question.

"I did. But I did not want this fight."

"Twelve on one, who would?"

"Indeed," he agreed, wiping the sweat from his brow.

The captain looked at the downed men, then at the faintly glowing runes visible through Korvin's ruined shirt. "You know the Chogul technique," he said with awe. "And you possess the runes for it."

"I do."

A murmur rippled through the crowd.

"Then you are no ordinary Nimenni. You are one of the Bohdzee Guard."

Korvin merely gave the slightest of nods.

The police all lowered their weapons, each giving him a little bow of respect and deference as they realized who, and *what* he really was.

The captain looked at his officer and gestured to the fallen men. "Call a conveyance to take these fools away," he instructed, then turned back to the imposing man before him. "We thank you for all you have done for the Conglomerate. I cannot state enough what an honor it is to meet you. May I inquire your name?"

"I am Korvin."

"And your companion?"

"She is called Nyota," he replied.

"And you are new to Molok, clearly."

"Clearly."

"Then the magistrate will be most honored to have you as our guest. Have you acquired lodging yet?"

"We were about to."

"Then please, if you will come with me, I will escort you to meet the magistrate myself. While you talk, the lodgings for distinguished visitors will be readied for your stay."

"You do not need to—"

"Thank you," Nyota interjected, stepping in front of him.

"We appreciate your hospitality and would be delighted to meet your magistrate."

Korvin looked at her with a mix of annoyance but also a hint of respect. She was standing up for herself, albeit at a somewhat inconvenient time. He wanted to simply bathe, eat, sleep, and continue the search for his general, but it seemed he would have to play at diplomacy a bit first.

"As my companion said, we appreciate your hospitality. Please, lead the way."

Walking out of the small side street whispers fluttered through the crowd. All eyes were upon them, now, and the women who hadn't given him a second glance were now staring with open interest. Nyota couldn't help but feel a flare of what? Jealousy?

He's just a man, she reminded herself. *And he's an alien, no less. Let it go. Just let it go. We've got more important things on our plate. Like meeting an alien magistrate.*

As they walked, she felt the jealousy fade, and her emotions calm. He was just the man protecting her, nothing more. And that was a good thing, right?

In the back of her mind, she couldn't help but wonder.

CHAPTER TWELVE

Word about what had happened in the relatively quiet city spread like wildfire, the news of an actual Bohdzee Guard in their midst drawing even the most cynical of the residents out to catch a glimpse of the man. There were so few of them, the odds of actually seeing one with your own eyes were slim to none.

There was also an old saying. *If you witness a Bohdzee in the flesh it will be the last thing you ever see.*

Of course, that was an exaggeration. They were not randomly killing death machines. But the legends served them well, so no effort was made to correct them.

The Bohdzee were among the most elite of fighting forces, sent into harm's way in seemingly impossible situations to restore the balance of power. Nimenni, all of them, they were marked with a special set of runes, the hidden alterations to the normal designs only known to a very select few Skrizzits—the artists who applied the powerful pigment to their bodies trained in secret to grant their runes the requisite enhancements.

And now one was here in Molok. It set the entire community abuzz.

It would also serve as a warning to any other ruffians with

thoughts of criminal behavior when they learned what happened to the band of thugs who had foolishly accosted the newcomer and his companion.

It was for that reason the police captain chose to walk them she short distance to the magistrate's chambers rather than fly there. Not only would it afford curious locals an opportunity to see what all the fuss was about, but it would also spread the word and thus make the job of policing the city much easier, at least for a short while.

"That is the magistrate's residence," the captain said, pointing to the brightly lit, domed building ahead.

It was transparent on the top, and the material seemed almost as if blown like a bubble, though it was anything but delicate. Housing the overseer of the city, it would undoubtedly possess numerous safety elements not visible to the naked eye.

And then there were the guards posted around the building at regular intervals. Not so many as to give the impression an attack was imminent, but a large enough contingent to be more than able to leap into action should the need arise.

"We are going to the magistrate's private chambers?" Korvin asked.

"She retires from her offices as the sun sets. In the longer daylight of our summer months she works until late, but the sun lowers a bit earlier this time of year."

"An interesting schedule."

"Fitting with the nature of this world and setting an example for those living and working here that there is a natural order to things. Working late into the night may be normal for taverns and the like, but she hoped her actions would convince others to imitate her and shorten their days accordingly. And so they did. And in so doing, stronger social bonds would form, better sleep would result, and an overall healthier, happier populace has been the ultimate result."

Nyota gazed at the staring throngs watching them pass and realized that indeed they seemed at leisure, not work. "Amazing," she said. "A place where the pursuit of money is not the most important thing on everyone's mind."

"Oh, that is still important to most," the captain said with a chuckle. "But it is balanced with a healthy, sustainable form of living."

She spun a slow circle as they walked, taking it all in. "I can see. But why a magistrate? Isn't that a legal position, like a head judge?"

"Do not mind her query. Her translation rune is in need of a touch-up, nothing more," Korvin interjected. "The word you hear as magistrate is the head of all matters legal, but also those of a civil nature as well."

"Oh, got it," she replied, taking his cue, and making sure she was properly covered.

The captain looked at the newcomer with a questioning glance. "Were her runes damaged?"

Korvin flashed his charm once more, this time using his celebrity status to add to his persuasive appeal. "Not damaged, but the pigment the Skrizzit used was somewhat inferior. I intend to remedy that situation straight away."

"Ah, I see," the captain replied, satisfied with the answer.

Nyota stepped close to Korvin. "What do you mean, inferior? You said your general was a talented artist," she quietly hissed.

"And he is. But the Raxxians only provided him with the most basic pigments to work with. Do not fret. We will deal with your shortcoming before we continue our search."

Nyota wasn't so sure how she felt about a flawed tattoo that she hadn't even wanted being called a shortcoming, but she kept silent as they were led toward the entryway. This was clearly not the time or place to get into it with Korvin about manners.

"Captain," the lead guard at the door said with a little bow of his head. "The magistrate is expecting you. Torpa will escort you."

A small creature with bright yellow skin, striped with faint green lines in addition to its rune tattoos stepped forward and bowed deeply. "This way, this way!" it said in a high, sing-song voice, then scampered ahead on all fours.

It was no bigger than a mid-sized dog, but it clearly possessed higher thought and was wearing pants, but no shirt. It also shifted from two legs to four with ease, almost as apes did back on Earth. But this was unlike any creature Nyota had ever seen at home.

Torpa hurried along, looking back over its shoulder to make sure they were following, then stopped at a large, ornately framed open doorway. "In here, in here!"

The captain guided them into what looked like a large library or study. The ceiling was high and domed, showing the sky above, which was a neat trick since they were well below the top level of the building. Clearly a projection of some sort, but to Nyota's eyes it looked as real as if they'd been standing on the roof.

The walls were adorned with marvelous artwork, the designs not hanging but actually built into the walls themselves. Landscapes, still lifes, and abstract designs the likes of which she'd never seen brought warmth and color to the room.

A slender, robed figure rose from a plush chair and walked toward them. The captain and Korvin bowed their heads. Nyota quickly followed suit.

The magistrate was a rather humanoid looking woman, though taller than most and with a few curves under her clothing that belied her alien nature. Her skin was gray speckled with gold, and her hair was a radiant yellow falling below her shoulders.

"It is so good to meet you, Korvin, is it?" she said, stopping before her guests.

"It is, Magistrate," he said, accepting her outstretched hand in greeting. "And it is my pleasure to make your acquaintance."

She glanced at the officer. "Thank you, Captain, that will be all."

"Magistrate," he replied with a bow then stepped out.

Her attention shifted back to the Nimenni soldier before her. "A Bohdzee Guard in my city. Admittedly, we boast a wide range of races here, and even a Nimenni from time to time, but never one of your status."

"We are grateful for your hospitality, Magistrate."

"As am I grateful for your presence. Word of your arrival will undoubtedly calm the rabble for some time. I hear you had a run-in with some of the more unsavory residents of our city."

"It was not a problem."

"Not for your like, I'm sure. But tell me, how did you come to find yourself in Molok? You are a long way from home."

Korvin took a deep breath. Now knowing he was an elite soldier, Nyota realized how painful it must have been for him to be captured. And now he had to put ego aside and admit as much.

"My general was leading a small group on a mission when we were cut off from our main forces."

"Dohrags?"

"No. Raxxians."

The woman paled a bit at the word, a look of disgust clear on her face. "Foul creatures, the Raxxians."

"On this we agree."

"But they are not foolish enough to attack any settlements here. Yes, we have seen them pass through on occasion, but they leave us well enough alone."

"We were being held on their ship when it fell under attack."

"A Raxxian warship was attacked in our system?"

"No. It was not a warship but a transport vessel for livestock."

The magistrate nodded her understanding. "And Raxxian transports are designed to save as much cargo as possible in such an event. So, you and your friend here were dropped down on our world in one of those segments, yes? And in such an instance the Raxxians would undoubtedly brave our airspace to retrieve what they see as theirs."

"You know Raxxian capabilities well," Korvin said with an appreciative grin.

"In my position, one must be well informed."

"Indeed."

Nyota watched the exchange with great interest. This woman ran the whole city, yet she was almost deferential to Korvin. A powerful woman dealing with a powerful man. The dynamic was almost electric, and a little twinge of jealousy flared in her gut.

As if she could hear her thoughts, the magistrate turned her attention to the human, fixing her dazzling eyes on her with a curious stare.

"And you?" she asked. "I have never seen one such as you."

"I am Nyota, Magistrate. I'm not from around here."

"A refugee from Raxxian bondage under the protection of a Bohdzee Guard is always welcome in my city," she replied, extending her hand.

Nyota grasped it, noting the woman lacked the intense heat that radiated from Korvin's kind.

The magistrate studied her hand as she lightly held it. "Your kind has beautiful skin."

"Thank you."

In a flash her grip firmed and she turned Nyota's hand palm up, pulling in a way that slid her sleeve up, exposing her bare wrist.

"But where are your runes?" the magistrate asked, a curious look in her eye.

Korvin's body tensed ever so slightly but he did not move. "She was taken from a world outside of the Dotharian Conglomerate. She is unfamiliar with Dotharian law."

The magistrate calmly studied the human, assessing her with a steady gaze. "But the law is the law," she finally said, releasing Nyota's hand and turning her attention back to Korvin.

His eyes locked with hers, sensing curiosity but no threat.

"I agree. The law is the law," he replied. "And with your blessing, now that we are free of our captors and in a civilized setting, I would seek to provide her with her first set of runes. And as Raxxian bondage left lasting damage to a few of mine, I would also seek to have mine repaired." He pulled out his money pouch. "I have ample currency if you can just direct me to the nearest Skrizzit."

The magistrate laughed, light and cheery without a hint of threat. "Oh, nonsense. I would not hear of it. The Nimenni have long been our allies. And a member of the Bohdzee no less? Put away your coin. I shall send our finest Skrizzit to your quarters to service you both. After you have dined, of course. I am sure you are famished after your ordeal."

Korvin bowed low, Nyota following suit.

"That we are, Magistrate," he replied. "And we thank you for your hospitality."

"Good. Then it is settled. I will have Torpa escort you to the dining hall for a proper meal, after which you will be shown to your rooms. Torpa!"

"Yes, yes! This way, this way!" the little creature chirped. "Come, follow! Follow!"

The newcomers gave a parting bow then followed Torpa out of the room.

"So, I'm getting runes?" Nyota asked when they were clear of the magistrate's chambers.

"You are. Visit my chambers after we dine, and we will begin the process."

"I—uh..." Nyota found herself at a loss for words.

It seemed they had dodged a bullet, but in the process, she was going to get inked, like it or not.

CHAPTER THIRTEEN

The meal had been hastily prepared for the magistrate's guests, but even without much prep time a wonderful assortment of delicious foods was presented for them to indulge in.

Nyota was beside herself. Aboard the Raxxian ship she had been fed the same small assortment of boring food balls every damn day, and since they had arrived on this world, she'd been living off of what Korvin foraged and hunted. The fruits were delicious, no doubt, and the fish and meat had been glorious compared to the Raxxian fare, but they were still no match for actual properly cooked food.

And oh, how these delightful offerings were seasoned.

They were also utterly novel to the human. Amazing alien cuisine the likes of which she had never experienced—for good reason. She was the first human to ever partake of these delicacies, and she savored every bite.

By the time they had finished their meal, Nyota's belly was warm and happy. She hadn't eaten nearly as much as she thought she would, though, her stomach having grown smaller during her captivity. Raxxian food had nutrition to keep their livestock healthy and robust, but it came with a lack of anything extraneous. Very small amounts of densely nutritious food was what they had eaten, and their bellies had shrunk as a result.

The one benefit, however, was that despite a fantastic meal, she left the table feeling sated but not bloated.

"Bathe in your chambers," Korvin said as they were led to their separate rooms. "Ensure you are clean and relaxed. It is vital your body is fully at ease when you receive your runes. Any tension will make the process more difficult."

"A hot shower after all this time will do wonders," she replied, stepping into the door Torpa had opened for her.

"Indeed, it will. I have been informed the Skrizzit will work on us both in my chambers. Come when you are ready."

"Both of us at once?"

"Yes. My repairs are relatively minor, and they will be able to affect them during the pauses in the application of your pigments. But first we bathe."

"With pleasure. I'll see you soon."

She shut the door and took in the suite provided her. It was spacious, and frankly amazing. She just hoped she could figure out how the hot water worked. Fortunately, that proved quite intuitive, the system activating when she stepped over the small water collection device embedded in the floor.

As she washed, an invisible forcefield of some sort kept the water in one place, keeping the room from flooding, and the water at her feet was immediately whisked away by a mechanism she wasn't even going to try to understand. Probably a recycling device of some sort, but she was too busy enjoying the sensation of hot water on her skin to care.

She took her time, rinsing the dirt and grime from her hair and the sweat from her body until she felt like a new woman. Mostly, anyway. She was still a bit sore from all the trekking, and a small knot of worry gnawed at her belly. She was on an alien world, hunted by creatures that wanted to eat her, and about to be tattooed whether she wanted it or not.

It was a lot to process.

Nyota slid on the clean robe provided her and stepped out into the corridor. Korvin's chambers were just next door, so the walk was a quick one. She waved her hand over the panel next to the door.

"I thought that was the doorbell," she mused when no one answered, rapping her knuckles on the door instead.

"Yes, I hear you," Korvin said, pulling the door open.

Nyota felt her breath catch in her throat.

He was stripped to the waist, his delicious body scrubbed clean, his hair still damp from bathing. She could see his runes more clearly now, as well as the scars from the Raxxian torture that had damaged some of them. He stepped aside, gesturing her in. The thin trousers he had been provided barely concealed the thick cock swinging loose between his legs as he moved. Nyota felt her mouth water at the sight.

"Please, come in. The Skrizzit is not here yet. Make yourself comfortable."

She walked into his suite and spotted the twin tables set up side by side. They looked somewhat like massage tables back on Earth with a hole for them to breathe comfortably as they lay face-down while being worked on.

The lights were dimmed, and a few musk-scented candles burned, giving the place a cozy, comfortable vibe. Still, Nyota felt uneasy as she sat on one of the tables. Korvin noticed her tension, one very warm hand resting on her shoulder. He gave it a little squeeze.

"You are tense."

"Well, I have a lot on my mind."

"You must be properly relaxed to receive your runes."

"I know, you said. The shower helped, but I'm just a bundle of nerves, I guess."

Gently, but firmly, he pushed her down onto the table. "I will assist you. Lay here and relax," he said, picking her up and rolling her onto her belly as if she weighed nothing.

His long fingers deftly unfastened her robe and pulled it from her body. Nyota felt goosebumps spread across her skin as she lay there exposed.

Korvin took a vial of oil from the small table at the foot of the table and applied it to his hands, then poured some onto her bare back. It was warm and slightly musky in smell, comforting in the light tingle it induced.

He rubbed his hands together then began sliding them along her aching back, working the oil across her body, his powerful hands gently kneading the tense muscles with an expert touch.

"Just breathe," he said in a low voice, the sound of his words rumbling in her body. "The Skrizzit would normally perform this step if needed, but I am in your debt. As such, I will aid you in this."

His hands knew precisely where to rub, the knots in her back releasing with his long strokes and careful squeezes. Korvin worked her shoulders, arms, and back, before pushing down lower, his palms sliding delightfully over her ass as he pressed the muscles of her hips and glutes, spreading her cheeks with each stroke as she felt her core tension flow from her body.

That wasn't all she felt. Nyota was slick with oil, but the muscular alien's touch had moistened her in another way as well.

He slid his hands lower, stroking her thighs with even pressure, the sensation of his fingertips gently digging into the muscles as his palms moved making her nipples grow hard against the table beneath her. Nyota's breathing grew faster, but the large man standing above her continued his work at the same even pace.

Reaching her calves and finally her feet, he moved back up her body and slipped a hand under her waist, flipping her onto her back with ease.

Fully naked, her erect nipples taut and exposed, Nyota's pulse thundered in her chest as he worked his hands back up her body, sliding from her feet to her shins, caressing his way up her thighs, his warm hands feeling incredible on her bare skin.

He spread his hands wide, his long fingers enveloping her legs as he stroked higher. Nyota couldn't help but gasp as his fingers grazed her engorged lips before coming to rest on her lower belly.

She could feel herself almost dripping wet from his touch. Korvin's hands continued moving upward, massaging her hips and belly before sliding to her flanks. He rubbed higher, the sides of his hands barely touching the bottom of her breasts making her nipples strain with delight.

Shifting his hands, he cupped her fully, his oiled hands sliding up, her nipples shooting hot electric jolts of pleasure to her clit as she felt his palms slide against the sensitive skin.

Korvin rested his hands on her shoulders, assessing her body. She looked at him with heavy-lidded eyes, noting the thin sheen of sweat that shone on his body from the effort.

"You are still tense," he finally said. "Perhaps more than before, even."

"I—"

"Do not concern yourself," he said, cutting her off, his hands sliding lower again, his thumb and finger gently squeezing her nipples as he moved down her body. Nyota squirmed with pleasure, her thighs rubbing tight at the sensation. "Lay still. I will help you achieve the proper state of relaxation as best I can."

She was wondering what exactly he meant by that when his hands slid across her belly and down between her legs, the long strokes rubbing gently along either side of her labia, teasing her deliciously as he coated his fingers with her wetness.

Nyota's back arched as his thumb came to rest on her clit, the pressure sending a hot jolt of sparkling electric bliss through her body. She gasped, her breath ragged from arousal.

Nyota looked down but her eyes suddenly went wide, nearly rolling back in her head as two of his thick, long fingers slid into her. He was so hot-blooded; the sensation was unlike any she'd ever felt. Hot, but incredible. She couldn't help but wonder what his alien cock would feel like. Would it be even hotter?

The sudden rippling of his fingers inside her sent all rational thought from her mind. Pure ecstasy blossomed deep inside her as he put the extra joints in his fingers to good use. Pulsating, undulating, they moved inside her, putting just the right amount of pressure on her G-Spot while the unrelenting circling of his thumb on her clit pushed her over the edge in a rush of orgasmic delight.

She came hard, clenching down on his fingers, but Korvin did not slow his rhythm. Rather, he slid his other hand up her body until he reached her nipples once more, squeezing them gently, teasing them as his other hand coaxed her further into her bliss, the combination of sensations sending a whole different kind of delight to her already swollen clit.

"Oh, ffffuuuu—" Nyota gasped as she came again and again, her body locking up hard, trembling under his touch, squeezing his fingers still deep inside her as he coaxed out a series of orgasms so intense her vision went dark.

Nyota was in another place. All she could feel was wave after wave of climaxes crashing through her body, her hearing muffled, her vision nothing more than sparkling flashes as she came harder than she'd ever come before.

Korvin's fingers slowed their movement, and he gently slid his fingers from inside her. Nyota's body jerked as she felt the length of them emerge, lying still, breathing hard. Her vision began to return, and the ocean sounds filling her ears started to fade.

Korvin moved up to the head of the table and looked down on her with an assessing gaze. "There," he said, satisfied with his work. "Your tension is released. Your body will accept the runes properly now."

Nyota's body was tingling with lust, the desire flooding her from head to toe washing away any confusion she had harbored about her attraction to him. She wanted him. Badly.

Her eyes fell upon the outline of his cock, clearly visible through his trousers, her mouth watering fiercely at the sight. Without pausing to think about what she was doing, she reached out and grabbed his waistband, pulling it down with one hand while the other wrapped around his radiantly hot cock, squeezing it as she pulled him closer.

He began to thicken in her hand at once, growing hard at her touch. The ridges she had seen when he'd stood before her at the water's edge began to swell and enlarge under her fingers, the little rune on his pelvis seeming to glow slightly and shift as she pulled his length, a drop of precum glistening at the tip.

"Wait—" he began to say, but Nyota ignored him, leaning over and sliding his gorgeous cock into her mouth.

The salty taste of his precum coated her tongue, sending new waves of desire pulsing to her clit. She wanted him. Every glorious inch. Nyota pushed her head forward, letting out a happy moan as she took his impressive length as far as she could.

Large as he already was, she felt him thicken and grow in her mouth even more, his pulse throbbing hard against her tongue as she teased the ridges of his cock, coaxing out a trickle of delicious precum.

Korvin's body shuddered. He stood there, rock hard, the human woman latched onto his manhood, giving him so much pleasure.

"You do not have to do this," he said with ragged breath. "I was not intending to–" he groaned as she swirled her tongue around the swelling head of his cock. "Th-this is wrong. It is simply my duty to protec—"

She slipped him from her mouth with a wet smack as his thick head passed her suctioning lips, looking up at him with raw lust. "Shut up," she growled, driving him back into her mouth, sucking him harder, moving faster over his shaft.

The hot ridges along his length rippled under her lips as she moved, a delightful sensation to them both. He was so hard, and that glorious cock was all hers. He had relaxed her, sure, but he had also done so much more. She was ready for him. Wanted him inside her. *Needed* him.

And despite his stoic protests, she could sense his confused denials giving way to pleasure, his hand resting gently on her head as she worked his cock. He may not have intended to go down this path, but now that he was upon it, it seemed he was quite able to look at his human counterpart in this new light.

A chime rang out through the room. Someone was at the door.

Korvin took half a step back, a sticky strand of saliva and precum trailing from his cock to her lips.

"The Skrizzit is here," he said, his beautiful eyes dilated with arousal.

Nyota leaned forward and licked up the glistening strand and gave his cock a final squeeze.

Korvin twitched hard, his cock pulsing under her grip, then stepped back, tucking his manhood flat up against his belly as he pulled his trousers back up. Long as he was, his cock still protruded from above the waistband so he quickly tied a towel high around his waist, hiding his erection as best he could.

He opened the door as casually as he could. The Skrizzit was a somewhat round bodied creature with thick upper arms but delicate lower ones. Large green eyes stared out from a flat face. The Skrizzit was carrying a tray with needles and an assortment of pigments. Korvin saw at a glance that the magistrate had spared no expense. These were some of the most powerful and hard to come by varieties.

"I am Dahrag, your Skrizzit for this session. May I come in?"

"Yes, of course," he replied.

"Thank you." Dahrag's gaze fell upon the nude human, her skin devoid of any markings beyond the small translation rune behind her ear. "Ah, good. You are both prepared, I take it?"

Nyota smiled a not-entirely innocent grin. "Oh, I'm ready for it," she said, flashing a wicked glance at Korvin.

"Excellent," the Skrizzit said, oblivious to her double entendre. "If you would remove your towel and trousers, and if you would please both lie face down, I will begin."

Korvin turned his back to the Skrizzit and did as he was asked, his erection slightly diminished but only just, then lay face-down on the table.

"Yes, I see the damage was not too extensive," Dahrag said. "I will start with your companion first, if you do not mind. She requires far more work."

"We are in your hands," Korvin replied.

"Then I shall begin."

Dahrag laid out the supplies and dipped the first needle into the jar of pigment. "This will pinch a little, but it won't be bad."

With the endorphins flowing through Nyota's body, she was confident the Skrizzit was right.

CHAPTER FOURTEEN

The Skrizzit's hands were steady and strong. They'd need to be given the amount of effort it would take to ink the human woman's entire body with the runes and connecting lines all adults in the Dotharian Conglomerate were required to possess.

To do it all in one sitting would take time, and a lot of it. Fortunately for Nyota, the pigment naturally soothed the skin as it was applied. It was still uncomfortable, having tiny needles rapidly jabbed into her flesh over and over and over, but all told it was far less painful than she'd expected.

Of course, the massive rush of sexytime endorphins Korvin's extremely talented hands had flooded her body with could also explain that. He had said he would prepare her, and he had sure as hell done a magnificent job of it.

Nyota had watched with a wicked gleam in her eye as he did his best to hide his beautiful erection when he lay down on the table. Seeing it press into his stomach as he lowered himself face-down, she couldn't help but think of all the wonderful things she wanted to do with it.

"Ow!" she gasped, pulled from her erotic daydream.

"Apologies," Dahrag said with a little shrug, pausing for only a moment before continuing the detailed work. "Some areas of the body are more sensitive to my needles. This section will only take a little longer."

"I hope so," she replied through clenched teeth. "That really sucks."

"Every race reacts differently. Yours, it seems, is a bit more sensitive than most. I will endeavor to speed this portion of the work, but one does not want to rush a Skrizzit."

"A rushed Skrizzit means lesser runes," Korvin said, turning his head to watch the master artist at work, his eyes lingering on Nyota's bare flesh a bit longer than he'd intended.

His own damaged runes had only begun to be repaired, the Skrizzit opting to direct the majority of their attention to the human requiring so much work. The Nimenni man, on the other hand, was a relatively easy fix, and the needles used for the initial repairs lay neatly lined on the table beside Nyota's far greater assortment of implements.

She was having larger swaths as well as fine work done, and that required the Skrizzit to switch tools and techniques frequently. The results thus far, however, were impressive.

"They look good on you," Korvin admired. "Your natural lines are well suited for them."

"Thanks, I guess. I'd never planned on getting any tattoos, but I suppose after alien abduction, a little ink isn't nearly as big a deal as the rest of all this."

"Indeed."

The door chime softly sounded, announcing a visitor. Dahrag sighed, finishing a line with an expert touch before setting the needles down and crossing the room to the door. A uniformed guard stood at attention when it opened.

"Yes? What is it?" the Skrizzit asked, annoyed. "I am in the middle of a session."

"I am aware," the guard replied. "The magistrate has directed that the Admani pigment is to be provided to you for our guests."

At this Dahrag's eyes widened. "The Admani pigment? Really?"

"Yes. But you will need to come sign for it in order for it to be released from the vault."

"Oh, I see," Dahrag said, glancing back at the Nimenni and human lying naked on their worktables.

A lot had already been done, all of it freehand, applied with expert skill. But to have some of the Admani pigment to work with? It was an exciting honor to be permitted to use it.

"Are you coming?" the guard asked.

"Yes, yes. Of course." Dahrag turned back to the others. "I need to step out for a few minutes. I will be back as soon as I am able."

"We'll be here," Nyota said with a relieved little chuckle. "Honestly, it's good timing. I could use the break."

Dahrag simply nodded once and shut the door, following the guard to the heavily fortified vaults.

"What's that all about?" Nyota asked, pushing up on an elbow to better look at Korvin's gorgeous body.

His violet eyes met hers with a smoldering but conflicted look. She'd unsettled him earlier. Somehow, this little woman from Earth had affected this alien warrior like no one else had, and that made their brief interlude even hotter.

"The Admani pigment is an extremely rare extract from a powerful flower. It can only be harvested in full moonlight, when the pigment must be extracted within minutes of the flower being cut."

"Powerful?"

"It is a pale shade, used to enhance certain runes. Possessing even a tiny amount in your designs will ripple through your entire body, boosting the potency of all the connected runes you possess, not only those that are marked with the pigment. Consider yourself very fortunate. Few ever receive such an honor."

She eyed his naked body, a renewed flare of heat growing between her legs, spreading through her belly as she admired every inch of his chiseled physique.

"Oh, I do feel lucky," she purred, sliding from the table to her feet and reaching her hand under his hips.

"What are you doing?"

"What does it look like?" she said with a grin as her hand found its target, wrapping tight around his semi-erect cock and squeezing firmly.

Korvin let out an involuntary gasp, his pulse pounding hard in his rapidly swelling cock. "I told you. We cannot."

"We have time," she countered, moving her hand beneath his prone body, stroking his length as he lay on the table.

"It is not about time," he said, his voice ragged with conflict and lust. "I am your protector. I have an obligation."

"You're damn right you do," she said, sliding her thumb over the head of his manhood, coaxing a droplet of precum out and using it as lube to work over the ridges now engorged in her hand.

"No, this is wrong," he protested as her hand pumped faster, coaxing him until he was rock hard.

"Your mouth says no, but your body is saying something else."

She was reveling in the moment, flexing her newfound sway over this powerful man. Korvin rolled to his side, his erection snapping to attention, released from beneath him.

"Yeah, that's more like it," she said, leaning forward and wrapping her lips around the pulsing head of his cock.

Korvin's hands grasped her gently but firmly around the neck.

"Oh!" she groaned, her clit swelling with delight.

"No," he said, pulling her eager mouth off his straining manhood. "This is not to be," he said, his gold-rimmed eyes conveying that as turned on as he clearly was, this was not going to go any further.

He had grabbed her neck, all right, and that was sexy as hell, but it had been done to avoid her new tattoos still fresh on her shoulders.

"But—"

"No." He was clear in his meaning. This stopped here and now.

"I don't under—" Nyota began to protest when the Skrizzit's voice was faintly heard talking to the guard in the corridor. "Shit!" she blurted, spinning and hopping back to her table, bumping into the tray of implements in her haste.

Nyota grabbed the jumble of needles and did her best to separate them back into their respective places. There were a lot of them, though, and she could only hope she'd gotten it right.

She lay down flat in a hurry, Korvin doing the same, just as the door opened.

"I have the pigment!" Dahrag said with clear excitement. "This is a momentous day. Momentous!"

"We appreciate your hard work," Korvin said, then lay flat, turning his face away from Nyota.

"Oh, I am thrilled for this opportunity! To work with the rarest of the rare? What an honor!"

The Skrizzit opened the tiny bottle of almost white pigment and placed it on the tray with the others, pausing for a moment with a confused look. "Strange."

"What's strange?" Nyota asked.

"Nothing," the Dahrag said, nimble fingers straightening out the tools of the trade until they were neatly laid out. "I must have left these out of place. It is unlike me, but I was in such a hurry when I learned you were to receive the Admani pigment, I clearly forgot."

Nyota felt a flush of relief wash over her. "But everything is all right?"

"Yes, all is fine," Dahrag replied, picking up a fine-tipped needle. "Now, let us not delay. There is a short time to work with this pigment when the bottle is open. One must not delay."

"As you wish, Skrizzit," Korvin said with no trace of his earlier arousal in his calm, steady voice.

The artist dipped the needles in the bottle. "I will highlight your human first. Her tiny Infala will be the perfect place to start and will act as a powerful conduit for it to flow through the rest of her body."

"A sound choice," he noted.

"And then I will apply it to your Infala as well."

"But mine is complete. Grown to maturity," he said, hoping his erection would fully subside by the time he had to roll over to receive the new ink.

"Yes, but it is also the most powerful rune on your body, and we want to make the most of the Admani, do we not?"

"Your reasoning is sound."

"Of course it is," Dahrag said with a happy grin. "Now, let us continue."

CHAPTER FIFTEEN

The Skrizzit's work finally done, the night passed swiftly for the weary travelers, both of them sleeping soundly in their separate chambers. Not only had the efforts of their adventures caught up with Nyota's overtaxed muscles, but the ordeal of having her entire body marked with special pigment had left her utterly wiped out and in need of self-repair.

A solid night's sleep was precisely what the doctor ordered.

As for Korvin, he was in fine shape, and the touch-ups on the damaged parts of his tattoos were minor enough that he felt no ill effects. He was also a soldier and had learned long ago to sleep wherever, whenever, because there was no telling when he might be able to rest again.

In this case, however, he was safely ensconced in luxurious surroundings with no chance of a Raxxian reclamation team disturbing his sleep. As a result, he had his first truly restful night's sleep in longer than he cared to remember, and when he woke, he felt wonderfully refreshed.

In Nyota's case, when she roused she wondered if she had moved at all in her sleep, so sound had it been.

"Oh, this is going to suck, isn't it?" she wondered as she

carefully pulled the thin sheet from her body and rose to her feet.

Amazingly, the crusting tattoos did not stick to the delicate yet warm material. What's more, there was no flaking or peeling of note.

"Huh. Maybe not," she said with a relieved chuckle.

Her next stop was the bathing area. Now *that* she was sure would not be pleasant. But cleanliness was important when you were the guest of the ruler of an entire city, so she put on her proverbial big girl panties and stepped into the alien shower.

"Here we go," she murmured, tensing as she activated the water flow.

Incredibly, the water, while warm and cleansing, seemed to somehow detect the delicate skin and fresh ink where she had been so recently marked, redirecting on what appeared to be a molecular level as she was sprayed, avoiding any direct contact with those areas.

How the water was being directed like that and what mechanism was keeping it not only from hitting the new ink but also from running down her body across the fine lines the Skrizzit had marked her with was beyond her. Alien tech, obviously, but more than spaceships and blasters, which she understood on a basic level from old sci-fi movies, this felt *truly* alien. Like, something she couldn't even begin to fathom.

She shut the water off with the wave of her hand, the system immediately shifting to gently blowing her with warm air, the invisible force again aiming the flow everywhere but directly on her new ink. In less than a minute she was completely dry.

"Damn. Now that was impressive," she mused just as something new happened.

A gentle spray of fine mist coated her body, but this time it was layered upon the healing skin rather than around it.

Immediately, the itching she had begun to notice faded and the heat of her tender flesh diminished.

"Aloe vera?" she wondered. "Or, some kind of healing ointment?" She carefully touched one of the fine lines on her flank with a finger.

Not oily. Not greasy. It felt perfectly dry, protecting the pigment embedded in her skin from irritation. Nyota gave an impressed nod to the invisible alien machinery. "Not bad, guys. Not bad at all."

She carefully dressed in her new attire, no longer having to focus on keeping every bit of her body covered, checking herself out in the mirror she had discovered when curiosity had gotten the better of her and she started touching random things in her room.

The image of herself was projected in space in front of her, not reversed like an Earth mirror, but as others would see her. A true and correct representation of her appearance, and something she wondered why Earth hadn't come up with. They had the technology after all. Or they could at least achieve a similar result using the tech they did happen to have.

Regardless, she looked herself over, admiring the healthy glow she seemed to exude. She looked good. Better than good, truth be told.

"Maybe there *is* something to these runes after all," she admitted.

She was re-adjusting her hair when the door chimed.

"Coming," she called out, tucking a wayward strand in place then moving to the door.

She opened it to find Korvin standing quietly outside. He was clean shaven, washed, and dressed in some very flattering clothing. A warm tingle fluttered in her belly, but this was a new day, and whatever shenanigans they'd been up to the prior evening, there were people around. That discussion would need to wait.

"Are you ready?" he asked, the low-hanging fruit of that question too easy for her to take a swing at.

"Yeah, I was just freshening up. Do I look okay?"

"You look well," he said, failing that little test. "Let us move to the dining hall. Your body surely needs significant sustenance after so intense a session."

Nyota bit her tongue, knowing he was merely talking about the Skrizzit's work and nothing more interesting. "Are you saying calories don't count after you get tattooed?" she asked with an amused grin.

"Calories?"

"Ugh. Says the man with the washboard abs."

"Washboard? Why does one wash a board? Your world is quite strange."

"Just let it go," she said with an exasperated groan. "We'll go get some food, leave it at that."

"Yes, that is the plan. The magistrate expressed an interest in seeing us this morning."

Nyota stepped out and closed the door behind her. "Then we'd best not keep her waiting."

"Indeed," her guardian replied, turning and leading the way. He paused a moment and turned back to her.

"What?"

"Your hair. It looks nice today."

Without another word he turned and continued on his path.

Nyota's mind whirred. *What the hell was that?* she wondered, falling in step behind him. He had denied her, but maybe, just maybe, the thought of *what if* was now creeping into his mind.

As they walked, something felt very different from yesterday. Drastically different, in fact. Everyone they passed was turning to look at the borderline celebrity in their midst. And the women who wouldn't have given Korvin a second glance previously were now openly showing interest, giving him come hither looks and batting their eyes at him—even those who possessed more than one pair.

He simply walked on, ignoring them, impervious to their stares and uninterested in their advances. He did, however, periodically glance over his shoulder at the human woman following close behind. And even when he wasn't looking at her, Nyota felt certain he knew exactly where she was and who was around them.

A protector, that was his role, come hell or high water, and regardless of what had happened between them the day before, or his new social status, it was his duty of honor to ensure her safety, and a task he took *very* seriously.

Nyota felt the looks of jealousy from the women they passed but they bounced right off her, she was feeling so good. A bit sore, perhaps, now that she was up and moving around, but good. Her legs had renewed energy and the aches that had sprung up from head to toe were largely gone.

Whether it was the new runes she'd been given or just the regenerative nature of good, sound, stress-free sleep, she was unsure. All that really mattered was that she felt human again. Better than human in a way.

But that was probably the living alien pigment now a symbiotic part of her anatomy.

A disconcertingly soft-spoken guard with beautiful pale green skin and a form-fitting uniform accentuating her musculature quietly made her way to the newcomers. "The magistrate is expecting you. Please follow me."

Korvin nodded once to the security professional with respectful professional recognition and fell in behind her. Nyota followed suit, the crowd parting as the sturdy woman led the way.

The magistrate was dining in a large, public setting, but her security detail was casually spread out, each of them unobtrusively keeping a close eye on every last guest.

Must be the safest room in the city right about now, Nyota mused.

"Ah, my guests! I trust you slept well," the magistrate said, offering her hand in a warm greeting.

"Refreshed and rested," Korvin said. "We greatly appreciate your hospitality."

"Yes, I feel like a new woman," Nyota added, shaking the woman's hand.

The magistrate held her grip a moment longer, turning it over, exposing the new markings on her wrist and forearm.

The magistrate smiled wide. "The Skrizzit did a remarkable job. I must see that they are properly commended for their efforts."

"It did come out pretty good," Nyota agreed.

"Pretty good? For an unfamiliar race, the application of the pigments was expertly done."

"About that," Korvin interrupted. "You provided us with a most generous gift. The Admani pigment is really too much."

"Nonsense. Only the best for a Bohdzee Guard. And your woman deserves no less."

"She is not my woman."

"Oh, you are already mated?"

"No. My Infala remains unbonded. But one in my line of work, well, you understand."

The magistrate nodded solemnly. "And we appreciate your sacrifice. But a life alone is no life at all."

"I am not alone. My general, my colleagues—"

"Are not the same. But who am I to lecture one who has experienced as much as you have? I know as a man who has seen so much death that you appreciate life more than most."

Korvin's jaw flexed slightly. "Perhaps so," he said with a slight nod.

A team of serving staff swarmed the table, a delightful assortment of food, both savory and sweet, piled high.

"Sit, eat," their host urged. "We have much to discuss."

Nyota was silent for some time while Korvin and the magistrate spoke. She might have had one or two things to add to the conversation, but she was too busy sampling the amazing spread in front of them. And the others seemed to be doing just fine without her.

"You do not have to head out so soon," the magistrate protested when Korvin expressed his intentions. "Rest, heal, enjoy our city. You are most welcome in Molok for as long as you wish to remain."

"I thank you for your hospitality, Magistrate, but my general is still out there somewhere, and I would do all I can to find him sooner than later."

"I understand your sense of urgency. But you have had a difficult run of luck thus far, and sometimes a pause can ultimately move you forward faster than if you hurried ahead. I think I can assist your search while you fully restore your energy. We are cautious not to enter certain areas—we cannot afford to go starting a conflict with the more hostile factions on this world—but if you allow me just a few days, I will send our scouting craft in all directions to compile as much data on likely crash sites as possible."

Korvin hesitated, something Nyota had not seen him do before. His drive was clear. Find his general and friend. But this offer? While it would require a day or two of down time, during which he would undoubtedly be all but climbing the walls, eager to continue his search, if the magistrate's team could accurately map out other crash sites, it would dramatically speed the actual search and recovery process.

Of course, there were planetary politics to consider, and the magistrate would have to act tactfully in that respect, but even if he was to continue on foot, at least he would be able to save many days of searching thanks to such a map.

"I appreciate your generous offer," he finally said. "And I accept with gratitude."

"Wonderful," she replied, nodding to an aide standing quietly nearby. "The process will commence at once."

The aide hurried away to carry out the command. It seemed his response had been expected, though she had at least waited for him to verbalize it before setting her plan in motion.

"I will use the down time to gather supplies I will require. With your permission, I would acquire weapons as well."

The magistrate nodded her approval. "Of course. Normally, most weapons are well regulated among our residents. But for you an exception can be made."

"It is greatly appreciated."

"Think nothing of it," she replied, turning her gaze to the quiet woman seated at the table just as she took a large bite from her plate. "And your friend? Healing well, I take it?"

Ugh! Right when I stuff my face! Nyota thought, amused at the idea that the magistrate would have made a fantastic waitress with her choice of timing.

"She is," Korvin replied for her while she chewed. "And with your permission, perhaps she could remain here under your care while I—"

Nyota nearly choked on her food. "Hang on!" she blurted, forcing it down in a hurry. "There's no way you're leaving me behind. There are humans out there as well. Maybe not close friends, but the only other people from my world in this galaxy so far as I know. I'm coming with."

Korvin fell silent, staring hard at her, sizing up her drive and conviction. It seemed the weak human had more fire in her belly than he'd given her credit for. Slowly, he nodded. "Very well," he said, his lingering gaze abruptly stirring something within her.

Nyota shifted slightly in her seat, her legs crossing, sending a little jolt through her body. *What the hell was that?* she wondered.

He had always had stunning eyes, and she was more than pleased to stare into them, but this felt different somehow. Like a tingling heat crawling under her skin as well as the usual flare of arousal.

Whatever it was, she was coming with. And no matter how things turned out, she would have time to further assess this confusing new reaction. Did the tattoos make her hyper-sensitive to sexy men? She had no idea, but if all went well, she'd find out soon enough.

CHAPTER SIXTEEN

For the next two days Korvin and his strange companion from an unknown world were in high demand in Molok. While Korvin had received the initial surge of interest when word of him spread through the city, soon enough tales of the woman from a race called humans shifted an equal amount of curiosity Nyota's way.

Together they were the newest *"it"* couple, though they were not actually anything of the sort. But for the masses seeking to tell their friends they had met the hottest things in town in years, that made no difference.

Nyota stayed close to Korvin the entire time, not daring to venture out on her own, especially with the throngs of people and all the newfound scrutiny directed at her. Also, that would have been utterly unacceptable in Korvin's book. His honor dictated he keep her safe, and that was what he would do no matter what.

Fortunately, along with word of who and what he was spreading like wildfire, so too was the tale of his taking apart a dozen armed thugs with ease. Had it been merely one or two or even three, perhaps some overzealous musclehead would have stepped up to challenge him in an ill-advised attempt at earning street cred. But having laid out twelve full-grown men? And without breaking a sweat? Even the most foolhardy were not *that* stupid.

Interestingly, while Korvin still remained unmoved by the increasing number of women and men coming on to him, the new ranks of interested parties curious to get a piece of his novel human counterpart seemed to rankle him. Nyota noticed the subtle shift in his reactions after the first day. It was not a big reaction, but it was definitely there.

He'd always been cool and aloof where she was involved, but now there seemed to be an almost possessive flare in his demeanor. It was odd. Flattering, but odd.

She started consciously paying more attention to his attitude, and sure enough, his holier-than-thou affect was diminishing by the day. On top of that, the looks they shared sparked a strange heat in her chest, as though maybe, just maybe, something more might be brewing.

But no, he had made his intentions abundantly clear. She was a duty, nothing more. An annoyance, on top of that, one hindering him from his quest to find his general. But even so, Nyota couldn't help but wonder as every time their eyes locked, she felt an increasing tugging sensation deep within her.

He got you off, that's all, she chided herself. *Sure, it was hot as hell and the hands down best orgasms I've had in years, if not ever, but don't go letting yourself get confused by it. He broke your dry spell, nothing more.*

It sounded good. Logical, even. But Nyota had one little problem.

She didn't believe herself.

Regardless, Korvin carried on with his preparations.

By the end of the second day, with the magistrate's assistant making the right introductions and ensuring a fair price, Korvin had arranged for the acquisition of nearly all the tools and equipment he felt he would need for the rescue attempt. Many, but not all, were neatly laid out on the bed in his chambers, where he had been carefully going over what to do and what not to do with his human tag-along.

Surprisingly, he had only requested a few knives and a small pistol, though Nyota knew size could be deceiving when it came to guns. A small one could kill you just as much as a big one could.

"Nothing larger?" she asked as he examined the small gun, her eyes briefly flitting to the outline of his manhood tucked in his trousers along with the blade now fitted to his hip.

"If the magistrate is correct in her initial assessment and the downed segments of the Raxxian ship are indeed in hostile territory, then we will not wish to make any undue noise. Weapons tend to produce the opposite effect of what we desire."

"Yeah, but if we're out-gunned—"

"Then I will acquire one from our adversaries. Hearing the sound of their own weapons will usually not raise much suspicion, if any. Use of another type, however, will. Keep this foremost in your mind. Stealth is our greatest asset until there is no other option. Do not let the enemy know you are there until it is too late."

She realized he was talking about the basics of guerilla warfare. It was something she'd barely paid attention to in history class her senior year in high school when Mr. Dunlop, a veteran and military history buff who had wound up teaching history to a bunch of unruly kids somehow, would delve into details of the events they studied that weren't in their books.

One of those tidbits was something he'd said about the Vietnam war. How it was the first real conflict where you didn't have clear-cut adversaries. Worse, there was no visibility to speak of in the jungle. As a result, every little thing could make or break a mission, from noticing a sandal print in the mud instead of that of a boot, to smelling the different sweaty body odor different sides of the conflict gave off due to their drastically differing diets, down to the sound of their weapons fire.

It was during that war that some of the special forces teams began carrying the enemy's weaponry. Not only did it make securing additional ammunition easier as they simply took it from those they killed, but the guns they employed also had a very distinct sound belonging to their adversaries, and for that reason it didn't raise an alarm when heard close to their locations.

And now, it seemed Korvin was thinking along those same lines. If they couldn't fly all the way into hostile territory to save the day, he would have to do it the old-fashioned way on foot.

Nyota eyed the additional wicked looking knives he had laid out beside their sheaths and shuddered. If things went the way she was afraid they would, there would be violence, and it would be ugly.

"Excuse me," a quiet voice said at the door. "I hope I am not intruding."

It was Minnix, one of the staff they had come to know during their short stay.

Korvin looked up from his inventory. "Please, come in."

"Thank you. The magistrate asked me to inform you that our aerial reconnaissance units were able to obtain a fair amount of intelligence pertaining to your objective. A great many sections of the Raxxian vessel came down on this part of the continent."

"This is excellent news! And what of survivors?"

"Unfortunately, the direction in which the crash and landing sites lay is well within the no-fly zone. Our long-range optics were sufficient to plot a basic map, but for such things as life signs and the sort, the density of the woods prevented us from seeing, given the angle of approach."

"You're saying that your people were too low on the horizon compared to the height of the trees around the downed ships," Nyota interjected.

"Yes, that is precisely the issue."

"Can't they just fly higher?"

"Normally, yes. But as there are Dohrags active in that airspace, we do not risk it. They have a transit hub in orbit above the planet and this is a common route. Tensions have run high for some time, but they no longer bother our city. But to fly between it and their terrestrial forces would be ill-advised."

"We appreciate the efforts, regardless," Korvin said, gathering up his gear into a compact pile. "I suppose it doesn't much matter anyway. By now any survivors would likely have either scattered, died, or been captured. Few would linger around the downed ships unless they had no other choice."

"And that would be wise of them," Minnix noted. "There have been reports filtering in from travelers that some traces of unusual foot traffic were stumbled upon in the woods. Creatures unlike any they had seen before."

"Humans?" Nyota blurted. "Are you saying there might be others out there?"

"It is indeed possible. But Raxxians have also been sighted roving the area in small groups. Everyone has been avoiding the region for obvious reasons. In all cases it is best to avoid them than engage."

"And by steering clear, the magistrate avoids provoking a diplomatic issue."

"Or an all-out war, for that matter," Minnix added. "No one wants that. Even if it is a fight, we could ultimately win. Warfare is such a drain on resources, none want to bear the burden, and the Raxxians are so brutal the cost in lives alone would negate any real sense of victory."

"Wise words," Korvin acknowledged.

"I have seen war in my day."

"And those who have do not glorify it."

"Indeed," the aide said with a familiar, respectful stare. He may not have been a Bohdzee Guard, but all warriors shared the bond of combat. That, and the respect for life that came with surviving it.

"So, Raxxians are afoot."

"Yes. Our intelligence experts posit they are survivors of the crash who have joined up with one another."

Korvin scowled. "A recapture party, then."

"That is what we have assessed as well. Undoubtedly, they are scouring the area looking to corral the escapees before their recovery ships arrive."

"And let me guess. They are located in Dohrag territory as well."

"Yes, they are. An astute guess."

Korvin stroked his chin a moment, glancing at Nyota. "Not so much of a guess. This explains who killed the Raxxians we saw at the crash site we discovered. Dohrags, almost certainly, and in fair numbers if they took on armed Raxxians head-on."

"Two aggressive races with a penchant for shooting first and asking questions later, for certain," Minnix agreed.

"It makes things difficult, but not impossible."

Nyota threw her hands up in the air. "Hang on a sec. Just hang on. So, if I understand you correctly, what you're saying is we've got *bad* guys, and *worse* guys out there fighting one another. And *that's* where you want us to go?"

"It is where the downed vessels are, so yes."

Nyota felt her face flush. "A real chance at recapture, if not a brutal death, and you want us to just go traipsing in there, wandering about the forest?"

"We will not be wandering. We will have a map."

"Screw the map! We should get a *ride*. I mean, if we're doing this, I mean *really* doing this, then fly us in fast and get us close. At least then we'll stand a chance."

Minnix shook his head. "I am truly sorry, but the magistrate was quite clear. We are to abide by the perimeter set by our military advisers. I wish I could do more to help, but I'm afraid her decision was final."

Nyota began pacing, a knot of anger in her belly. There were humans out there. Possibly the very same people she called friends during their short imprisonment aboard the Raxxian ship. And if that was the case, every hour counted. And here they were, being forced to march into the lion's den on foot, and from a distance no less.

Korvin glanced at her. She could see in his eyes that he sympathized with her frustration. His friend was out there too. His general. And every delay hurt his odds of finding who he sought just as much as hers.

Nyota forced herself to take a deep breath, then another.

"I'm sorry I blew up," she said calmly. "We really do appreciate all you've done for us."

"And I sincerely wish I could help you further."

"No, that's okay," she said, a look of hard resolve sliding across her face. "We'll do this ourselves."

CHAPTER SEVENTEEN

Nyota slept fitfully at best, visions of Raxxians and worse running through her mind, pulling her from any hope of a restful slumber.

Am I really doing this? she asked herself lying awake in the dark of night? *I mean, I'm no soldier. I could just stay in Molok.*

A flare of discomfort twinged in her chest, radiating to her limbs. The new tattoos were unusual in their healing process, and this wasn't the first time she'd experienced a weird feeling since receiving the living pigment.

Whatever the cause, the irksome sensation pulled her from her ponderous, depressive state, setting her sights back on what really mattered. Staying close to Korvin and finding the other human survivors. It was a very real possibility she would never see home again, and she'd be damned if she didn't do everything she could to ensure she wasn't the only human living wherever the hell they were in the galaxy.

"Well, looks like sleep isn't an option," she grumbled, rolling out of bed after only a few hours rest.

She activated the dimmest lighting setting and took what would likely be her last hot shower for some time, then slowly clothed herself in the light but protective attire Korvin had acquired for their trek.

It felt far too thin, not remotely sufficient for their needs, both against poking thorns and uncomfortable weather. But Korvin had assured her it was far more robust than it appeared.

"Costly, but worth the expenditure," he had said before explaining the function of the material.

It made sense, she supposed. Where her kind were still infants in the galactic sense, struggling to simply make it into space without freezing, burning up, or exploding, these cultures were hundreds if not thousands of years more advanced. As such, it was only natural they would have developed materials that could insulate and regulate temperature without requiring the sheer bulk of a clunky Earth space suit.

And if there was Kevlar and other types of flexible, protective fabric back home, it stood to reason that whatever these people had developed would be lighter, thinner, and more flexible than anything she could imagine. And as it turned out, while that was the case if you had money, most common citizens wore relatively regular materials akin to what one would find back on Earth in their daily clothing.

It seemed that just like anywhere else in the world, while the good stuff existed, it came at a price.

Fortunately, with the sizable haul from their salvage trade, along with friends in high places, Korvin had acquired them a respectable and lightweight kit for their needs.

Nyota looked at herself in the mirror projection, admiring the fit of her pants.

"Damn, I need to get another pair of these. They make my ass look *fantastic*," she said with a grin, moving around, enjoying the stretch to the fabric that seemed to hug and lift in all the right places.

She gave her outfit one last look then took a seat, sliding her feet into her new trekking boots. They weren't actually boots, though. At least not in the normal sense. These were entirely alien in design.

Nyota stepped down on the wide open footbed, the pressure making the sides all fold upward around her foot to just above her ankle. The material then quickly shifted and forced itself into a snug but comfortable unit supporting her quite nicely.

They were not overly supple in feel, but had flex in all the right places, just right for hiking. The boots were designed to protect from rocks and whatnot while also supporting the foot and ankle, the fastening mechanism automatically detecting the species and shape of the wearer's foot and adjusting the boot's shape to best accommodate them. No laces, no half sizes not quite fitting right and cutting off circulation. These boots fit like a glove, albeit for the feet.

Nyota rose and took a few steps.

"Nice." She jumped up and down, shifting her weight this way and that. The boots felt almost like a part of her body the way they moved comfortably on her feet. "I could get used to this."

She looked around the room. This was it. There was nothing else to do but wait. She paced back and forth for a few minutes, bored.

"Screw it."

Korvin was just next door, so the walk took her only a few seconds.

"Good, you are prepared," he said when he opened the door. "Come in."

She'd been half hoping, half expecting him to greet her largely undressed due to the hour, but he was fully clothed and bright eyed.

"Did you sleep?" she asked.

"Of course. And you?"

"Oh, yeah. Slept great," she lied. "Just feeling a bit antsy."

"It is normal before an undertaking such as this. You are still welcome to remain in Molok. The magistrate has graciously offered to provide round-the-clock security to watch over—"

"No, I'm coming with," she blurted, that strange flare in her chest forcing the words out in a rush.

He looked at her a long moment then nodded. "Very well," he said, picking up a small knife from the assortment of blades and gear he had laid out on his bed. "Here, I wish for you to have this."

She reached out and accepted the offering, pulling it from its sheath, admiring the craftsmanship. It was a fine knife, well-balanced, and strong, but light, made from some material she'd never seen before. The grip was a composite of some sort with a texture that felt extremely secure in her hand. The blade itself was a deep green with wavy lines barely visible in the metal. Metal, or whatever the substance was.

Looking closely, the pattern kind of reminded her of a gift she'd received a few years back, a faux Damascus chef's knife resting in her kitchen drawer back home. Only, these people were undoubtedly far too advanced to rely on folding and hammering over and over to make a knife. She re-sheathed the blade, feeling how securely it held it in place for so smooth an action.

"Thank you, it's lovely."

"It is a weapon."

"Obviously. But it's still a nice knife. What's the occasion? It's not my birthday, you know."

"I would prefer you armed."

"Aren't we trying to *avoid* the baddies?"

"Ideally, yes. But in any case, please, wear it."

"Okay."

"And the pointed end goes *toward* your enemies."

"Ass," she said with a chuckle. "I know how a knife works."

He met her chuckle with a twinkle in his eye and an amused grin. Like, *genuine* amusement. That was something new. Actual humor? What was going on with him?

As quickly as it had appeared, the smile vanished, replaced by his usual all-work-and-no-play demeanor. Korvin began re-checking his equipment with cool efficiency.

"We depart before dawn. It is a short flight, but I wish for us to be on the ground and well clear of the landing site before sunup. We leave for the transport shortly. Are you absolutely certain you wish to come? Once we take off, there will be no turning back."

"You're not leaving me behind."

He grunted, nodding his head but saying nothing more. Not long after, a member of the flight team came to escort them to the ship. It was a small craft, maneuverable and with a diminutive visual signature. Perfect for making a quick drop-and-run at the edge of hostile territory.

They loaded up, settling into seats that molded to their bodies, holding them in place without the need for straps or safety belts, then took off. The interior lighting was deep red, ensuring their night vision remained intact. They would be landing in the dark, and every little detail mattered.

It was a quick trip, the flight lasting only a few minutes, but Nyota didn't let that deceive her. The faint glimpses she saw flashing by in the darkness from the observation display showed the high rate of speed at which they were flying.

Apparently, the Dohrags had been spotted flying additional sorties in the area the night before, and while they were not typically active at night, the increased activity meant a shift in plans. The flight crew had absolutely no desire of accidentally bumping into them and drawing all of Molok into open conflict. That meant speed, and lots of it.

The ship came in low and fast, dropping to a hover just above the ground in a tiny opening in the trees.

"Watch your step, there's a steep drop not far to your right," the crewmember at the door warned.

"Thank you for your assistance," Korvin replied, hopping to the ground and reaching up to help Nyota down.

She slid into his arms, a flare of heat flooding her body, and more than just what she felt radiating off him. Her tattoos were tingling, a pins and needles sensation that seemed strongest in the rune on her chest. Korvin put her down and stepped back, waving to the ship as it silently lifted off and darted away into the night.

Nyota looked around the area. There was limited moonlight but somehow her night vision seemed better. Sharper. And that was regardless of the ship's red lights.

"The runes are healing," Korvin said, noting her reaction. "Good. It is but a small enhancement, but your senses will be improved moving forward." He turned, quickly surveying their surroundings. "We go this way."

"Is it all going to be like this?" she asked, following his lead as he quietly pressed forward. "Hearing? Smell? What else is going to happen to me?"

"It varies from person to person and species to species. Some individuals feel little change, while others display startling reactions. Only time will tell."

They walked silently for some time, Nyota keeping pace with Korvin's long strides far easier than when they first arrived on this world. She followed close, studying him as he moved through the brush with careful prowess. He was so quiet, not just for a man his size, but for anyone. The way he stepped, pivoting his foot to spread the weight and silence his footfall, how he gently pushed aside small branches to keep them from snapping, all played into his economy of movement.

Nyota did her best to copy him, mimicking the way he moved, although not nearly as successfully. Still, when he glanced back at her and saw her attempts, he actually seemed pleased, going so far as to give her a reassuring nod of encouragement.

Again, not like his usual dour persona of earlier days. It was a shift Nyota could get used to. That is, if he didn't slip back into his dismissive ways.

Korvin slowed and came to a stop. "Come," he said, waving her closer.

Nyota moved up next to him to see what caught his eye.

"Do you see it?" he asked.

She stared where he was pointing with her newly enhanced eyes. A small clear spot in the brush where animals seemed to have passed. At first nothing stood out, but after a moment she saw what he was talking about. A fine loop of wire was camouflaged by leaves, the end of it trailing off into the brush.

"Is that a trap?"

"A snare," he replied.

"Is that bad?"

"No, this is designed for prey, not people. A hunter lay this here."

"So we're safe, then? Or at least safe-ish?"

He let out an amused chuckle. "Oh, not hardly. Similar designs are used against people, and if Dohrags are present, you can be sure some are out there."

"Shit."

"Do not fret. You know what to look for now, so keep your eyes open. And above all, do not stray from the path I walk." With that he continued ahead.

"Wouldn't think of it," she said, taking care to step where he stepped.

She gently rubbed her arms and torso through her clothing

as the thin sheen of rapidly cooling sweat tickled her skin. She would warm up again as they moved, but the sensation at the moment was not exactly pleasant.

The air temperature had increased notably in the last half hour as the sky brightened, and while it wasn't hot, it was certainly no longer bordering on cold as it had been when they landed. But now the sun was cresting the horizon at long last, and with it would come a lot more perspiration.

Nyota reminded herself that she'd have to make sure to hydrate regularly as they walked. Cramping up and slowing their roll was simply not an option.

They covered a fair bit of ground in short order as the terrain shifted from dense growth to more rocky ground. Trees still towered above them, but the spacing was greater, allowing more freedom of movement. It also meant they had to be extra careful where they walked as the ability to see anyone in the area from farther away went both ways.

Nyota's hands rubbed the fabric of her sleeves, her nails making a little friction noise as they passed over them.

"Shh," Korvin quietly chided.

"My tattoos itch," she replied in a hush.

"As they do. Now stop scratching them. They take time to heal."

She dropped her hands and carried on. They walked in renewed silence, but now that she was actively thinking about *not* scratching her new tattoos, the tingly, itchy sensation seemed so much worse. Like telling someone not to think about an elephant, directing her to ignore her itching had much the same effect.

Nyota used her open palm to rub rather than itch, the desire to devolve into full-fledged fingernail scratching glory rising inside her. "How can you stand it?" she asked. "Don't yours itch too?"

"Of course. But I had far less work done than you. Also, I have experienced this sensation before."

"But it tingles."

"Yes."

"And there's that tugging feeling, if that's the right word for it. It feels weird."

Korvin shrugged, not slowing his pace. But now that she mentioned it, he realized that his own tattoos felt a bit different this time. Almost a tugging sensation, as she had described. He pushed the thought aside, attributing it to the Admani Pigment they had received. He'd never had so powerful a pigment blended into his runes before. That was likely the cause of the sensation.

Little did he realize, something more was at play. Something that would change both of their worlds forever.

CHAPTER EIGHTEEN

By mid-morning Korvin had led them a good distance into the hostile territory. As they walked, Nyota found that, as he had predicted, her senses were indeed sharpening even more as her new runes healed, and as the sun rose, it only improved. The pigment was bonding with her body perfectly, it seemed, and as a result she was discovering each of her new enhancements as they unobtrusively did their thing.

Her hearing could now fine tune and focus on distant sounds, for one. The initial realization came when she jumped back fearing the crashing she heard drawing near.

As it turned out, it was merely an animal reacting to their presence and running away. The interesting part, Korvin pointed out, was it was still a fair distance ahead.

"You heard that?" he asked.

"Yeah. It sounded like it was right in front of us."

He gave a satisfied grunt. "Hm. You are adapting faster than most."

"That's a good thing, right?"

"It is. But I will need to instruct you in some basic control techniques so you are not caught off guard like this in the future."

"Okay. What sort of things were you thinking?"

"When we stop for the day, I will walk you through them. For now, we need to focus on our progress. The map of the landing sites the magistrate provided us shows our best options for reaching segments of the downed Raxxian ship."

"Right, I saw. But there were a bunch of them, and they seemed pretty spread out from what I saw."

"Yes, they are. And we are going to have to make a thorough survey of the ones that came down intact." A look of determination and concern spread across his face. "It has been days, and anything could have happened in that time, but one of these locations will be where my general is. I know it."

"Sure, I get your sense of urgency. But remember, he's not the only one who may have survived. There could be other humans out there."

"Yes, as you have already said," he replied almost dismissively.

"Yes, as I said," she shot back. "Hey, just because they're not some military big wigs doesn't mean their lives are any less important."

"I was not saying that."

"Not in so many words, but you sure don't seem to care about finding them."

"As you know, my general is my priority."

"And that's fine, but the humans are mine, okay? We search for everyone. They're my only link to home."

"But you said yourself that you barely knew them. They are not your friends. Your comrades."

"That's not the point. Sure, I may not have known them all that long, but they're still my friends in a way. The others in my holding cell? We supported each other during our captivity, and I owe it to them to do what I can to help if I can."

Korvin stopped in his tracks, turning an annoyed glare at the little human woman. His jaw flexed slightly, but he kept his tone level. "The general is a great man as well as my friend and leader. Compared to civilians? And non-Dotharian subjects at that? He is the clear priority."

"And I'm going after the humans," she shot back, fearlessly staring up at the massive man. "And if I recall correctly, you're supposed to be protecting me, right?"

"It is my duty," he grumbled, knowing where this was heading and grudgingly respecting the power over him she was now flexing.

"Then we look for the humans too. I'm not saying we aren't trying to find your friend as well, but *everyone* is a priority."

Korvin took a deep breath, relaxing his shoulders as he slowly exhaled. "Of course," he said. "I will do as you ask."

"Thank you."

"But we are deep in Dohrag territory, and with Raxxians likely in the area as well. I will abide your request, but you must also do as I say. If I tell you to hide, you hide. If I say run, you run. Do not hesitate, and do not ask questions. Are we in agreement?"

"Sure. You're the expert in all that sort of thing. So long as we're on the same page I'm all good."

"Very well."

"So, which way do we go?" she asked, peering at the holographic map displayed as a small projection from the pocket-sized device the magistrate had provided them.

Korvin studied it a long while, adjusting the angle of the image, zooming in as close as possible on several of the locations marked by the scouting party. A few of the sites appeared to be burned up crash downs. Those would be ignored for now as anyone aboard them would have perished either during the fiery re-entry into the atmosphere, or upon impact. The remaining ones, however, all held the possibility of survivors.

"What do you think?" she asked. "Do we pick one based on proximity?"

He spun the image assessing their options a moment longer before shutting off the projection and tucking the device back into his pocket.

"No. There are signs that the closest has already been picked over."

"You saw that? I didn't—"

"It is subtle, but I have spent many years learning to identify these things. A smaller ship hovered, likely sending a scouting party down to the surface. Treetops were slightly bent, but not from the downed ship."

"You could tell?"

"The angle was different from that caused when the segment landed. A careless mistake, but one I am not surprised a Dohrag would make."

"You really don't like those guys, do you?"

"They are thugs," he sneered. "Brutish, aggressive, without tact or nuance. Yes, a formidable adversary in numbers, but one that lacks the refinement of a proper foe."

"You sound like a samurai with all that 'worthy adversary' talk."

"What is a samurai?"

"It's an old Earth thing. An aristocratic warrior class who served under feudal rulers in a place called Japan. They were often attributed with a sense of honor, justice, and that sort of thing."

"They indeed sound like their morals aligned with those of the Bohdzee."

"Well, yes and no. A lot of that stuff was exaggerated, and from what my ex told me, they were often pretty brutal."

"War is brutality, there is not always a means to avoid that."

"Sure, but he was really into that stuff. Made me watch a ton of old sword fighting movies when we were together."

"Combat by sword is indeed an honorable test of one's skill."

"Yeah, I get it, but the point is, sometimes the legend is not exactly the truth of what really was. You know, like the old saying, history is written by the winners."

Korvin's eyebrows raised slightly. "Oh, I like this saying. A very astute observation."

"Well, you're welcome to it. Let's just hope any run-ins with the Doorags—"

"Dohrags."

"Right. Dohrags. Let's just hope we're the ones writing the history of any encounters."

Korvin patted the large blade sheathed on his hip. "Do not fear. We are no longer walking this world without direction. And we are no longer unarmed." He pointed off in the far distance toward what would have been west on Earth. The direction the sun would eventually set. "We will head to the second closest landing site. A long trek, but our best option for the moment. Any competent survivors would have moved away for the safety of the woods, but I can track them."

"And if there are no tracks?"

"Then we move on to the next, and the next after that, until there are."

CHAPTER NINETEEN

The trek had started out relatively consistent in its difficulty. Ups and downs, some minor gullies, and occasional streams to cross, but otherwise nothing that would have worried Nyota or hindered her keeping up. As the afternoon stretched on and the heat increased, however, the terrain took a turn for the difficult.

On more than one occasion Korvin had been forced to slow his pace so his human tag-along wouldn't fall behind even with her rune improvements. Striding across marshy gaps hopping from rocks to logs was easy for his long, muscular legs, where hers were simply shorter, requiring a bit more finesse.

Then there were the rocky obstructions they hadn't seen in the aerial imaging. Nothing insurmountable, but Korvin had to physically lift her up to grab a hand hold and crest the stone face more than once.

Nyota was torn every time that happened. Frustrated she couldn't quite do it by herself, but excited as his long fingers and powerful hands wrapped around her body tight, carefully holding her securely as he hoisted her up.

"Do you feel it?" he asked of her grasp on the stone above.

"Uh, yeah," she replied, the warm fluttering in her belly

spreading to delightful places the longer his hands lingered on her body.

And linger they seemed to do, holding her perhaps a bit longer than necessary. She figured it was just to make one hundred percent sure she wouldn't fall, but whatever the reason, she enjoyed his touch, regardless.

They trekked on, the most serious of rescue missions at hand. But even so, Nyota had questions. Everything here was so new. So alien. And he took time to answer them, though he rarely slowed his pace.

"Okay, what's that?" she asked, pointing to yet another unfamiliar thing.

"That is a Grommix," he replied patiently as the small animal scurried into the brush.

"Herbivore?"

"Yes. A prey animal for many species. Normally, they do not grow so large."

"Maybe there aren't a lot of predators here."

"Or perhaps they have been driven off by something more dangerous," he replied, his gold-rimmed eyes scanning the area as they had been the entire day.

As of yet, however, they had not come across any sign of the Dohrags. Nor had they encountered a single Raxxian. The fates, it seemed, were on their side. For the time being, at least.

"Korvin?"

"Hm?"

"Can I ask you a question?"

A slight grin tickled his lips. "Is that not what you have been doing all day?"

"Fair enough," she said with a chuckle. "I'm feeling, I don't know, *different* since I got inked. I was wondering. How exactly does this enhancement work?"

"It varies by race. Different abilities are boosted, new ones given."

"I know that part, you've already told me. But some things don't make sense. Like, I get how my legs can feel stronger. As if this pigment could somehow direct more nutrition to my muscles so they work better."

"That is not how the pigments function."

"I get that, but in terms of understanding, thinking of it that way makes sense for me. At least, for muscular things. Even for sight and sound it kinda works. But I saw you make fire with your bare hands. Not rubbing sticks together, but literally making fire from nothing."

Korvin actually slowed a moment, sizing her up with an appraising gaze.

"It is the pigment now bonded to your body. As you become familiar with the way it reacts to your wishes, you will gain the ability to draw from the energy it stores and shares with you."

"Like how it powers my legs."

"Not exactly. That is diverting energy to a large area. A muscle group. To make fire it is the opposite, focusing energy to a point, that concentrated spark igniting into flame."

"So you think fire and it makes fire. Got it."

"It is not so simple. I admire your enthusiasm, and you do possess the runes for it now. Not to mention, healing as quickly as you are, you will soon have the strength. But it will take time to learn to focus and control the power that is now part of your body. Do not become frustrated. It is this way for the newly marked. Some master their skills faster than others, but all require time. This is the natural way."

"Huh. Okay, I think I understand. Kind of like that Qi Gong class I took a few years ago."

"Qi what?"

"It's an Earth thing. Same idea about focusing your body's

energy, but totally different, I guess. We don't have alien microorganisms living in our bodies, after all."

"We all have foreign life forms in our bodies, from our stomachs to our skin. The pigments are just an intentionally placed variety. But we dally and there is much distance to cover yet. Are you capable of increasing your pace now that the terrain has leveled out?"

"Yeah, sure," she replied, not thrilled about speeding up, but also actually feeling pretty good.

"Very well. Stay close."

They pressed on, faster, yes, but not truly pushing the pace. It seemed that despite his declaration, Korvin was still taking her needs into account.

Nyota appreciated it more than he could know, not just for the break it gave her body, but also because it afforded her the opportunity to try something. Something Korvin said she shouldn't even bother attempting for now.

Nyota did not like being told what she couldn't do.

She brought her hands close in front of her body, low and relaxed but not quite touching. She breathed deep, recalling the lessons she'd learned way back when.

Just focus on your gut, she reminded herself. *Picture inhaling a stream of energy, gathering it in your belly, then push it to your hands on the exhale.*

She took steady breaths, imagining a ball of warm power building with every inhalation. After several minutes, she actually started to feel something. Was it energy gathering, hunger pangs, or just her body reacting as she watched Korvin's well-muscled frame as he walked in front of her?

Whatever the case was, she felt ready to try something.

Focus on your hands. Exhale and envision the energy you gathered flowing from your core down your arms and out your hands.

When she'd done the exercise in her Qi Gong class, she

would often feel a warm sensation in her palms as more blood flowed to them from the effort. This, however, was something new.

A slight prickle made her palms begin to itch. Not a tingle, like she expected, but an uncomfortable feeling of tiny needles poking her hands.

Well, that's interesting, she mused, trying again, this time imagining it focusing just from the center of her palms.

The sensation shifted, narrowing a bit, but it was still covering most of her hand.

Practice makes perfect, she reminded herself.

"Are you okay?" Korvin asked.

"Yeah, why?"

"Your pace slowed."

"Oh. I didn't realize. Sorry."

He just grunted and continued on. Nyota kept at her practice, but also focused on staying close. As long as that marvelously sculpted ass was in front of her, she was more than happy to lock her gaze on that target and keep pace.

On and on they moved, the time passing quickly for Nyota as she now had something to take her mind off the actual hiking part of it. Korvin was the eyes and ears of this outing, and she felt entirely confident relying on his years of training to be their warning system. Anything she might see or hear, he would have noticed long before.

The heat grew substantial as the day wore on but eventually the sun passed its apex and began to lower in the sky. They had been trekking all day without her needing to stop once, she realized. This newfound stamina was proving to be pretty amazing.

No sooner had she thought that than Korvin held up his hand, signaling her to stop as he had several times that day. This time, however, his shoulders were relaxed as he sniffed the air. He was scanning the area, but for something else.

"Follow me," he finally said, leading the way deeper into the brush.

They pushed ahead, their boots compressing the dark soil feeding the lush foliage in this area. Finally, he stopped.

"What is it?"

He pointed to the low tree in front of them. "Quinx fruit," he said, pulling a yellow-green orb from the tree. "High in protein as well as minerals and liquid. It has been called the traveler's friend. Here. Taste."

She took the offering and wiped it on her sleeve, then took a bite. A tangy-sweet rush of juice flooded her mouth, her body feeling a surge of energy as soon as the liquid trickled down her throat.

"This is awesome!"

"Yes. One of the core Dotharian crops within the conglomerate."

"How do you mean?"

"The Dotharian Conglomerate is an amalgam of many worlds, and many policies within them, all under one central rule. One of the core tenets is that all habitable worlds are to be seeded with edible plant life. Not all varieties will take hold, naturally, but the idea is that no one within the conglomerate should ever go hungry."

"They literally just go and plant food everywhere they go?"

"It's not quite as simple as that. There are indigenous varieties to take into account which they do not wish to drive to extinction. But as a basic idea, yes."

Nyota marveled at the idea. On Earth, politicians were all about themselves, it seemed. Here, some good was actually being done for the common people.

"It's idyllic," she marveled.

Korvin chuckled. "Not all conglomerate policies are. But the common good of the citizens is of vital importance. It is believed that even those who lack currency should not face the possibility of starvation. If they but use the sweat of their labor, even the poorest among us will have a full belly."

Nyota reached for another fruit. Korvin's warm hand wrapped gently around her wrist. "No, only when they begin to turn yellow are they ripe. The juice of the green ones is still somewhat caustic."

"Eek, my bad," she said, trying to reach for a yellowing one instead. His grip remained firm.

"And you must only eat one a day. Due to the high nutrition composition, one can develop digestive issues if one eats too many."

"Seriously?"

"Trust me. Many hungry parties have learned this lesson the hard way. But I smell Orgla berries nearby. They are delicious and pose no such threat. Come."

"Lead the way."

The berries turned out to be growing on a loamy hillside not far away at all, and as they grew near, even without her newly enhanced sense of smell Nyota would have been able to pick up the gloriously sweet aroma.

Fallen overripe berries squished beneath their boots as they walked to the thick vines.

"Dark ones are best," Korvin said, picking a plump, deep purple specimen and handing it to her.

She popped it into her mouth and bit down. A flavor explosion the likes of which she'd never tasted before washed over her tongue. It was like all of her favorite berries combined in one.

"More!" she said hungrily, plucking several berries and shoving them in her mouth with glee.

"Slowly. There are plenty. No need to rush," Korvin chuckled, picking a few for himself.

They picked and ate as they moved along the snaking vines. Unlike so many berries back on Earth, this plant lacked nasty thorns at every turn, and that lack of prickly pain made the impromptu feast all the more delightful.

Korvin moved just downhill from Nyota, picking some of the less ripe, and thus less likely to go *smoosh*, berries to carry with them in their supplies for later. Better to eat fresh than tap into what they'd brought from Molok if they could.

Nyota, on the other hand, was simply reveling in the moment, flitting about the hillside with a belly full of wonderful, sweet nutrition, her legs re-energized for it. At least, until the ground at her feet broke loose, sending her airborne.

"Shit!" she blurted as she fell.

Korvin moved in a flash on pure instinct, covering the distance faster than she thought possible, wrapping her up in his arms, absorbing the impact. It was a chivalrous move, and it set free the butterflies in her stomach. Unfortunately, it also collapsed the loose soil beneath him, sending them both tumbling down the hill.

Nyota and Korvin rolled for several seconds before coming to a stop. They had managed to avoid any rocks or stumps, but they had seemed to land on every last fallen berry on their descent. As a result, they were quite a mess.

Nyota sat up, her arms held out in disgust as she looked at the dripping, purple mush she'd managed to coat her body with. Korvin just lay there laughing.

"It's not funny!"

"It is at least a *little* funny," he countered, likewise smeared with sticky goo.

Nyota hesitated a moment before the absurdity of the situation sank in. A chuckle rose from her belly, then another, until she was laughing along with him. They lay there, their mirth slowly diminishing until the laughter faded, tears of amusement in their eyes.

Nyota felt wonderful. It was a release of a different kind she hadn't even realized she needed. But this? It was absurd, but also so intimately comfortable and safe. She looked over at Korvin with a happy gaze.

"So, it looks like we're going to be purple from now on."

"Do not worry. The juice does not stain."

She reached for her water container.

"Wait," he cautioned. "The map shows a water source not far from here. And as the day is winding down, and we are in need of a wash, perhaps it will make a good site to bed down for the night."

She put down the container. "Okay, but how far is it?"

"Not too far. A good hike, yes, but nothing you cannot handle. So, do not wash. Conserve your water for drinking."

"But this stuff—" she started to say when he abruptly scooped up a handful of dirt and rubbed it on her arm. "Hey!"

"The dirt will bind with the juice."

"Great. Now I'm purple *and* muddy," she griped.

"It will cover the scent, which we most certainly need to do. It will also diminish the sticky sensation while keeping bugs at bay. Trust me, this will make the rest of the journey easier."

"Ugh, okay," she grumbled, rubbing more dirt onto her body.

Korvin rose and reached down. She accepted his assistance, helping her to her feet. "Look at us," she said with a reluctantly amused grin.

"Yes. Look at us, indeed," he agreed.

Something new was in his eyes. Interest? A degree of care beyond mere duty? She couldn't quite tell. But as quickly as it had appeared it vanished, forced down by his efficiency and drive. He began their renewed trek.

"This way."

They walked for hours, far longer than she'd anticipated, and both worked up a good sweat in the process, the muddy juice forming rivulets on their bodies. By the time they reached the stream he had spotted on the map it was nearly dusk.

"There," he said, pointing to a rocky grotto. "Protection from the current and a wind block."

She followed him down to the shore where he dropped his pack and waded right into the water, clothes and all. Nyota followed suit without hesitation.

The water felt amazing, washing the mud and sticky berry mess from their bodies and clothes. Korvin quickly undressed, thoroughly rinsing his clothes and setting them on the rocks at the shore to dry.

Nyota stripped as well, following suit. She couldn't help but admire his body as he scrubbed himself clean. His muscles gleamed as rivulets of water ran down his body. A now-familiar heat began to grow low in her belly. She turned away, focusing her attention on washing her clothes.

A hot hand gently touched her shoulder, examining her, sending goosebumps across her skin. Her nipples hardened, the skin tight and tingling with enhanced sensations, a static charge running down to her clit.

"Hmm," he said in a low rumble that made her legs feel weak. "Your runes are truly healing faster than expected." He traced his finger along one of the connecting lines until it met a rune on her hip. "Remarkable."

Her body quivered a moment. She turned, looking deep into his violet eyes, the folds between her legs growing warm and wet instantly. His beautiful cock twitched to life, rising as if it had a life of its own.

Nyota reached out without even thinking, instinct taking over as she wrapped her hand around it, feeling the ridges throb with his every heartbeat as he grew even harder. The rune on her chest twinged, sending a new sensation through her body. Deep. Tugging. She felt her cheeks flush.

Korvin's deepened as well. "We must make camp," he blurted, pulling away from her, flustered and confused as he quickly strode to the shore.

She watched him go, wondering what that sensation was and if he had felt it too.

Korvin gathered wood in the nude as his garments dried, the exercise lowering his erection and giving him something else to focus on. Nyota sat waiting for him near the grotto, wearing her panties and top but nothing more.

He dropped the wood and walked to his drying clothing, avoiding her gaze like a shy schoolboy. Something was eating at him, but she had no idea what. Nyota piled the wood into a little teepee then held her hands to it.

Just breathe, she told herself.

The uncomfortable itch in her hands swelled into being but she kept focusing, imagining a pinpoint from each palm directed into the wood. A whiff of smoke rose.

"Holy shit! Did I do that?"

Korvin looked at her, shocked, distracted from whatever was bothering him and actually impressed. "You should not be able to do that so soon. This is highly unusual."

"So that was me?"

"It was," he said, holding his own hands over the wood and starting a proper fire. "You are a quick study, Nyota. *Very* well done. You will be able to make fire far sooner than anticipated."

He turned away from her, letting the heat fully dry his clothes. Her eyes were on him. He could feel it, and his body began to react against his will. He once more forced his erection to subside, then spread a meal out before them.

They ate in silence until it fell dark then lay down to sleep, drawn to each other but not touching. Lying there quietly they both tried to nod off.

They both failed, the uncomfortable tension hanging between them until, at long last, they finally drifted off to sleep.

CHAPTER TWENTY

Though they had only trekked for a day, the combination of distance covered on foot along with that which the Molok transport had taken them had left the travelers a fair distance from the comforts and newly familiar climes of the city. More than that, the weather patterns in this new area were a bit different, thanks to the changes in topography.

As a result, the days were hotter and the nights more temperate, lacking the chill of their earlier arrival. Even so, Nyota and Korvin roused from their slumber to find themselves wrapped up in each other's arms.

Nyota smiled, feeling his warmth radiating over her whole body as she nestled into him. *This* was a good way to start the day.

"Mmmmorning," she purred, stretching languorously, rubbing her ass along the bulge pressing up against it.

Korvin's cock twitched and swelled, his breathing shifting from slow and steady, increasing as he snapped awake.

"What is—" His body tensed, quickly pulling away and leaping to his feet.

"What's the matter?" she asked, rolling over to look up at his confused face.

"I—we need," he stammered. "I must scout a route."

Without another word he turned and jogged away, his sleep thoroughly wiped from his body, whatever restful state he had been in gone entirely. Nyota watched him disappear into the woods upstream from the little grotto they had sheltered in.

"What the hell?"

Her own state of cozy happiness was fading as well, but nowhere near as abruptly as the tattooed alien's had. She lay there a long moment, listening to the gentle flow of the water nearby, wondering what in the world had just happened.

Korvin had his ways, sure, but recently there had been telling moments of warmth as opposed to the way he had treated her when they first met. He was hot and cold with her where before he'd only been on the chilly side. Something was up, but she had no idea what it might be.

Nyota sat a long time in the little grotto, watching as the sun slowly rose higher, raising the temperature and clearing the remnants of mist clinging to the water. It was nearly an hour before Korvin silently appeared at the shoreline.

He stood there a moment, watching, then walked back to join her. He seemed less unsettled than earlier, and frankly she felt a lot better for it. He was her protector, but if he was distracted, she couldn't help but worry he might be hindered in that regard.

"I have reconnoitered and plotted a route," he finally said.

"You were gone a long time."

"I required higher ground. The map shows much, but not all. We are deep in hostile territory now and require a more detailed assessment of our situation."

"Which you got?"

"I scaled a nearby hill and climbed the tallest tree atop it."

"And?"

"And the path is clear. The first landing site on our path is just shy of a day from here."

"I thought it was much closer."

"It is. Or, it should be. But due to the angle from which its images were acquired, the map did not reveal something of importance. Our route must change."

"Raxxians?" she asked, paling at the thought.

"No. This obstacle is natural in origin. Geological. A deep gorge traverses the land ahead of us. It is hidden from sight from above unless one is almost directly atop it. The trees growing nearby create something of an optical illusion, making it seem the ground is level."

"But it's not."

"Correct. Water has formed a break in the terrain."

"Can we cross it?"

"That is our delay. We will have to divert, traveling to a narrower section to make our attempt at crossing."

"Attempt? You're not sure?"

He looked at her a long moment. "I could risk the more difficult section. But you?"

"I get it. I'm just not big and strong enough."

"Do not be upset by it. This is simple physiology. You are not built for this, nor have you trained for it. But we will make the traverse. It will just require a bit of work."

His gaze lingered on her a moment longer then he gathered up his pack and began walking. Nyota hurriedly scooped up her own gear and followed.

It was a relatively short walk, at least compared to the prior day's outing, and they reached the gorge in no time. Nyota saw at once why they had to go around.

"Damn. That's deep."

"And the stone walls are wet and slick with moss. A challenging climb for any who should fall into it."

She listened to the rushing water down below. "If you don't break your neck or drown first."

"Yes, there is that to consider as well," he acknowledged. "Come. Upstream appears to be our best option."

Korvin had packed light for their trek and as a result had not brought any implements for crossing a gaping chasm in the ground. There was no need, the aerial images had not shown any such obstacles from the angle of their vantage point.

But now they were facing precisely that sort of hindrance and Nyota wondered how he planned on making it across. Sure, for all she knew his superpowered runes could allow him to leap across in a single bound. But hers, she was quite sure, could not.

Korvin's matte-bladed knife was put to work as they trekked, slashing down the slender dangling roots from a tree that seemed to pull its water from the moist air. The roots appeared to eventually grow to support the tree itself as well once they reached the ground. It reminded Nyota of what she'd seen on some nature show back home, only these roots were much thinner, almost like string bundled together.

Korvin knotted each to a stick he tucked into the strap of his pack. When he had gathered several, he then began tightly braiding them.

"Tell me you're not planning on us swinging across a gorge with *that*," Nyota said.

"Of course not."

"Good."

"I must add several more layers before this will be thick enough to properly grasp for our crossing."

Nyota did not like the sound of that. Not one bit.

"I'm sorry, but that seems like a really bad idea."

He glanced at her but kept walking and braiding. "We have no rope. As such, I am making one."

"Out of tiny little—"

"Try to break this," he said, cutting her off a piece no longer than her arm.

Nyota wrapped the ends around her hands and pulled. The root dug into her hands but held fast a long moment before finally snapping from the strain.

"The Zuduku's roots have long been used for fashioning all manner of implements, rope being among the most common. I have done this on many occasions when the need arose. Just a few of these strands, when braided, can support an adult's weight. I am merely crafting a rope that will be thick enough for you to grasp more easily. Rest assured, it will not break."

She processed what he was saying, and it made sense, but the idea of swinging across certain death like some alien Tarzan was not her idea of a great plan.

"What if my hands slip?"

"The runes should be giving you greater grip strength by now."

"Fine. But what if? That's a long way down."

"The fall would likely be fatal, yes," he replied matter-of-factly.

"Not helping."

"Apologies. I merely stated a fact. But I can see you are concerned by this relatively simple task."

"For you, maybe. Me, I'm not used to this sort of thing. Back home I try to keep my feet on the ground, not flying through the air above it."

"Do not fret. You will be fine."

Korvin turned his attention back to the lengthening rope in his hands, his long fingers nimbly braiding more of the root fibers into it, adding girth as well as length. It was something he continued for several hours as they walked, cutting more of the hanging roots as they encountered the Zuduku tree, never taking more than a few at a time.

"We do not wish to cause harm to the tree," he explained. "Nor do we wish to make our passage obvious. A few taken from the layer underneath will not raise suspicion, but a larger quantity would reveal our presence to any knowing where to look."

It made perfect sense. It also didn't put Nyota's mind at ease one bit. All she could think about as the coil of rope draped over Korvin's broad shoulders grew longer was the *what if*. What if her hands *did* slip? What if she fell? Lying at the bottom of a gorge, her body broken on the rocks, was not how she envisioned her life ending.

She ruminated on her fate a long while as they trekked, and her fear only grew deeper.

"This is a good spot," Korvin said well into the afternoon, stopping at a somewhat narrower gap in the ground.

"Here?" she replied, looking at the gaping chasm. "Why here?"

"The roots of these trees, do you see the angle at which they grow?"

"Sure, I guess."

"This is what I have been looking for, along with a narrower gap for us to traverse. The roots are positioned in a manner that will give the trees closest to the edge more than adequate leverage to support the force exerted when we cross."

"You mean when we *swing* across."

"Yes, clearly."

Nyota carefully crept toward the edge and peered over. She hurried back, tripping over her feet in her urgency. Her stomach did a flip-flop, and she nearly vomited.

"Nope. Can't do it."

He took her hands in his, a jolt of heat rising in her belly at his touch. Korvin, if he felt it as well, managed to show no signs of it. He turned her hands over in his, squeezing and feeling them in his own. "Of course, you can. Your body is sound, and your hands are strong and unharmed."

He released his warm grip and slid the rope from his body.

"You don't get it. It's too high. I can't."

"You can," he said, tying a thick length of wood as long as his forearm to one end of the rope. "Stand clear," he instructed, then spun the rope a few times before lobbing the weighted end high through the air.

His aim was true on the first attempt, the rope sailing right through a Y-shaped crook in a stout tree's branches on the other side. He tugged hard, making sure the rope was secure, then, when he was satisfied, drove a stake into the ground and wound the other end around it.

"We should not delay," he said. "Come, I will show you how to best hold the rope."

Nyota felt her legs tremble in spite of herself. "I-I can't. I just can't."

"You can."

"No. I really can't." She sank to the ground. "Go on without me. I'll try to find another way."

He stared at her hard a long moment, then sighed. "Very well. I will not leave you behind. It is my obligation."

"But you need to cross."

"And I shall. *We* shall." He bent down and grasped her firmly, one hand around her back, one under her ass as he lifted her easily. "Hold tight," he instructed, pressing her chest to his.

Instinctively, her legs parted, wrapping around him and squeezing tight. She could smell the musk of his sweat, spicy and clean from the day's exertion. His body was hot to the touch, her arms and legs absorbing his heat as they held him in a strong embrace.

"Why—"

"I must keep my pack securely on my back for proper balance."

"But won't I—"

"You will not throw off my movement," he said, his breath hot on her cheek, his lips so close to hers.

Nyota felt a surge of electric tingling between her legs as he gathered up the end of the rope and walked toward the split in the ground, her clit pressing hard against him with every step he took.

Her nipples were hard, jutting out and pressing into his chest. She could feel his heartbeat thundering against her body, so powerful, yet so calm and steady. Just like he was. She turned her face, looking him in the eyes. He met her gaze, a twinge shooting through her chest, running deep into her body when he did.

Nyota swallowed hard. Korvin did too.

His expression shifted abruptly, his eyes moving to the chasm. "Hold firm," was all he said before leaping into the air.

The sensation of weightlessness was less disconcerting pressed against his muscular body. In fact, the feeling was actually enjoyable as she rode him across the gorge. Her heart was pounding hard and fast, but the traverse was only part of the reason.

Korvin's feet landed firmly on the other side of the gap, the impact jarring her from her reverie. His free arm squeezed her tight, making sure she was safe and secure. He glanced down at the woman pressed against him, her arms and legs wrapped around his body. A spark flashed in his eyes. And with it, something different. Something tender.

She felt the swelling in his trousers press up against her and shifted her position slightly, grinding against him with the most delightful pressure. Korvin's pupils dilated as he let out a soft groan.

Abruptly, he released his grip and peeled her from his body, setting her down gently on the ground.

"We, uh... We need to be going. Come along."

He retrieved the rope and wrapped it around his pack then started walking.

What the hell? Nyota wondered as she stood there, her body full of endorphins, scared, aroused, and confused.

She took a moment, composing herself and settling her churning emotions and forcing down her raging libido. Her body did as she told it, thankfully. Walking when that turned on could be uncomfortable to say the least.

"I honestly don't know what his deal is," she said, then with frustrated resolve, she followed him into the brush.

CHAPTER TWENTY-ONE

Nyota found her legs moving with a renewed vigor after her not-so-near-death experience in the arms of her brooding alien companion. The adrenaline, along with whatever the hell they had brewing between them, had left her feeling exhilarated and the day flew by quickly as a result.

It was still going to be a long trek to the downed ship, of that she was certain, but picking up the pace a bit, it was looking like they'd make it there well before night began to fall. At least, she hoped that would be the case. Bumping into Raxxians in the dark was not high on her list of things to do. In fact, it wasn't on it at all.

Fortunately, Korvin had been demonstrating just how keen his sight and hearing really were as they walked. The things he saw and pointed out that she would have missed entirely gave her a feeling of extreme confidence in his abilities. That he was also a highly trained warrior didn't hurt either. But as he had clearly stated, the best fight was the one you could avoid entirely.

If you did have to fight, however, be fast, brutal, and efficient.

Lucky for her, he excelled at all of the above.

They walked mostly in silence, but it seemed more than tactical to Nyota. Yes, they were being cautious of the Dohrag presence, as well as making sure to avoid any Raxxians who might be nearby, but the overall feel was one of communing with nature. As if, after so much time trapped aboard the Raxxian ship, reconnecting with the beauty of the plants and animals was healing them both.

When he did speak, Korvin quietly showed her what other edible plants the Dotharian Conglomerate had seeded the world with, providing a history lesson while also gathering them a moving buffet of sorts as they continued toward their destination. Berries and tubers, edible leaves and stalks, by the time they came upon the broken trees and flattened shrubbery of the landing site, both were full of belly and renewed of spirit.

Korvin held up his hand as they drew close. Nyota crouched behind a bush at once. He flashed an approving nod, then vanished as he moved toward the landing area. Only a few minutes had gone by when he returned.

"You may stand," he said.

"What did you find?"

"Nothing. The compartment landed intact and seems to have avoided any damage on its descent."

"So good news."

"Not exactly. It is also empty."

"Did they make a break for it? Or were they captured?" Nyota wondered, a surge of adrenaline entering her bloodstream.

"Neither. From what I can tell, there was no one aboard. There are no signs of passengers. No footprints. Nothing."

Nyota pondered what the odds were that more of the sections that had made it down in one piece might also be lacking occupants. She had no idea how many prisoners the Raxxians had been holding. For all she knew, the total numbers could have just been a small amount of the ship's capacity. They were all segregated, after all, and aside from a select few aliens, she'd really only mostly seen humans during her imprisonment.

Korvin shook his head ever so slightly in what she assumed was frustration, then turned and walked back into the woods.

"Wait a minute," she called after him. "Don't you want to, I don't know, maybe scavenge for more things to trade? Stuff we can use? You did it before."

He stopped and turned back to face her. "We have a very long trek ahead of us across potentially difficult terrain in hostile territory and with no trading outposts to speak of. Not only are we unlikely to secure any trade, but the additional weight of any salvage would not only slow our progress but also hinder us in the event of attack."

"But what about things we can use, then? Weapons, maybe?"

"We have all we need. As I have said, I will take what we require should the necessity arise."

Nyota looked through the brush at the empty craft just sitting there waiting to be plundered, then sighed and let it go.

He was right, of course. She had been thinking in terms of what they needed as if they hadn't already secured ample currency and equipment. But they had done just that, and to attempt to scavenge more, jeopardizing their situation only to acquire just a little more money would be akin to the old adage about the hierarchy of needs. Namely, at what point are you just accumulating for the sake of it rather than out of genuine necessity?

They needed nothing.

Well, except for the location of the ships that had come down with actual survivors aboard. That bit of information would be worth a pretty penny if only it were readily available information.

But that sort of info wasn't, and thus they were left with precisely what Korvin had said.

A long walk.

And walk they would. All. Damn. Day.

Due to the need for a slower and more cautious approach now that they were in truly hostile territory, it would be one, if not two days before they reached the next section of the Raxxian ship. At least, that's what it seemed from what his map said. Adding insult to injury, it would be getting dark sooner than later, so Korvin reluctantly shifted his focus from covering as much ground as possible to making good headway while also moving somewhat off course but in the direction of protection from the elements where they could bed down for the night.

"We have enough light to make it to those rocks," he said, stepping close and pointing to a distant break in the trees. "Do you see it?"

She felt his heat right beside her, the scent of his musky-sweet sweat filling her nostrils. Nyota's whole body felt the strange pull toward this man, as if he were some undeniable force of nature she simply had no power against. It was crazy, but she almost couldn't help herself.

With every bit of willpower she had she forced those thoughts down, peering along his arm to their eventual campsite.

"Yeah, I see it," she said. "What do you think? A couple of hours?"

"No more than that. And a good thing. It will afford enough time to properly shield ourselves. And then we can work on your firemaking, if you wish."

"Oh, I wish," she replied, turning to face him directly.

Their bodies brushed against one another, a jolt of electricity running through them both, and unlike any static either had ever felt. Suddenly, their trek was the last thing on either of their minds as their bodies asserted their will, urging them closer.

Korvin's cock quickly began to rise of its own accord, the bulge in his trousers swelling in a flash, drawing the fabric tight over his length. Nyota's own arousal spiked at the sight, the ball of heat in her belly quickly spreading lower with a delightful tingle.

Pressing up against him her nipples sent jolts of pleasure to her clit from the contact. Without a thought her hand slid into his waistband, her fingers wrapping around his length, pulling him free in one swift motion, exposing his beautiful cock to the fresh air.

Korvin froze, torn at what he should do as she squeezed and gently pulled. Nyota coaxed a droplet of pre-cum out where it glistened from the tip.

"Oh, yes," she cooed, rubbing her finger in it, sliding up and down his shaft using his own fluids as a warming lubricant.

A low groan was all he could manage, his pulse quickening, thundering in her hand, readily apparent in the raised ridges of his cock as they pulsated under her touch.

Nyota's other hand reached out, wiping a drop from his glans and bringing it to her lips. It was so salty, so masculine, but it also tasted so right. She felt herself nearly dripping with excitement. Tasting him was hot as hell, sending her body temperature spiking with arousal.

Korvin's hand slid down between her legs, his long fingers coating themselves in her juices, curving to slide up inside her. Nyota's body jerked and twitched as his fingers did that delicious rippling thing again, pulsating against her G-spot while his thumb stroked her clit almost on instinct alone.

Both of them were on auto-pilot now, their bodies reacting to each other's spiking arousal, feeding off the increasing desire, working both of them into a frenzy.

His fingers moved strong and steady, hitting the perfect rhythm, and sticking with it as if he somehow knew precisely what she was feeling, certain what to do and what not to do to bring her to climax.

Nyota felt him swell even more in her grip, his cock now rock hard, the raised ridges encircling it hot and firm under her pumping grip. Korvin reached out, grabbing her hair as his body tensed, his balls tightening against his body as a massive load sprayed out of his engorged cock. His right leg nearly buckled from the force of it as wave after wave of pleasure shot through his body.

In sync, Nyota's own orgasm exploded, the bliss flowing through her seemingly linked with his. Her vision went fuzzy and her legs weak as her sopping wet pussy clenched down hard on his fingers. Korvin held her upright and close, his strength easily keeping her on her feet even as they both came together in body-shaking climaxes.

Nyota fell forward into his torso, her head nestling against him, feeling his pounding heartbeat against her cheek, the heat of his body warming her despite the warm sunlight already on them.

Korvin's twitching leg and pulsing cock slowed their contractions as her own bliss finally began to subside. As if they were linked. As if they were feeding off one another, connected through their ecstasy.

They stood there, holding one another close as they both reeled from the moment. It had been so fast. So hot. And most of all, so totally unexpected.

"What the hell just happened?" Nyota managed to say when she regained the power of speech.

Korvin slowly pulled his fingers from inside her, the sensation threatening to make her come yet again. She felt him harden as well, linked to her as her body reacted, her runes tingling and moving within her skin.

She looked up at him with a sex-sated gaze then followed his eyes to their entwined bodies and noticed something odd. His pigment. His runes. She could see them glowing ever so slightly inside his clothes. And they seemed to be shifting. Moving in unison with her own.

Korvin's gaze abruptly went cool, almost panicked.

"No. No, no, no! This cannot be happening," he muttered in shock.

"What? What is it?"

"I thought it was only the Admani Pigment."

"You mean that powerful ink stuff they gave us. Is that what just happened? Did it just do that to us?"

"Yes, perhaps," he said, his demeanor calming a bit. "That may be all it was." The concern, however, was still in his gaze. "But perhaps something more."

Nyota wasn't sure what to make of his cryptic words, but whatever had just happened, she was quite certain she wanted it again. And much, much more of it.

"What do you mean, something more?" she asked, leaning into him.

He pulled back, quickly tucking his still-hard erection into his trousers. "I-I need time to be sure."

"Are you okay?"

"I am fine. I am always fine. But we should not have done this. Not here. Not now."

"What's going on, Korvin? Talk to me."

"Do not worry yourself, Nyota. Just carry on as before and let me worry about it. We must not lose focus. Carelessness will get us captured again. Or worse."

She sure as hell didn't want that to happen, no matter how hot their little tryst might have been.

"So, what do we do, then?"

"Do? We make shelter. We eat. We sleep. Come sunrise, we move out, fast and quiet. We have a mission to complete. My general is out there, and we cannot afford distractions."

She followed close as he led the way, watching him with piqued curiosity as he did exactly what he said he would. He found them shelter just as the sun began to set. He laid out a small assortment of food to eat. Then he helped her focus her power to ignite a small fire around which he built a stone barrier, focusing the heat back towards them while blocking the flames from view.

Then, despite both of their bodies wanting much more of the delightful sample they'd had earlier, they restlessly drifted off into an uneasy sleep.

CHAPTER TWENTY-TWO

Korvin was up before the sun, quick to rise and get ready. The abrupt lack of his body's warmth against her roused Nyota from her slumber. She rolled over, watching him slide into a clean tunic in the dim pre-dawn light.

He was beautiful, the solid curves and lines of his musculature clear even without full sun. His runes, once a mystery to her, now almost made sense in a way, the lines gracefully connecting them, tracing all across his body, the runes themselves strategically placed enhancing all sorts of aspects of his physique.

She thought back to the previous day's little tryst and wondered, *What does the one nestled just above his cock do?*

Korvin glanced at her, and his look told her at once she would not be getting an answer to that question anytime soon. Something had shifted overnight. He was all business. Driven and single-minded in his purpose. Gone were any signs of passion and lack of control she had seen the day before.

But something *had* changed. It was subtle, but she'd spent enough time with him by now to perceive the shift, and it went beyond whatever their little tryst of the other day was. There was a little something in his gaze. Not raw lust or want, but something else. Curiosity, mostly. Pensive wonder, cautious and perhaps a little aroused, but all restrained by his years of training and self-control.

The rune on her chest twinged slightly and she could have sworn he flinched as it did. But that was impossible, wasn't it?

In this strange alien world, it seemed anything was possible, so who could say? Something was up. With them both. What it was didn't matter, at least not at the moment. He was right about one thing. They had to go, and that was that.

Nyota rose to a seated position, peeling off the top she'd slept in and rummaging through her pack for her spare. They traveled light, but not so light that they didn't have one to wear and one to wash.

Her nipples hardened to twin peaks in the cool air. She felt the chill, but also a flash of that familiar arousal that seemed to be constantly lingering just below the surface lately. It was odd, actually. She had always had a healthy libido, but this was becoming almost distracting at this point.

She glanced up. Korvin's gold-rimmed irises faintly gleamed as he watched her, not shy, not looking away. She raised her arms over her head, stretching out long before slowly slipping the clean shirt over her body, pulling it tighter as it descended over her breasts.

Nyota felt a tingle inside as the material grazed across her nipples, and for just a moment she could have sworn she saw the dormant length hanging between Korvin's legs rouse, at least a little.

He broke the stare, quickly shifting his attention to loading the remainder of their things into his pack, which he slid onto his shoulders with ease. Reluctantly, Nyota did the same, the weight settling into place, comfortable for now, but cementing the reality of this morning's task.

They would walk.

A lot.

The terrain was easier than the prior day, and even better, there was no Tarzan routine required as they made their way toward the location of the next downed section of the Raxxian ship. Better still, the trees thinned as they hiked, providing them a much better view of any potential threats as they stayed in the denser portions of the tree line scanning the area.

There were native birds of a sort, colorful and large, gliding on the thermals in the not so far distance, seemingly at ease. Korvin said that meant no Dohrag ships had flown here recently. The skies were a warning system, just like everything else around them, if only one knew where to look.

Crossing from the thicker woods, the footing here was a bit on the rocky side, which hindered larger trees for the most part, but did allow smaller ones to take root. Nyota veered deeper into the shady part toward a cluster of somewhat out-of-place trees.

"Varxin nuts?" Nyota asked as she plucked a large yellow pod from a low branch.

"*Vorxin*," Korvin corrected. "But yes, one of the edible crops placed by the conglomerate.

"And yellow is ripe, right? Orange means not ready, and brown can't be eaten but is good for disinfecting scrapes and cuts."

"You remember all of that from the other day? Good recall."

"When you're stuck on an alien world and someone tells you how to survive, it's probably a good idea to pay attention," she replied with a flirty smile.

Korvin, stoic to the end, nevertheless seemed to have a slight blush rise to his cheeks, and damn if it wasn't the sexiest thing she'd seen in ages.

"You want some?" she asked, ripping open the waxy skin to reveal clusters of small tan nuts the size of small grapes.

"Yes, thank you," he said, accepting the half she offered him. He popped one in his mouth and chewed with gusto. "You picked a good one."

"Of course I did."

He chuckled. "It is more of an art than a science. Vorxin are notoriously fickle about their bounty."

"Hey, I was the gal who could always tell the ripest, sweetest watermelon back home, so you're in good hands."

"A melon that produces water?"

"It's just called that. It's actually really good. Sweet and full of juice."

"Hence the name, I take it?"

"Yeah, that's my guess, though I never actually Googled it."

"What is a Google?"

"Tell you what. If we ever make it back to Earth, I'll teach you all about it."

"A generous offer."

"He says, not knowing what Google is. Now that's a rabbit hole you don't want to go down."

"Nevertheless," he said with a warm look in his eyes. "And this watermelon. You would show me this as well."

"If you can find a way to get me home, I'll show you whatever you want."

Korvin looked away as his cheeks began to flush again. Not what you'd expect of a rough-and-tough soldier by any means.

"Oh, wait! I didn't mean like that," she backpedaled.

Korvin glanced at her, a curious look in his eye as the gears churned behind them. Something was up, definitely, but he wasn't ready to spill what it was. For now, it seemed, she'd just have to wait.

It was late in the afternoon when they arrived at the open clearing where the Raxxian compartment had landed. No trees were broken in this instance as there had been ample room for it to touch down unhindered. This time, though the air was still and quiet, the ship's door stood open.

Korvin gestured for her to stay low as he scouted the craft. Nyota crouched behind cover, watching him dart forward, somehow almost blending in with the landscape despite lacking any actual camouflage. Perhaps it was the way he moved, or maybe his runes were playing some kind of trick on her eyes. Whatever it was, the last thing she saw was his knife in his hand before he vanished into the open door.

She stayed there silently for several minutes, her ears straining to filter out the sounds of nature her enhanced senses were now picking up. It was distracting, but she was just starting to get the hang of it when Korvin squatted down beside her.

"Jesus! You scared the shit out of me!" she hissed.

"Apologies. And thank you for keeping your voice down."

"How the hell did you do that? I didn't see you come out. You're good, but you're not *that* good, are you?"

A slight grin of amusement creased the corners of his lips. "Nothing like that. There was a damaged section of hull we could not see from here further up on the craft. I exited through it and circled back."

"A hole in the ship? So everyone was dead, then?"

"No, actually."

Nyota felt her heart quicken. "You're saying there are survivors?"

"There were, yes. The compartments inside, if sealed, would have survived the extremes of re-entry. And from what I have seen, well, it would be best to show you. Come."

He rose to his feet, taking her around the ship via the tree line before cutting back into the clearing. He stopped well short of the ship on a slightly muddy patch of ground away from the rocks.

"Why'd we stop?"

"Look," he said, pointing at their feet.

She saw the footprints almost immediately. Big, clawed ones stood out, the weight of their owners sinking them deep into the soil. But there were others as well.

"Are those running shoes?" she gasped, bending down for a closer look. "These are from Earth. Humans made these!"

"Indeed. And they headed into the woods in that direction."

"Were they captives or were they escapees?"

"The ground is still wet from what must have been a regional storm, but it would seem the prisoners made theirs first, fleeing the downed ship before the Raxxian retrieval team arrived."

"Then we've got to find them."

"Agreed. But there is something else," he said, pointing toward the rockier ground.

Nyota looked hard until she saw what he was talking about. A boot print, larger than a human's and shockingly familiar. She'd seen that same pattern before, left by her companion when they first arrived.

"One of your people?"

He nodded.

"Is it your friend? Your general?"

"That I cannot say. But a Nimenni survived this landing and is out there somewhere and I must find him."

"So we go looking," Nyota replied, energized, terrified, and shockingly ready to face danger if it meant finding another human.

"We shall. But we must be exceedingly cautious. The Raxxians are tactless brutes aboard their ships, but on the ground they are fierce and skilled adversaries. We would do well not to underestimate them."

"I'm following your lead."

He nodded once then trotted toward the trees, his feet silent on the soft ground. They pushed deep into the woods, tracking the footprints until they diverged at a small boulder.

Nyota looked at the prints, human, Nimenni, and Raxxian. At the landing site she could make sense of them, but here? Here it was beyond her skillset.

"They go both ways. What do we do?"

Korvin cocked his head and listened a moment. "I hear something, but I am not sure what. Remain here. There is a space between this rock and the shrubbery. You will be concealed there."

"Where are you going?"

"Do not fear, I will be back shortly. But I require a tall tree from which to get a better view of the area. We are at a disadvantage here, one I would seek to negate."

With that he turned and jogged off into the woods, leaving Nyota on her own.

"Well, fuck," she grumbled, then slid into the hiding place he'd shown her to wait as long as it took. "This is not how I pictured today going. Not at all."

CHAPTER TWENTY-THREE

Nyota sat as quietly as she could for nearly fifteen minutes, nestled in her cramped hiding place, more than a little irked at Korvin's insistence she not come with him. She understood his concern, but she wasn't the same person he'd carried from the crashed ship. Not by a long shot.

Nyota was new and improved now.

She focused hard, forcing her ears to pick up more sounds than she was normally used to. The enhanced rune behind her ear had definitely gained extra potency from the Skrizzit's repair job and she actually discovered she could sort of zoom in on certain sounds even better than before.

Animals, birds, the wind, all of them were slowly separating from one another as she strained her senses.

There were sounds of nature, but that was all.

"This is stupid," she grumbled. "He shouldn't have just left me behind like that."

She hesitated a moment. He would be annoyed with her, even mad, perhaps, but just sitting there doing nothing, she felt useless. Helpless. And as she had just learned, her new runes were giving her abilities she hadn't even realized she had. It made her confident, wondering what other things she could do now.

"Screw it."

Nyota slid around the rock and back into the open. She looked at the ground in the direction Korvin had headed off following the tracks. Naturally, he had chosen the path that had Nimenni footprints.

While his own prints quickly vanished into the trees, she knew where he would have been going, and this was an obvious enough trail that even she could follow it with relative ease. She took a moment longer to really consider her actions, then made a decision.

"This shouldn't be too hard," she muttered to herself, then headed into the woods, following the remains of the muddy prints.

The terrain shifted from dirt to stone a few times, each of them forcing her to scour the area for where the footprints picked up again. A few times she nearly panicked, wondering if they were gone entirely. But she eventually found traces at the edge of the rocky area.

"Shifted direction," she noted, wondering if this had been a pursuit or a natural, meandering change of course.

There was only one way to find out. That, and Korvin had surely followed the trail with far more ease than she had. He was up ahead, somewhere. All she had to do was catch up.

Nyota walked quickly, pivoting her feet as she stepped as she had observed him doing, the motion spreading her weight as she moved, quieting her footfall. Amazingly, even without actual training, it seemed to work, at least to a degree. She was nowhere near as quiet as he was, but she didn't sound like some beast crashing through the woods.

She walked a good ten minutes when a faint rustling caught her attention. It was just ahead behind a patch of dense foliage.

"Korvin?" she quietly called out.

The sound ceased.

Nyota felt the hair on her neck stand up as she began to think maybe this was not such a good idea after all.

"Got one!" a gruff voice shouted as a meaty, green-scaled hand grabbed her arm from behind.

"Get off me!" she yelled, pulling hard, kicking the Raxxian in the leg as she spun away. With her newfound rune-enhanced strength, she almost slipped free of the brute's grip.

Almost.

"Squirmy one, this is," he growled with malice. "And a pain in my ass."

"Your leg, more like it," his two accomplices said, emerging from the brush. "In any case, more trouble than she's worth. I say we eat this one first. I am hungry from the hunt, and the others have more meat on them anyway. They'll be more appreciated when we rejoin the group."

"Yeah, but we need to bring her back alive first. Ormax will be upset if we don't."

The annoyed Raxxian glared at their captive with open dislike. "She'll still be alive if I just take an arm for now."

"You know what I mean. No cutting off bits until Ormax sees her. The rules are the rules."

"He's right. You don't want to risk angering him," his companion said.

Her captor looked at his two comrades and seemed as if he was about to fire off a retort, but he thought better of it. "Fine."

They started walking, pulling her along by her arm, not even bothering to bind her hands or search her for weapons. They outsized her by a lot, and she was clearly not carrying a firearm, so her threat potential was considered minimal at best. Nevertheless, his grip remained firm.

"What about the rest of the livestock?" he asked.

"This kind are slow and weak. We'll just come back to the search after," was the reply.

Others? That means there are survivors out there. More like me!

"Keep moving," the Raxxian hissed, yanking her arm. "Keep up. Don't make me carry you."

Nyota was about to fire off what was likely a very ill-advised reply when a flash came streaking down from above, landing square atop the two Raxxians leading the way.

"Korvin!"

He ignored her exclamation, already in motion, his knives in his hands, flashing out with deadly intent.

The Raxxians, to their credit, reacted immediately, all three shifting to a fighting stance, though the one holding Nyota was at a bit of a disadvantage. His friends, however, were not.

Korvin spun toward them, blades a blur of deadly kinetic energy. The Raxxians didn't even try to unstrap their larger firearms. There was no time, and the attacker was too close. Instead, they pulled their own blades and engaged as best they could.

Korvin's knives sliced deep into their tough flesh, parting the scales as only a trained warrior could, his aim impeccable. The Raxxians bellowed in pain. At least, they tried to. One found his words cut off as the knife in Korvin's left hand drove up under his chin, piercing the thinner scales and ramming straight through his skull into his brain.

His arms and legs twitched and went limp, pulling the knife from Korvin's hand as he fell. The Nimenni warrior immediately retrained his focus on the other Raxxian before him. The third seemed to be sitting this out. At least for the moment.

Nyota's frozen panic snapped at the sight. She was in the middle of a fight to the death, and unlike the meek prey they perceived her as, she was also armed. Armed and dangerous. Or so she hoped.

Her fingers felt for the small knife strapped to her lower back. The Raxxians hadn't even searched her, missing what would have been obvious had she worn it on her hip.

She felt the texture of the grip and wrapped her fingers around it tight, pulling the knife free and driving it into her captor's shoulder in one fluid motion. The Raxxian cried out in pain, his grip releasing as the blade forced his hand to open, his arm's nerves firing in shock.

Nyota felt her runes pulsing, pouring strength into her limbs, enhancing her speed and stamina as they did. The Raxxian yanked her little knife free and threw it aside.

"I'm going to rip you limb from limb!" he bellowed.

Korvin tried to get between her and her attacker, but his own adversary was proving more difficult than the first. He had been right. They were formidable adversaries, and only a fool would underestimate them.

He dodged a vicious swipe of the alien's clawed hands, doling out a few small cuts as the Raxxian's beefy arms flew past him. He glanced at Nyota, concern clear in his eyes.

But she was feeling good. Better than that. She felt *great*, the strength in her body so much more than any she'd ever experienced. Her captor reached out to snatch her, but she dodged him easily, landing a solid punch to his ribs as she did. In fact, it was so hard she could have sworn she heard a crack. Her hand throbbed from the impact, but the move she'd learned in her cardio kickboxing class had stayed with her in the form of muscle memory.

If she'd done damage, the Raxxian was good at hiding his pain. He shifted his strategy from simple capture to disabling violence, his claws whipping through the air. Again, Nyota evaded his attacks, kicking his legs viciously as she did.

The bones were obviously too strong to break, or even damage from her kicks, but the muscles were taking a beating nonetheless and the Raxxian actually faltered on his cramping legs.

Korvin's expression had shifted from one of worry to one of confused elation—at least until his opponent landed a powerful elbow strike, sending him flying. Korvin tucked in mid-air, rolling out of it as he hit the ground, his feet digging into the soil and launching him right back at the Raxxian, redirecting the momentum at his foe.

The Raxxian blocked the fist coming right at his face with ease. It was only as the other hand—the one holding Korvin's *other* knife—slammed into his chest, that he realized his mistake. It had been a decoy attack, and he had taken the bait.

The tip of the knife sliced deep, penetrating his sternum and opening up his heart as if it were soft butter. The Raxxian looked at him, stunned, then the light went out in his eyes.

Korvin didn't pause to enjoy his victory. He turned his attention immediately to the remaining adversary.

Nyota was fending him off well, or at least as well as an untrained human could, and her blows were seeming to have some effect. Unfortunately, the Raxxian was simply too big, too strong. She was fighting with incredible ferocity, drawing power that should have been beyond her from deep within her runes, but even so it was only a matter of time.

The Raxxian's meaty hand finally made contact, sending the much smaller woman flying. She hit the ground with velocity, the wind knocked out of her, but scrambled back to her feet, her runes glowing faintly as she charged the larger alien.

Korvin watched with awe even as he moved to help her. Abruptly, his own runes twinged, tugging hard through his whole body as he felt a fraction of his impressive power abruptly surge and vanish. But he didn't have time to think about that. Nyota was in jeopardy.

The Raxxian saw her attack a mile away, a wicked grin on his face as he readied his lengthy dagger. The others were dead. That was bad, but it also meant there was no one to complain if he gutted this troublesome creature and dined on her flesh.

Nyota flew through the air. The Raxxian tensed, waiting for just the right moment to impale her and slice her wide open.

Korvin's body slammed into hers, sending her flying into the brush just as the Raxxian swung his blade. The edge skimmed Korvin's shirt, but the robust material managed to survive the cut, although only just. He hit the ground and rolled to his feet, the runes on his arm and wrist churning in his flesh as he rebounded and drove his fist into the Raxxian's throat.

The alien's body was strong. Thick. Protected. But that one spot, while covered with scales like the rest of his body, was susceptible to impact injuries. And Korvin had just delivered one of epic magnitude.

The alien fell to his knees, gasping for breath that would not come as the man who bested him loomed tall above. Korvin bent down and picked up the dropped knife and plunged it into the creature's skull without hesitation.

The Raxxian went limp, crumpling to the ground.

Korvin wiped his hands on the alien's clothing then gathered his knives, cleaning them and resheathing them before retrieving Nyota's blade.

"You have fight in you," he said, a sparkle in his eyes. "You fought well."

She met his gaze, knowing she had just screwed up massively, but feeling a crazy surge of arousal flow through her as well as she stared into those beautiful violet orbs.

"Not well enough," she said, electric sparks surging through her body when her fingers grazed his hand as she accepted the knife.

His pupils widened. She could see his pounding pulse in his

neck, its intensity and rhythm matching hers. This wasn't just exertion. And, clearly, *whatever* this was, he felt it too.

A glimpse of the bodies at their feet quickly snapped Nyota from her reverie.

"What do we do with them? Did I just mess things up big time?"

"No," he said, dragging one of the dead aliens into the brush and covering him with leaves. "You did not. This was a scouting patrol."

"That's bad."

"Not as bad as you might think. Look at the uniforms. These Raxxians are from our downed ship, not a retrieval squad. They were survivors, like us. It is most probable that they have split up and spread out to recapture as many of the escapees as possible. It is their usual tactic, and that means a team like this can go many days without contact with the others. No one will miss them. Not yet, anyway. We still have the advantage."

"Then what now?"

"Now?" he asked, looking up at the sky. "Now we follow the trail while there is light, then if we do not find them before nightfall, we rest and begin again in the morning. Beyond that, I do not know."

CHAPTER TWENTY-FOUR

The fight was done, but Nyota still felt her heart pounding hard in her chest. That sensation, however, was elicited not by combat, but rather by the crazy rush of stimulation she felt every time she grazed up against Korvin's firm physique.

He seemed distracted by the contact as well, which for the seasoned warrior was both unusual as well as a little disconcerting.

They made quick work of the location. Rather than burying the bodies, Korvin arranged them spaced out and in different positions, simulating what the aftermath of an animal attack might look like. His plan was to let the local wildlife cover their tracks, providing them a meal while they provided a plausible cause of death that would also leave no trace of the knife wounds.

After that, they continued on their way. The trail was clear enough for Korvin, and the mud had dried and hardened at this point, preserving the footprints for his skilled eyes. There was no rain on the horizon, so when the inky darkness of night fell it seemed they would be able to bed down with the confidence they could resume their pursuit in the morning.

Korvin led them to a small stream as the last light faded to clean the blood and dirt from themselves. They then dried off as best they could and ate a cold meal, not risking a fire. After that they disposed of the remnants of their food by burying it all, then washed off their hands and headed back toward the trail away from the water where it would be a little warmer that night.

Without the benefit of a fire, it would likely get a bit chilly, and Nyota found herself wet at the thought of feeling his hot body radiating its warmth onto her as they slept.

Or while they were awake.

The stirring heat in her belly had been growing steadily, spiking every time he came closer. Pheromones, survivor's attraction, whatever it was, she wanted him. Needed him. And despite his stoic behavior, she noticed the glances the sexy alien was casting her way, along with the bulge he was trying to hide in his trousers.

Korvin found them a secluded spot near a downed tree, then quickly arranged some fallen branches to provide them proper shelter and windbreak. After layering branches and leaves thickly, it was almost as good as a tent by the time he was done. A tent that would not only help keep out the cold but also keep in any sounds. Perfect for a night in hostile territory.

"So, this is where we sleep?" she asked as he laid out the auto-inflating pads that would keep their bodies safe from the chill of the ground and the poking ends of any loose sticks or rocks.

He surveyed the area with a satisfied nod. "This will do. We are well protected here."

Nyota could feel his heat standing so close to him, smelling the manly aroma of his clean, musky sweat wafting from his body. Her mouth watered a little and her legs shifted, rubbing together. It was intoxicating. Distracting.

"So, it's still early," she said, moving close, pressing up against him.

Her body sparked with joy at his touch, absorbing his heat while her runes sang with wonderful energy. She nestled her head into the welcoming scent of his chest, her hands sliding into his trousers without her even realizing what she was doing.

This was right. This was good. And it was so natural she didn't feel a single conflicting thought in her body.

She squeezed his hardening cock firmly, pulling it up so the tip jutted above his waistband, tugging gently as the pulsing ridges swelled in her hand. Korvin groaned, then made a feeble attempt to push her back.

"I cannot."

"You can. You should."

"No. It is not right."

"It *feels* right to me. And to you too, from what I can tell," she replied squeezing a little harder and coaxing a droplet of pre-cum from him.

He gasped, swallowing hard. "No, I must not. My honor—I am duty bound. I am your protector."

Nyota looked up at his gorgeous eyes, a lustful gleam in her own. "No, you aren't," she said, her desire clear and raw. "You saved my life back there. The debt is repaid. We're even now."

"But—" he tried to protest.

"No buts. That excuse is long gone."

Nyota was not taking no for an answer. Her body was positively vibrating with arousal and there was no way she was not getting what she wanted. It was so unlike her, giving in to raw desire, but the glowing heat had spread from her belly, and she was positively dripping wet, her clit engorged with want, her nipples hard and sending jolts of pleasure through her every time they moved against him.

Korvin put his hand on her shoulder and half-assedly tried

to push her away. Nyota replied by pulling his cock free of his trousers and sliding to her knees, taking his length into her mouth in a single movement before he could protest further.

He was already hard, his impressive manhood firm from her touch. But now, as her tongue swirled across the ridges on his cock, teasing more of that salty, delicious pre-cum out of him, she felt him swell even more in her mouth. His arousal made hers even more intense, his every pulse in rhythm with hers as she sucked him deep, sliding her lips over the ridges, each of them quivering as she pushed his cock to the back of her throat.

She'd never been able to do that before, especially not with someone so big, but her gag reflex somehow seemed to shut down, her mouth and throat receiving him as if every inch was bringing her as much pleasure as she was to him.

Nyota's hand gently cupped his hefty balls as she worked her mouth on his cock, coaxing him to steel-bar hardness. His pulse was pounding under her lips, the heat delicious in her mouth. She felt the rune on his pelvis tickle her nose, the design gently churning, glowing ever so slightly as she increased her pace.

She felt his balls tighten, drawing closer to his body.

"Mmm. Give it to me," she begged, pulling her mouth free just long enough to make her wants clear before taking him back deep into her mouth with the gusto of a starving woman promised a glorious meal.

He groaned, his fingers in her hair. She reached around and grabbed his ass, feeling the chiseled muscles contract hard as he spurted a massive load of hot cum across her tongue, his body trembling beyond his control. Whether it was pheromones or something else, the taste, the sensation, sent her over the edge as well, a climax of her own surprising her, making her body shake as she sucked down every last drop.

Nyota licked her lips greedily. He was delicious. Salty, manly, and perfect. She looked up at him as she licked the underside of his cock, teasing out the last droplets of cum and sucking them off the head with a wet smacking sound.

His body twitched, a fire blazing in his eyes like she'd never seen before. Ravenous. Untethered. And entirely focused on her.

In a flash he had her on her back, her bottoms pulled free in an instant by his powerful hands. She gasped as he buried his face between her legs, his mouth lapping up her juices with gusto sending her entire body trembling with delight.

He latched onto her clit, sucking gently while his tongue worked her nub until it swelled even more in his mouth. The sensations were unlike any she'd ever experienced before, sending bursts of tingling bliss coursing through her body from her head to her feet as she orgasmed again.

Korvin did not relent, coaxing her body as if he knew her every need, her every desire.

"Oh, fuck!" she gasped as he slid his thick fingers inside her. "Oh fuck!"

He looked up at her, a thrilled, wicked gleam in his eyes as he licked his lips then dove back to work, bringing her to even higher levels of arousal than she thought possible.

His tongue, she somehow managed to think. *It's split.*

That explained the incredible sensations she was feeling. At least partly. The two sides of his tongue were working her up into a frenzy, her belly positively radiating sexual heat as his fingers pulsated and undulated inside her, drawing out a half dozen chained orgasms as he stroked the rippling flesh of her G-spot while greedily lapping up her juices.

Nyota's vision blurred, her fingers grabbing tight in his hair, pulling his face against her hard as she bucked with uncontrolled bliss. She stayed there in a near out-of-body state, reveling in the sensations crashing over her before slowly coming to her senses.

Somehow making her eyes focus, she looked down at the gorgeous man gently licking her pussy.

"How did you—" she started to say, but her words fell short as he lifted himself up onto his arms and moved up her body, his slick lips pressing hot and hard against hers, their tongues intertwined in delight, sharing each other's taste with relish.

"Oh!" she gasped when his cock grazed against her thigh, settling atop her quivering clit.

He had just orgasmed minutes before, but he was hard again, his erection at full mast, thick and ready from the taste of her, turned on, throbbing, and wanting so much more.

He looked deep into her eyes, the gold rims of his irises gleaming with bare lust. Their gazes locked on one another, he shifted the angle of his cock and pushed his hips forward.

"Fffffffuck!" she groaned as he slid between her folds, his girth stretching her in a painful pleasure, his own fluids mixing with hers to make the hottest, almost overwhelmingly warming lube she'd ever felt.

He growled with pleasure, pushing himself deeper into her, each ridge of his cock making her body thrash and buck as it pressed inside, the heat and feeling of them making her come all over him as soon as he buried himself in her to the hilt.

Nyota almost couldn't take the pleasure. It was so intense, so visceral, that she worried the atoms of her body would denature into nothing if she came any harder. Then she felt it. The incredible sensation pressed against her clit, drawing out bliss she didn't know she was capable of.

The rune on his pelvis had locked onto her somehow, its power bound to her in wave after wave of ecstasy as he began thrusting hard inside her. Every movement made the ridges of his cock press her G-spot in just the right way as he took her, claiming her with his length, driving hard and fast, his arousal uncontrollable.

His fingers grasped her hair tight as he pounded into her, his girth spreading her delightfully wide with every stroke.

"Mine," he growled, his voice rough like a feral beast.

"Yes! Whatever you want, I'm yours!" she managed to gasp.

His cock swelled even more, another climax fast approaching. Nyota felt his bliss link with hers as her vision went dark. All she could see were swirling spots, all she could hear was the dull thundering of her pulse in her muffled ears. Her body was a thing of ecstasy, her orgasms forcing her out of her right mind as she felt Korvin's cock explode another gush of hot cum deep inside her, sending her right over the edge.

Her hands clawed at his back, her legs wrapping him up tight, holding him deep inside, her grip that of a woman ten times her strength as she bit down on his arm, stifling a scream as her body locked up in a ball of ecstasy.

Even lying still, the orgasms kept coming. Every subtle shift, every beat of his pulse, seemed to coax yet another from her. She'd never experienced anything like it, and had she possessed enough awareness to try to count them she would have lost track after the first few dozen. It was as if a tsunami of sexual perfection had washed over her, powerful, unstoppable, taking her where it wanted without any thought of being denied.

They lay in each other's arms a long time, faces close, breathing each other's breath as they gradually came back to their senses. But rather than move, they stayed that way a good while longer, reveling in the smells, the sensations of their embrace.

Finally, Nyota broke the silence.

"What the hell was that?" she asked, her voice trembling in spite of herself.

Korvin traced his finger up her side, running it under her breast, sending new feelings of arousal through her even as she wondered if she would literally die if she came just one more time.

His touch did not progress to her taut nipple, but rather drew his fingers across the faintly glowing rune in the middle of her chest.

"Infala," he replied tenderly.

"What? The bonding thing you talked about."

He nodded. She looked down at the design embedded in her skin. It seemed to have grown further, if that was possible, the pigment spreading and shifting. And it had begun to change design as well.

"What is this, Korvin?"

He stared at her with none of his usual aloofness. No distancing. He was *present* with her. Fully there, open and raw.

"I believe the Skrizzit commingled the implements during our marking session."

"Commingled?"

"Our blood, our pigment, has mixed."

"What does that even mean?"

"Honestly, I am not sure. We are linked, you and I, though a Nimenni and a human sharing pigment, let alone blood, is unheard of. And to be Infala mates? It should be impossible."

"So, it's weird, is what you're saying. Taboo, even?"

"Yes," he replied, a hungry look in his eyes. "But it is *good*. And I desire more."

Any further questions Nyota might have had were silenced with his lips, and soon enough she was in another world, giving herself completely to this strange, alien man, to the sheer bliss he brought her as they reveled in one another again and again until they were so exhausted, they simply could not continue any longer.

CHAPTER TWENTY-FIVE

With the sun rising and spreading its warmth the following morning, something else rose as well, eager and replenished after a restful night's sleep.

"Again? Can you?" Nyota asked, amazed at the rigid erection rising to greet her pressed against her ass as the big spoon of her lover held her close.

His hands slid to her breasts, teasing her nipples with the expertise none of her former lovers had ever shown. Nyota was wet in an instant, the tingling jolts of pleasure shooting from her nipples to her clit with the most delightful intensity.

No one had ever been able to turn her on like this. So quickly, so deeply. But Korvin was no ordinary man. Not only was he an alien, and a hot as hell one at that, but he could very well be blood and ink bonded to her as well. Feeling that connection blossom now that they had consummated their attraction, she only found herself more eager for his touch.

Korvin's cock was rubbing against her ass, a hot, ridged length of delicious manhood radiating heat and want. She pushed back instinctively, her lips spreading as she moved.

He rubbed against her a moment longer, squeezing her

breasts, his hot breath on her neck just below her ear as she felt him throb with lust. Then his hips shifted, changing his angle and directing his cock between her legs.

Spooning her, he slid back and forth, the thick ridges now coated in her wetness, thumping across her clit delightfully as they both reveled in the intimacy of the moment. Electric jolts of bliss raced through her belly to her toes as they spooned, grinding on one another. Korvin sensed her wants instinctively, one hand sliding to her head, his fingers running through her hair, pulling back firmly, arching her back as his thrusts continued relentlessly.

He was edging her, his cock sliding between her lips and over her clit bringing her to the brink then just barely pulling back, the lust welling up inside her until she almost couldn't take it anymore. From the ragged sound of his breathing, she could tell he couldn't wait much longer either.

The mixture of her wetness and his pre-cum coated them both, heating and lubricating them as they rubbed against one another, spreading over them both.

Nyota's lips curled into a little smile as she felt him angle his hips differently, the head of his cock now grazing her begging hole, her folds sliding around him, enveloping him, pulling him inside.

Korvin groaned, his grip tightening in her hair. He could wait no longer.

With delightful restraint he pushed himself inside slowly, the ridges throbbing against her as each passed her tight threshold and buried themselves deep. She gasped, her body convulsing involuntarily as he filled her with his length.

"Not yet," he whispered in her ear. "Hold it. Hold it for me."

"Yes," she muttered, teetering on the precipice of orgasmic bliss, held back only by his command.

Korvin reveled in their play, in the power of their dynamic, taking her, controlling her, bringing her to the highest peaks of ecstasy as she did the same for him. Their bliss was linked now, the two of them joined in a much deeper way than mere vows could achieve.

Their blood had commingled, their pigment as well, and with it, she now drew from him as he did from her in a mutual exchange of power and want.

His thrusting remained slow, holding her at the brink as he toed the line of release for himself as well, both of them so close to climax it threatened to overwhelm them.

Korvin tightened his grip around her body, squeezing her close as he finally gave in, driving his cock deep into her hard and fast.

"Now," he commanded with a primal growl.

She felt the head of his cock swell even larger as he exploded inside her just as his words unleashed her own orgasm ripping through her body like an earthquake, sending her trembling and shaking in his arms as they rode the climax and crested that peak in unison.

Korvin was still rock hard when he finally pulled out, both of them slick and coated.

"More," she begged, pushing back against him until she felt the head of his cock nestled against her asshole.

"Is this what you desire?" he asked softly, pushing the tip forward as she relaxed into it, allowing him inside as she had taken no other man before him.

"Yesssss," she gasped as he gently slid his cock forward, their juices lubricating it as he buried his length deep in her ass. "Oh, ffffuuuu—" She groaned as his fingers reached down and teased her clit while his cock pumped slowly, tenderly inside her from behind.

"You are mine," he growled in her ear. "And I am yours."

"Yes. All yours," she moaned, her head spinning as she

nearly passed out as a new kind of bliss rose up hard and fast inside of her. Korvin began to thrust faster, working her clit with his expert touch, tingling pleasure spreading though her body yet again as she felt like a pressure cooker about to burst.

Her orgasm hit hard, a variety she'd never felt before, his cock stretching her ass in the most wonderfully filling way, causing every nerve in her body to come alive in an instant.

She jerked and thrashed, climaxing in a way she didn't know possible, the overwhelming sensations of pleasure and pain washing over her, tumbling her senses in a spin cycle of bliss. A burst of heat suddenly shot through her as he somehow came inside her yet again, his body twitching hard as his seemingly endless reservoir of cum had perhaps finally tapped out.

They lay there, breathing hard for a long while before finally pulling apart, dazed in their bliss. At long last, they collected their wits.

The pair wiped themselves off, then picked up their clothes, making their way to the small stream nearby to properly clean up. They held hands as they walked, passionate glances cast between them threatening to interrupt their progress with yet another round.

Miraculously, they reached the water's edge without stopping. Once in the water, the cool splashes seemed to calm their raging hormones, at least for the moment. Somewhat rational and quite sated, they made their way back to their shelter, packed up their gear, and tore the whole thing down, making its parts blend back in with nature, leaving no sign they had ever been there.

Nyota stepped up on a rock, bringing herself level with him, planting a kiss on his sensual lips.

"Where to?" she asked, deliriously happy and not afraid to show it.

He smiled at her and gave her ass a little squeeze. "We go

this way, following the tracks of the Nimenni. Hopefully, it is my general."

"For your sake, I hope so."

"Thank you. We should move quickly. The Raxxians do not like to travel in the cooler air of early morning."

"So, we're safe for a bit."

"Hopefully. We will need to be on our guard, though."

"I've got faith in you," she said with a happy grin, then hopped down with a cheerful bounce and slid her pack over her shoulders. "Lead the way."

Korvin picked up his pack but not before he bent down and gave her a scorching kiss. "Follow me."

The two trekked for a few hours, following the Nimenni bootprints through the woods. It was only when they reached a small clearing that things suddenly became confusing.

"What is this?" she asked, staring at the jumble of tracks. "Wait a second."

Some of the imprints she was quite familiar with by now—the markings of Nimenni boots, as they'd been following all morning. But there were now others as well. Also familiar, but in a far different way. Bootprints, as well as a few bare feet. And all of these prints were human.

Korvin bent and examined them closer. "It would seem two parties of survivors came together in this clearing. I do not, however, see any Raxxian or Dohrag tracks."

Nyota was overflowing with excitement. "You know what this means? There are human survivors out there! Korvin, there are people from my world still alive!"

"Yes, it would seem that way, and they apparently headed away from the area we encountered the Raxxians," he noted. "The Nimenni headed that way," he added, pointing to a different trail.

"Well, obviously we have to find the humans. They'll be lost without help. Your general sounds more than capable of evading the Raxxians."

"And Dohrags. Remember, there are multiple hostile forces in play in this region."

"Right, whatever. The point is, we should get going, like, yesterday. The longer they're out there, the more danger they're in."

Korvin stared at her a long moment, torn, then slowly shook his head.

"My duty lies with my general."

Nyota flinched as if she'd been struck. In a way, she had.

"What do you mean, your duty? I thought you were honor bound to protect me."

"I owed you my life, yes," he replied, a pained look in his eyes. "But as you pointed out, I have returned the favor. The debt is repaid."

"B-but you've got to come with me."

"I cannot. My remaining obligation is one of honor. I must find my general at all costs. But you have grown strong. *Very* strong. And your tracking skills are greatly improved. In addition to that, your new runes will help you as you seek out your friends."

Nyota felt rage and disappointment surging within her, mixing into a potent cocktail of angry spite. "You're seriously going to ditch me? After all that's happened? After this morning? After last night?"

"I—"

"You son of a bitch. I thought you were different. Special."

"I do not mean to disrespect you, and what we have *is* unique. But you fail to grasp that my general is a great man. A warrior of unmatched skills. And having more Nimenni in our group will only serve to strengthen us. To benefit our cause. Adding Heydar to our numbers will provide us a great advantage, whereas, no offense to you, humans tend to be small and weak. They will not provide benefits toward our continued survival."

She stared at him cold and hard, her silence cutting him with every second.

"Please, say something."

She held her tongue a moment longer.

"Nyota—"

"Fuck you, Korvin," she spat. "Fuck you and your general."

With that she spun on her heel and stormed off in the direction the humans had gone. Korvin watched her go and sighed, then turned to follow the Nimenni tracks. She hesitated as she reached the tree line, turning back to take one last look at him, then plunged into the woods.

Korvin stopped a few seconds later, looking over his shoulder at her shrinking figure. A painful tug in his chest pulled at him, but he merely looked at the Infala rune loosely covered by his tunic and sighed. They were close, yes, but the pigment's connection was not yet complete.

Nevertheless, *something* was there between them. A connection of a different sort. He turned back to his path and started walking. Whatever the case, he would have to put that aside and do his duty. It was the Nimenni way.

CHAPTER TWENTY-SIX

Nyota's anger simmered a long while as she trekked through the woods, and with it her runes seemed to pour additional energy to her limbs.

From what she'd seen and felt during their fight with the Raxxians, as well as the revelation that they very well may be sharing blood and pigment, she had to wonder if she was possibly pulling power from Korvin's body rather than her own.

"Serves him right," she grumbled, leaping over a fallen tree with her newly powerful legs.

If indeed they were tapping the same wellspring of energy, she was damn well going to make the most of it. He actually had the gall to say humans were inferior. Weaker.

She had to admit that the others actually *were*, but that was beside the point. They were in a place where other people of his kind existed. But her? These could be the last humans alive outside of back home on Earth, and finding them was paramount.

She stopped in her tracks, head cocked as she listened to the wind. Her hand slid to the hilt of her knife, ready for a fight.

Stock-still she remained for nearly two minutes as the faint sound grew nearer.

"Oh, son of a bitch," she groaned when a small animal no larger than a lamb trotted across the path. It took one look at her and turned tail and ran.

"Yeah, you'd better run before I make lunch out of you," she jokingly muttered.

But now that she thought about it, she actually *was* getting hungry. All of this exertion, stolen energy or not, was taking its toll.

Nyota pushed on, sipping her water as her eyes now scanned the area beyond the faint prints she was following. Korvin had taught her the basics of his tricks of the trade, and she found that she actually had a knack for it. The footprints were becoming easier and easier to spot, allowing her to split her focus as she looked for something other than survivors.

After nearly a half hour a smile spread across her face. "Gotcha."

She pushed through the low brush, careful not to break the small branches or leave any other overt signs of her passage, and made her way to the cluster of fruit. Korvin had pointed out a great many edibles on their journey, and she was now putting that knowledge to good use. And by good use, she meant in her belly.

"Oh, yeah. That hits the spot," she murmured, slurping down a mouthful of juicy fruit.

The sugars and amino acids in the plant hit her system almost immediately, renewing her sense of wellbeing and boosting her energy levels back to normal. She had let her blood sugar fall low, clearly. A mistake she would take care not to let happen again.

She tucked some of the less-ripe fruit in her pack, careful not to pick any that might make her sick but also making sure they weren't so ripe they'd go *squish*, then closed her eyes and sniffed the air.

It was a trick she'd seen Korvin do on occasion, not knowing how in the world he could find fresh water like that. But she was embracing this new power she wielded, and if it really did come from her bond with him, then maybe she could do it too.

A strange sensation tickled the back of her nose. It was almost like walking into a fog bank mid-breath. She turned her head, focusing on the source of the feeling. She opened her eyes, the path now directly ahead of her.

"Water! Holy shit, it actually worked!" she exclaimed.

In less than ten minutes she found herself at a small spring feeding into a slightly larger brook. Korvin had said the water in this area was fresh as long as they drew it close to the source, and this was about as close as she could get. She dipped her finger in cautiously.

"Ow!"

It was hot. Not scalding, but enough to get her attention.

"Lesson learned," she said, filling her water vessel and setting it aside to cool a bit before taking a big drink.

She repeated the process, filling it to the top then heading back to the trail she had been following. Just a few days prior she'd never have been able to find the faint markings of the passage of her fellow humans, but she was not the same woman anymore. Not remotely.

Refreshed and hydrated, Nyota focused once more on the task at hand. "Now, where did you get off to?" she wondered quietly, picking up the trail and following with a keen eye.

The survivors had been walking aimlessly, or so it seemed. What she now saw as obviously edible plants were left untouched and the short game paths leading to fresh water were bypassed entirely. Whoever these people were, their survival skills were clearly lacking.

Reluctantly, she had to admit, perhaps Korvin had been right about them. He was a total dick for saying it to her face, but the guy had a point.

"Don't think about that. Focus," she chided herself. There was still an unknown distance to cover if she hoped to catch up to the survivors. Maybe their slow human bodies would actually be a plus in that regard.

The footprints seemed to follow a thin game path that appeared to weave around a long trail snaking up to a rocky hilltop from what she could see. It would be quite a walk, but what if she could shorten it?

Nyota strode off the trail and grabbed ahold of the rock face.

It was solid, her grip firm and sound.

She looked up. Maybe forty feet or so. Nothing crazy, and scaling it could cut a lot of time off of her pursuit.

She stood there, psyching herself up for the risky climb. "Come on, you can do this. It's not that far, and you're a lot stronger now."

Her body heeded her urging and before she could think twice, she began climbing. The handholds were a bit small, but her grip was more than adequate for the task and in short order she had scampered up a good thirty feet. She was cutting a huge amount of time off her trek, and every foot higher got her that much closer to her fellow survivors.

Thirty-five feet up she could almost feel the top, she was so close. But it was there the rock face had degraded from weather, water, and wind wearing down the surface, leaving it hard to grasp and unstable. Nyota felt the stone in her left hand crumble under her weight.

"Shit! No!" she exclaimed, frantically swinging her leg in an attempt to get a better foothold.

Her feet scraped the rock but could find no purchase as her

hand flailed for a new grip. Then, without warning, she felt her stomach rise to her throat.

She was weightless.

She was falling.

Her mother had always said your life flashes before your eyes when you face death, so live life to its fullest and make sure it would be a show worth watching. But as she plummeted toward the rocks below, all she could think was how little she had done.

How there was still so much more to accomplish.

How she was on an alien goddamn planet, something people on Earth had only dreamed of since the beginning of recorded time, and now her adventure was going to be cut short.

The impact jolted her body hard. The fall was no little thing. But as she lay there, she realized she was still thinking. Breathing. She was still alive. A little sore from the impact, perhaps, but definitely alive.

Then she felt something else. Something familiar. A comforting warmth enveloping her.

Nyota opened her eyes to find the most wonderful sight she could imagine.

"You are all right," Korvin said, a look of deep worry in his violet eyes. "You are safe. Just breathe."

Her heart was racing, adrenaline pretty much taking the place of her blood, so great was her panic. But she listened to his soothing voice and did precisely that, slowing her respirations, feeling the bruises in her ribs where his meaty arms had caught her ache with every breath.

There was no way to avoid injury from a fall that high. Not even with her new runes. But all told, having no broken bones and just some contusions that would surely turn all manner of pretty colors as they healed wasn't so bad.

One other thing she felt loud and clear. Distractingly so, in fact.

Her Infala was thrumming with their joined energy, positively glowing with warmth at his touch. Korvin moved to set her on her feet, but she latched her arms tight around his neck, kissing him hard. His worry quickly shifted to something far warmer as he returned the sentiment.

Nyota finally pulled away, sliding from his arms down onto her feet. "You came back."

"I did."

She studied him for a moment. He was truly worried about her. There was a hint of lingering annoyance, but whatever he might have been feeling when he came after her, seeing her nearly perish had pretty much put that on the back burner.

"I thought you were going the other way. After your friend."

Korvin chose his words carefully when he spoke. She felt he had probably practiced them as he followed her trail.

"For the moment I will help you on your quest. But after we find your friends, I will seek out my own."

"And your oath of honor?"

A pained look flashed across his face, pushed away in an instant. But she had seen it. Korvin was torn. Torn, but had chosen her. Over his friend. His general. His oath.

"We should get moving," he said, ignoring her query.

"But the trail looked like it—"

"I observed wisps of smoke that appeared to be coming from a small fire not far from here."

"How do we know those aren't the bad guys? We could be walking into a trap."

"Because, the Raxxians eat their kills raw, and the Dohrags would never be so careless as to make a smoking fire with damp wood."

"Well, shit. Point taken. Looks like I'm following you, then. Lead the way."

"Are you capable of moving quickly?"

"Why? Is there a reason to rush?"

"I have not seen traces of our adversaries, but if I can easily detect your friends, then they would be able to as well. We must reach them before that happens. If not, there is no telling what could occur."

He turned and began walking quite fast. Nyota, despite her aches, moved fast as well, keeping up with his much longer strides, concern and hope flowing through her. The only question now was who would they find around that campfire?

CHAPTER TWENTY-SEVEN

Korvin moved with speed and grace, weaving through the trees, silently avoiding obstacles that Nyota only saw when he pointed them out in passing, one hand or the other casually gesturing to them on the fly.

She marveled at the ease with which he filled his role of protector, guide, and warrior. He was a thing of beauty, a highly trained expert at ease in his element.

Nyota, for her part, managed to keep up, and aside from a few instances, she was just as quiet as he was, matching his speed and economy of movement as best she could.

He had a sense of restrained urgency to him. He wanted to get this over with as quickly as possible so he could return to his search for his general. And what was it that changed so drastically that he would put aside what he seemed to feel was a sacred vow? Nyota pondered that question as they drew closer to the campfire, the tiniest hint of smoke now reaching her sensitized nose.

He chose me over his friend, she marveled, watching his muscular body with a mix of lust, respect, and awe. *And not just any friend. No one's ever blown off so much as a Sunday football game for me, let alone some kind of war hero general.*

Sure, they'd clicked on a physical level in a way she'd *never* felt with anyone before. Hot damn, after what he'd done, she was sure no one else could ever come close. But even beyond that, here was this absolutely impressive specimen of a man, feared and respected, the sort women would fawn over—and had, back in Molok—and despite all of that, he had chosen her.

A contented glow warmed her belly at the thought. Actions spoke far louder than words, and there was pretty much nothing that could shout his affections for her greater than putting her needs ahead of his own. And while he had been torn at first, the more he committed to it, the easier it seemed to be for him. Natural, even. Instinctive.

And she followed him with that same confidence. There was no doubt here. Whatever had formed between them was real, and they both felt it. They just had to accept it and carry on.

Korvin's hand raised, signaling Nyota to be as stealthy as possible, but she knew his intent before he even gestured, picking up on the slightest shifts in his movement like their own secret shorthand.

They crept forward slowly, circling the source of the smoke. A small fire was visible flickering through the brush, but they could not see who was seated around it. Nyota listened. Silence.

She pointed toward the fire and Korvin gave a small nod. They would go closer.

The pair spread out slightly, approaching from about ten meters apart when they stepped into the small clearing. To Nyota's surprise, the fire was unattended. There was no one there.

"Kor—" she began to say when a war cry rang out from her side.

A scraggly human male charged at her, wielding a makeshift spear, his hair disheveled and his eyes wild.

Nyota spun, deflecting the weapon aside before she could even realize what her body was doing. A fraction of a second later the survivor was flat on his back, Korvin's boot on his chest, and his own spear, snatched from his hands, now pointing at his heart.

"Do you know this male?" Korvin asked. "Or would you prefer I end him?"

She could tell he was not serious, but his prisoner didn't know that. The comment was merely to make the man under his foot fully realize that he had lost. Fighting back would be of no use, so he would have to either use his words or perish.

The tactic seemed to have the desired effect.

"You-you're human!" the man exclaimed, staring at Nyota's clean, alien garb.

"I am." She glanced up at Korvin. "Let him live. I recognize him from the ship."

The man looked at the Nimenni warrior towering above him, his fear shifting to vague recognition. Korvin quickly extinguished the fire, putting an end to the thin plume of smoke this fool had been sending up into the sky.

"Hey, you're like that other guy on the ship. The one who gave us these tattoos behind our ears."

"I am Nimenni, yes."

Nyota was glad to see him coming to his senses, but she still had some pressing questions. "Why did you attack us? What were you thinking?"

"I thought you were one of them," he said, sitting up in the dirt and brushing himself off.

"You thought we were Raxxians?"

"No, not them. The other ones."

"What other ones?" she pressed.

"The ones hunting us. I don't know what they're called, but they have blue-gray skin and really flat noses. Broad foreheads too. When we crashed, we split up to look around. When I got back to the ship, we saw those things snatch Shalia and a few others. I stayed hidden as long as I could but finally came out when the rest of our people got back."

Korvin looked grim. He knew what it meant if the Dohrags had taken them prisoner, especially a female. "You were wise not to engage them," he said. "The Dohrags are formidable adversaries even when you are properly armed for a confrontation. Had you attempted to stop them you would have been killed."

"Oh, believe me, I realized that. The rest of us took off as fast as we could. Fortunately, there was some rain, so we had a bit of cover."

"And you left tracks because of it," Korvin noted. "It is fortunate that happened after the Dohrags had already surveyed your landing site. Had they seen your trail they would have undoubtedly captured the rest of you."

Nyota squatted down in front of him. "Hey, about that. You said there were others. We saw several sets of footprints on the way here. Where are they?"

"We split up to scout a bit. You know, cover a larger area. But that was a full day ago and I haven't seen them since."

"So, you just stayed here in one place?" Korvin asked. He left unsaid that what the man had done was make himself a particularly easy target in the process.

"I figured they'd maybe found something, but I know they'd come back. They wouldn't just leave me here."

"Unless they had no choice," the alien pointed out. "More likely than not, they encountered the crewmates of the Raxxians we came across."

The man paled at the mere mention of their captors. "You've seen them? The green ones, I mean?"

"There is a group of Raxxian survivors from the transport ship we were aboard. They appear to have regrouped into some semblance of organization and are now operating in this general area."

"To kill us?"

"No. They are attempting to retrieve us. We are valuable cargo to them, and it is their protocol to construct a central holding area and then reclaim as much cargo as possible before a proper retrieval unit arrives."

"You mean more of them are coming. Oh man, we're all screwed!"

"More are coming, yes. But it will take some time. From what we have learned, there are many races operating on this planet, and as such, even the Raxxians will have to exhibit a modicum of tact in their actions. They cannot risk blundering into a full-scale conflict. Not over a single transport vessel."

"But these Raxxians, they're out there, right? And they're looking for us?"

Nyota reached out and patted him on the arm. "Hey, it's okay. We already took out three of them. And they don't have a ship. They're on foot, just like the rest of us."

"You killed them?" he asked, shock clear on his face.

"They're tough bastards, but they're not invincible. And it sounds like they've got more of our people." She glanced over at Korvin with a questioning look. He gave a little nod. "We're going to do whatever we can to get them back. And if that means taking out those Raxxians, then so be it."

"What if it's the other ones? The Dohrags?"

"Then we fight them too," she replied. "Can you fight?"

A serious look spread across the man's face. One of grim

determination. Gone was his panic. He wasn't alone anymore. And his new friends had a plan.

"Yeah, I can fight," he said, getting up to his feet.

Korvin tossed his spear back to him. "Then take this. You will need it."

He nodded once. "I'm Steve, by the way."

"Korvin. And I believe you have already met Nyota aboard the ship."

"A pleasure. Well, as much as it can be given the circumstances."

Nyota couldn't help but chuckle. His panic was fading, and his eyes grew clear. This guy was going to be all right.

"Okay then," she said, looking to their de facto leader, "what's our next move?"

"Oh," Korvin said. "It is quite simple. At least in theory. We track them. We find them. We eradicate them and retrieve the others."

"You make it sound easy," Steve joked.

Korvin let out a cold laugh. "It will be anything but, I assure you. But our options are few and our time short. We do this now, or we don't do it at all."

CHAPTER TWENTY-EIGHT

By the time the adrenaline and shock of the whole situation finally began to wear off and realization of the scope of the danger had set in, poor Steve had already committed to the ballsy sneak attack on whoever it was that had taken the other human survivors.

Thinking about the sheer audacity of their mission, as well as the likelihood that they'd all be brutally killed, he had more than a few second thoughts sprinting through his mind. But they'd already covered a lot of ground and were close to the alien camp. To run away would likely mean capture or worse.

There was no turning back. Not now.

"How much farther?" he asked, his voice low, not only for stealth, but to hide the fear in it.

"The ground is rocky, but the signs of passage are clear enough," Korvin replied. "I believe it is Raxxians we face."

"Is that good or bad?" Steve asked.

Korvin gave a little shrug. "That all depends on their numbers. I also hear something akin to the mewling of animals."

"Animals? We're supposed to be looking for the others."

"And so we are." Korvin did his best to soften his next words, but he knew the impact would be substantial. "The sounds? I believe it to be the cries of the captives."

Steve's cheeks flushed. Whether it was fear, anger, or a healthy mix of both, no one was going to ask. He tightened his grip on his spear, his knuckles whitening from the pressure. "So what are we waiting for?"

Nyota watched their little rescue team's latest addition with interest. She didn't know how well he would fare once the shit hit the fan, but she was definitely a fan of his newfound zeal. Korvin's look told a similar tale.

"We will take stock of their positions and numbers," the alien said. "Then we will decide our next steps."

Nyota expected him to do what he usually did after making some sort of proclamation of that sort. Namely, turn and walk off, expecting them to follow. But rather than immediately beginning their final approach, he instead turned and stepped close to her, drawing her near.

She felt the pull of the rune in her chest drawing her to him, somehow sensing his pulse as if it were her own. He leaned down and rested his forehead against hers.

"Korvin, what's going on?" she asked, unexpected tears welling in her eyes, and not from sadness.

He gently wiped her cheek and kissed her tenderly. "You can feel it, I know."

"But *what* am I feeling?"

He pulled open the top of his tunic, then reached out and carefully did the same to the top of her shirt. At first, she didn't know what he was showing her, but then the Infala rune on her chest twinged, drawing her eyes to its shifting lines.

It had grown since just the day before. Changed. Evolved. And, she realized, so had his. Their Infalas were both reshaping themselves, becoming the same design on each of their bodies. They weren't quite identical yet, but it was plain to see it was only a matter of time. And with the speed this transformation had already occurred, it could be a short time at that.

Nyota felt a strong pull in her chest. One that spread through her entire body, drawing her closer to him. "What does it mean, Korvin?"

A genuine smile teased his lips, a tiny teardrop glistening in the corner of one eye.

"I had given up hope it would ever happen for me," he said, emotion charging his voice. "After so long, all these years, I accepted my fate. I never thought I would—"

"Would what?"

The fire in his eyes flamed bright as he stared into hers. "Find her. You."

"Me? What are you talking about?"

"It is certain now. Our Infalas are linked. They are becoming as one. Perhaps it was the Skrizzit's error mingling our blood and pigment. Perhaps it was just fate. Whatever the reason, we are very soon to become bonded mates."

"But—"

"You are my true love, Nyota. My only. My destined one. I accept that now. And I will *always* protect you. Keep you safe. I will never leave you again. Ever."

The look of raw emotion and passion in his eyes was positively smoldering, even in the dangerous situation in which they currently found themselves. Maybe even more so because of it. Nyota felt her knees almost weaken, but something else triggered in her even more strongly.

She shifted her legs, the hot tingle between them a distraction she could ill afford right now. They had a job to do, and she couldn't get derailed, not even for a quickie. And besides, with Steve there, they really didn't have the option anyway. That is, unless Korvin had an exhibitionist streak in him she didn't know about.

The thought made her arousal spike even further, though quite against her will.

Stop it, she told herself. *Down girl. Not now. Not yet.* She pinched her leg. Hard. "Are you serious? You're not fucking with me, are you?"

"We do not joke about the Infala bond."

She swallowed hard, wet and ready for him, as inappropriate as it might be given the circumstances. "Okay, then. We really need to find the others, kick some alien ass, and get back to Molok, because we have *things* to do, you and I."

The joy in his eyes relayed that he knew precisely what she was talking about. And he was very much on the same page. Poor Steve, however, was not.

He stood there quietly, confused by these utterly unexpected pronouncements of undying love. He was an alie; she was a human. And they'd only just met, no less. It was all pretty weird, to say the least.

But then he was a human abducted by lizard-like aliens, crash landed on another planet, and now fighting for his very survival at the side of a different alien and his human lover. Relatively speaking, *everything* was pretty weird right about now.

"Uh, guys?" he said, breaking the moment. "I hate to rain on anyone's fun time, but shouldn't we be going?"

Korvin gave Nyota one more passionate look then forced his emotions back into the strongbox in which he normally kept them locked away. There would be time for that later, oh yes. But right now they had work to do.

He drew one of his knives and pointed ahead. "Through there we will find what we are looking for. We do *not* let ourselves be known no matter what you may see. We will have one chance to do this. *One.* And we must make it count."

CHAPTER TWENTY-NINE

Steve handled the somewhat awkward third-wheel position he was abruptly thrust into as well as could be expected. He didn't know how or why the human and alien seemed to be so enraptured with each other—especially in so short a time span—but he wisely kept any questions to himself. They were in a dangerous situation and curiosity wouldn't help but could be a distraction that might hinder their rescue plan.

Plus, he really did not want to be recaptured or killed.

The trio crept along, staying low in the brush as they pushed forward, closing the distance to the murmuring voices and cries of the captives.

"Raxxians," he confirmed to his companions in a hush when they got close enough to make out the sounds of the voices better.

The Raxxians had a distinctive way of speaking that even with translation runes still came across in a very particular fashion. At least now they knew who they were dealing with. And from what he'd said earlier, while tough on their own, the Raxxians would at least not have the support of a proper retrieval team. Not yet, anyway.

Dohrags, on the other hand, appeared to control the airspace, and with a supply hub in orbit, they would have been a far more difficult adversary to overcome. The team continued on, not exactly at ease, but a bit more confident now that they had more information.

Sometimes not knowing was worse than the reality of a situation, no matter how difficult that might be.

Korvin froze abruptly, his hand up. Nyota froze immediately as well, her muscles tense, senses on high alert. Steve did his best to mimic her reaction though he nearly bumped into her with the sudden stop.

Korvin backtracked a step and pointed off to their left side. Nyota nodded but Steve shrugged his confusion.

"Trap," Korvin whispered, his fingers moving close to the fine wire loop coated in dirt laying right where someone might place a foot if they happened to be going this direction. If not for the recent rain making the ground muddy, then dry again, it might have been entirely undetectable, so fine was the wire's material.

"Raxxian?" Nyota asked quietly.

Korvin shook his head. "No. Possibly Dohrag, but possibly something else. This is old and has been here at least a month. And the design of it is not really Dohrag style."

She nodded her understanding. "So who, then?"

"I cannot say. Whoever set this trap, we must assume there are others. Step where I step. Do not stray. Frankly, it appears to have been blind luck the Raxxians did not stumble into one of these."

"Sometimes, luck favors the bad guys too," Steve muttered.

Korvin gave a little nod. "Well said. Now, stay close, stay alert, and from this point on stay absolutely silent unless it is of vital importance."

Nyota and Steve nodded their understanding, lips zipped tight.

They moved much slower now that Korvin had to scan the ground as well as look out for any Raxxian guards. They were fortunate that their adversaries tended to be brutish and overconfident due to their size, strength, and numbers, making them somewhat lax in the use of sentries.

Adding to that mentality was the fact that these particular Raxxians were survivors of the downed ship, and their mindset had been that of guards looking after a flock of livestock, not potentially dangerous prisoners. And now that they had regrouped with others who had come down in the same area, they were performing their duties as handlers rather than soldiers.

Retrieval of unarmed livestock was the order of business, and they were good at their job. Tracking, overpowering, and collecting the livestock for when the retrieval team finally arrived was not only their focus, it was absolutely essential for them to be well received by command when they were brought back to the fleet.

Their ship coming under fire was beyond their control. Capturing the escaped livestock was not.

Creeping as close to the edge of the protective trees and bushes as he dared, Korvin pointed to the Raxxians scattered around the small clearing. There were a lot of them. At least seven, perhaps more. But their demeanor was relaxed, almost casual, and their attention was focused on the makeshift pens holding the recaptured cargo.

Nary a perimeter guard was in sight. All they cared about was keeping this lot safely under lock and key until the retrieval team took them off their hands. A few were sitting in a small circle, tearing meat off of bones with their sharp teeth. As

Korbin had said, they did not use fire to cook their food. They ate it raw.

Nyota felt hot bile rise in her throat at the sight of a human leg, a woman's, by the look of it, with huge bites taken from it, laying in a pile of dismembered body parts. Whether this one had perished in the crash or been killed by the Raxxians didn't matter. Someone she might have known was now slowly digesting in these bastards' bellies.

Korvin remained calm, taking in every detail with his trained eyes. He noted the precise location of the guards, those merely resting, and where their supplies were staged. Notably, weapons were limited to small arms, blades, and only one heavier rifle. These Raxxians had been working simple guard duty when the sections they were in separated from the ship's core, and as a result they were only armed with what they had been carrying at the time.

The prisoners were separated into three crude pens, each with a guard sitting at its entrance. They seemed to have just shoved them in with little regard for gender or species, though the larger, stronger captives were spread between them, likely to ensure only one strong enough to be trouble could act up at any one time.

Korvin pointed at the farthest pen. Nyota's eyes widened. There was another Nimenni being held. It wasn't the one she'd seen before, Korvin's general, but someone else. Sitting with him were two human women.

Unlike the other prisoners, this Nimenni's hands appeared to be bound behind his back and he had more than a few bruises and scrapes. Someone, it seemed, had made their recapture difficult.

Three aliens she hadn't previously encountered were split up in the other pens along with one more human, this one a male. Sitting quietly, he appeared to be quite beaten up. All were wearing tattered clothes, but none of the man's injuries appeared fatal. Nevertheless, it was apparent that his recapture had been a violent one.

Korvin held up his hand and motioned for Nyota and Steve to stay there. He then crept through the brush, making his way to the far pen where his comrade was imprisoned, moving like a deadly cat, impossibly silent for a man his size.

Nyota and Steve couldn't see where he went, but the Nimenni soldier's head turned ever so slightly a few minutes later, as if he was listening to something just over his shoulder. The Raxxian sitting outside the gate to the pen didn't appear to hear a thing.

The slightest bit of movement became visible just behind the holding pen. Nyota squinted, her enhanced eyes focusing hard to track what she was seeing. It was a stick. A stick pushing something forward incredibly slowly. Its shape was familiar once she had it square in her line of sight. One of Korvin's wicked knives.

It slid right up to the Nimenni's hip, the stick vanishing in an instant. The Nimenni didn't look down. He didn't do anything but slowly shake his head, looking at the two humans sharing his confinement.

The women seemed to get his meaning and looked away. To Nyota it seemed a bit of overacting, but so long as it didn't draw attention to their penmate, it didn't matter much.

He shifted his hip, concealing the blade behind him, one hand casually sliding to the ground and palming the hilt, pressing the blade flat against his forearm, hiding it from view as he slowly worked the edge against his bindings until his hands were free.

All of this he did without a single change in his facial expression. In fact, he looked almost bored.

He winked at the two women who were watching him with a

mix of hope and confusion and whispered something, his eyes gesturing toward their guard. The two women, stressed as they were, took the hint and began bickering. Not too loudly, but enough to provide him a little cover for his own covert conversation.

"Who is here?" he whispered, not turning his head.

"It is Korvin. Good to see you, Halvax. Have you any word of our general?"

"Heydar? I have not seen him since our capture."

"No information at all?"

"I believe he lives. The one with the long blade hanging on the left of his belt is called Nimmix. He is this group's leader."

"And you believe he knows where the general is?"

"He mentioned Heydar's name soon after I was recaptured. I did not hear specific details, but I believe he has an idea where he was lost."

"Then we must interrogate him."

"Indeed."

"Are you injured, or can you fight?"

Halvax's lips creased into a little grin. "Brother, I can *always* fight."

A smile crept onto Korvin's face as well. His friend, his brother in arms, was alive, and it felt good having a trusted ally ready to fight at his side. And against this many armed Raxxians, he'd need all the help he could get.

"I will rejoin the others and devise a plan. Be ready to act when the time comes."

"Others? Are more of us with you?"

"Not exactly. Two humans, actually."

"Oh," the captive said, disappointed. "Too bad."

"There is much to tell you. But first things first. We must get you free and take this Nimmix captive."

Movement from the bushes caught both of their attention. A

Raxxian strode out, tightening his waist strap having apparently just relieved himself. From where he stepped into the clearing, he had a clear view of the Nimenni hiding just behind the prisoners' pen.

"Intruder!" he bellowed, his hand instinctively grasping his back looking for a slung rifle.

But the lone rifle possessed by the group was leaning up against a tree across the encampment. The guard immediately realized his error, drawing his knife as quickly as he could.

Korvin was already upon him.

The fight was short and violent with Korvin coming out on top, but the element of surprise was gone. The other Raxxians leapt to their feet, a call to arms echoing among them.

"Go!" Halvax urged. "I will join you momentarily.

Korvin didn't hesitate, rushing into battle against the superior forces. Halvax charged the gate, his knife slicing the cordage holding it shut with ease. The guard outside, however, was not going to be so easy, and he found himself locked in a pitched battle with the stocky alien.

"They need our help!" Nyota exclaimed.

"But he said—"

"Fuck that!" she cut Steve's protest short, grabbing her knife and bursting into the clearing.

"Well, shit," Steve grumbled, following her into the fray, his spear held at the ready.

Nyota raced to the holding pens, cutting the binding of the first gate as quickly as she could. Steve was moving for the other before he realized he was carrying a spear, not a blade. He quickly turned to face the Raxxian defenders, jabbing at them with the pointy stick, amazed it was actually holding them at bay. At least, for the moment.

Nyota moved toward the other pen, but the guard charged her, blocking the path and putting her on the defensive. Seeing this, the remaining Raxxians seemed to realize more action was needed than simply corralling these escapees into a pen and a proper fight broke out in full.

Steve did the best he could, though that consisted mainly of using his spear to keep the Raxxians from attacking en mass as Nyota fought the guard. She was drawing from her runes, pulling energy and skill from Korvin's as well as her own, and she was actually giving the Raxxian a run for his money. She had improved, and a lot, at that.

Halvax engaged a second Raxxian as best he could. He was good, but he was injured and moving at reduced capacity as a result. Handling two at once was the upper end of his limits.

Korvin, however, had no such handicap.

Nyota was focused on her own fight, but she caught glimpses of her lover mowing down his adversaries with brutal efficiency, disarming them both figuratively and literally as his blade flashed into action.

A lucky punch shook him, knocking him into another's kick, but that only seemed to enrage him, sending more force to his attacks. Korvin dove forward, plowing his hard elbow into the nearest Raxxian's temple, his pulsing runes helping drive the attack hard enough to crack the alien's skull.

Korvin didn't slow to enjoy his handiwork, spinning toward the next nearest adversary and gutting him from belly to neck in a single, vicious blow. The Raxxian fell in a twitching heap, a threat no more.

He glanced at Nyota, a feeling of pure joy washing over him as he watched her fight with far more skill than she ever knew she had. His runes twinged a bit, but he was enjoying the feeling, knowing his power was protecting his love.

Out of the corner of his eye he saw the one called Nimmix snatch up the group's lone rifle and charge straight toward Nyota.

"No!" he bellowed, leaping through the air just as Nimmix lined up a shot.

He slammed into the rifle just as it discharged, taking a portion of the hit while directing the bulk of it harmlessly aside. Nimmix didn't hesitate, dropping the larger weapon and pulling a smaller pistol free. He aimed at Nyota and was about to pull the trigger when he fell to his knees, the hilt of the long knife protruding from his chest. Nimmix looked at Korvin in disbelief, then collapsed, bleeding out on the rocky ground.

Korvin, Halvax, and Nyota closed ranks, working together to ensure the rest of the Raxxian guards soon met the same fate. Breathing hard and dripping with blood that was mostly not their own, the rescuers stood looming over the dead and dying, victorious, but at a cost.

Korvin and Nyota hugged hard, each wincing from their injuries.

"You okay?" she asked, worry and love in her gaze.

"I will live. And you, my love? Are you injured?"

"Nothing I won't survive, thanks to you."

The two stood there, quietly happy, satisfied they had won the day. Halvax, however, looked concerned. Concerned and *angry*. He rushed to examine Nimmix's inert body. He pulled the knife free and threw it to the ground at Korvin's feet.

"You killed him," he said with a marked chill in his voice.

"I did," Korvin replied calmly.

"The only one who might know where the general is. And you killed him. What were you thinking?"

Korvin glanced at Nyota then back to his friend. "She was in danger. There was no other option."

"But the general!" Halvax exclaimed, his exasperation almost palpable, his anger rising behind his frighteningly calm gaze. "Nothing takes priority over him. *Nothing*. And certainly nothing as inconsequential as an escaped human prisoner."

Korvin was clearly upset by his friend's words, but rather than rush headlong into an argument, his shoulders slumped ever so slightly. He looked at Nyota once more, then back to his comrade.

"As I said, there was no other option. I did what I did for her. And I would do it again without hesitation."

"What has gotten into your head? I have been at your side through countless battles and never heard such nonsense. This is not you speaking. What have they done to you?"

Korvin's expression was pained, but unapologetic. "They did nothing. But things have changed."

He pulled off his bloody tunic in a single motion, his sweat-glistening muscles pumped from battle. It wasn't that which caught his friend's eye. It was the glow of his runes. A glow he had never seen before.

Halvax stared, unsure what to make of this. "Your runes..."

Korvin nodded. "Yes." He then reached out and gently shifted Nyota's top, exposing her Infala rune. The transformation was complete. Both of them now possessed identical glowing Infalas. They were bonded for life in a way only death could end.

Halvax's demeanor flipped a full one-eighty at the sight. Suddenly, all was clear. No matter your duties, no matter your obligations, your Infala mate *always* came first. It was just he'd assumed Korvin would never find his, as was the case with so many professional soldiers. Especially members of the elite Bohdzee Guard.

"I had no idea."

"I know."

"Many apologies for my tone, my brother."

"You did not know. How could you?"

Halvax dropped his blade and gave Korvin a fierce hug, his anger replaced by nothing but happiness for his comrade. "This is monumental. Absolutely monumental. Many happy days and warm nights to you. To you both."

"Thank you, my friend."

"Yeah, thanks," Nyota added. "I'm Nyota, by the way. We kind of skipped the formal introductions, what with the whole battle and all."

Halvax chuckled, amused mirth in his eyes. "She has wit. Wit and fire. I can see she will be a perfect counterpart for you. I am Halvax. A dear friend of your mate. And now a dear friend of yours as well."

A throat cleared nearby. "Uh, I'm Steve," the spear-toting human chimed in. "Just in case anyone was wondering."

The other survivors, freed from their pens, gathered round as well, grateful for their rescue and unsure what to do now that they had their freedom. Korvin's answer was simple.

"We take all we can then leave at once, putting as much ground between ourselves and this place as we can."

"Okay, but what then?" the injured human asked.

"Then? Then we get you to safety. We have friends in a city not far from here. It will be a bit of a walk, but I promise, you will be safe and well-treated there."

The survivors glanced at one another. There was no other even remotely good option. And this guy had just saved them.

"All right," the man said. "When do we start?"

Korvin grinned. "We start *now*."

CHAPTER THIRTY

Despite their exhaustion, fear, and injuries, the rescued survivors kept pace as they fled the Raxxian encampment.

Fear was one hell of a motivation, and the revelation that their former captors were not the only nasty sorts roaming this area only served to make them move faster, their aches and pains fading away—at least until they finally stopped for the night.

They covered a lot of distance before the sun set behind the distant mountain range, but Korvin made it quite clear, this was still deep in enemy territory. As such, that meant a bit more discomfort for the time being. No fire would be lit, not after such a daring escape. Whether Raxxian or Dohrag, if anyone came across the remains of the slaughtered guards, a search for survivors—and with them a significant profit—would certainly ensue.

Fortunately, no ships flew over as they bedded down for the night beneath a dense copse of trees. Korvin and Halvax spread out, forming a moving sentry line to patrol the perimeter, while the aliens among the group—members of the Dotharian

Conglomerate, all of them—joined Nyota to search for what food they could scavenge in the area the Nimenni had declared their safe zone for the night.

All ate well, the taste of food, even just simple raw plants, was so much better without the shackles of bondage looming over them. And when sleep came upon them, it was sweeter than they'd felt in days.

At least, for most of them.

Korvin and Nyota were painfully awake, nestled close but unable to engage in the acts their bodies were screaming out for them to do. He was hard, pressed up against her ass, his arms wrapped around her tight. For her part, Nyota was wet and ready for him from the moment they lay down together.

But the safety of the group dictated they sleep close in a protective group. Should the enemy come upon them it would be far easier to defend themselves and less likely they'd lose contact with any of their number.

And so it was they spent their first night as Infala bonded mates in a most chaste manner.

It was not at all the way things usually went.

The following morning all were up with the sun and back on the move only a short while after, the cobwebs of sleep gone in a flash. The sense of urgency was not something that had to be reiterated to any. Freedom lay ahead, misery and death behind.

Korvin and Halvax took the front and rear of the group, respectively, handing off the salvaged Raxxian rifle to the new lead man and switching places periodically throughout the day to keep their eyes keen and engaged. Even for them, too many hours of the same old thing could sometimes dampen their sharp attention, and that was something they could ill afford.

Halvax appeared to take quite a liking to Nyota now that the drama of the prior day was behind them, and he did not show a single trace of irritation toward either of them since their big reveal. If anything, he almost seemed a little jealous.

"It must be amazing," he said during one of his and Korvin's swap overs. "To actually feel the bond. Tell me, is it all they say?"

Korvin's cheeks flushed slightly. "More, my friend. And I hope one day you experience it yourself."

"Not likely, for our sort."

"And so I thought as well, but here I am," Korvin replied, a smile spreading across his lips as he caught Nyota's flirtatious gaze upon him.

Halvax chuckled. "She wants to do things to you, you know. All sorts of things, I would wager."

"And I would let her, most willingly. But we are only just bonded, and this is not the time or place to complete our bonding."

"And how are you faring in that regard? Is it terribly uncomfortable?"

"What do you mean, brother?"

"I mean, the looks she sends your way. The comments. The grazing touches as you pass one another. It must be maddening for you, not consummating the bonding yet."

"With so many around, it is impractical," Korvin noted, glancing at the others. "But yes, it does grow...*uncomfortable*."

Halvax had sympathetic amusement overflowing in his grin. "Uncomfortable? Oh, Korvin. We have tended each other's wounds in the battlefield for longer than I care to admit. You do not need to mince words with me."

Korvin chuckled. "Well said, my friend. Well said. The truth of the matter is yes, it is becoming distracting. Almost painful, in fact."

"As one would expect of two Infalas denied their final bonding."

"Like I said, it is not practical."

"Practical has never been our strong suit anyway." Halvax's voice lowered as his eyes skimmed over their herd of wayward survivors. "Listen, I am moving to take the lead. We have not seen anything of concern all day. If you and Nyota were to fall behind a bit, I do not think any would notice."

Korvin felt his Infala flare and his cock twitch at the mere suggestion, but he forced them both to calm. "Thank you, brother. But with the Dohrags and Raxxians out there, the risk is far too great. I will tough it out until we reach Molok. It is the wisest course of action."

"As you wish, my friend. But remember, you are not the only one feeling the effects of this denial."

Korvin followed his friend's gaze. Nyota was walking with the others but staring at him. *Hard.* Her cheeks were flushed and her nipples visibly erect even through her shirt. He felt his body strain to respond, his cock abruptly pushing against the material of his trousers. He was tempted. *Very* tempted. But again his training kicked in. This was very much not the time or place.

His erection began to grudgingly subside.

Mind over matter. It had been drilled into him for years to the point it was second nature now. And no matter how miserable it might be at the moment for him, he was sure it resonated even stronger through his mate.

He watched her lovingly, his animal passion taking back seat to his simple, pure affection for her for the moment. She would be suffering indeed. And that was something he promised himself he would more than make up for when they reached safety.

Once they were once again in Molok, all bets would be off, and that lovers' game would most definitely be afoot.

The group walked on, all but Halvax oblivious to the drama in play between the newly bonded lovers. To the rest of them, any strange behavior was likely just a stress response to the situation. Little did they know.

It was late afternoon when a faint sound silenced the birds in the nearby trees. Almost in unison Korvin and Halvax called out for everyone to drop and get under cover.

The survivors had grown a bit complacent over the duration of the trek, but seeing these two toughened soldiers react in such a manner snapped them out of their collective daze.

All hit the ground, rolling under whatever they were nearest too, be it a tree, a shrub, or into a pile of leaves, as one of them did. The key was to blend in. At least, as much as they could.

The sound grew louder into a buzzing hum. Nothing ear-splitting, just enough of a noise to stand out in this place unmarred by artificial clamor. Nyota stared upward from her hiding spot under a prickly bush, wondering what in the world it could be.

Raxxian? Maybe. And if so, that would be bad. But they had made it a long way from the site of the slaughter. And if a search were to be started, it would take some time for it to fan out this wide. At least, she hoped so.

But what about the Dohrags? She really didn't know much about them other than the ships were crewed only by males, and they were a particularly nasty bunch.

Or maybe it was something else. Unfortunately, despite her badass alien mate, she was still the new kid in town and as such she simply didn't know a lot of things others might take for granted.

She watched a lone bird circle high in the sky. But it was moving a bit erratically, Not fluid. Not following the wind.

A moment later the spot abruptly dropped lower revealing itself to be something other than a bird. Something much larger and altogether different. The craft stopped its fall about three hundred meters above the ground, halting its descent abruptly then spinning a slow three-sixty.

Its hull was blue-gray, with small projections that could have been wings of some sort, though she couldn't help but think they'd never support a craft that size on such tiny things. Of course, if these guys possessed the technology for interstellar travel, maybe, just maybe, the simple rules of aerodynamics weren't much of a concern for them.

The ship hovered a moment, slowly drifting in the breeze. Then, as abruptly as it arrived, the craft powered up and moved away laterally in a flash. Korvin and Halvax counted to ninety as was their habit before sliding from cover.

"It is gone," Korvin said, dusting himself off.

Nyota found herself at his side, her hand wrapped around his forearm without even thinking about it. "Who were they?" she asked, feeling his heat warm her fingers, his heartbeat synching with hers.

"Dohrags," Halvax said, stepping between them, breaking their moment of unexpected reverie. "It was a standard transport ship, not a scouting vessel. If we're lucky, they'll just head on to wherever it was they were going and not even notice the Raxxians we killed."

"And if they do?" Steve chimed in, slowly emerging from under a pile of leaves.

"If they do, then they'll be on alert for Raxxians in their territory," Korvin noted. "But worse, with the Raxxian bodies, they'll also be on the lookout for whoever killed them as well. We need to keep moving. Our escape window may have just shrunk, and we have no way of knowing."

"I've got point," Halvax said, taking the salvaged Raxxian rifle from his friend.

"I'm on the rear," Korvin replied.

Nyota might have been tempted to make a flirty remark

about that under other circumstances, but her libido had just taken a very abrupt cold shower and she was all business now. The business of survival.

"Everyone's good to go," she said to Halvax, falling into step as he walked far quicker than before. "Lead the way. We're right behind you."

CHAPTER THIRTY-ONE

The mood among the survivors had changed after the Dohrag ship's flyover. They had been tense, wary, and a bit shell-shocked upon their rescue, but also hopeful with a sense of relief and a lessening of the traumatic memories with every step they took away from their former captors.

But now there was a new threat. One that came from above and could potentially drop in on them at any time if they weren't at their utmost vigilant. As such, every passing bird high above or strange sound carrying over the treetops brought an involuntary tensing of their bodies.

Korvin and Halvax were the only ones even remotely calm about the situation, but even they were moving with heightened awareness, their salvaged Raxxian weapons ready for action if the need arose. They were warriors, and there were now two of them, and they had faced difficult odds before. But protecting the others while facing an adversary could make things exceptionally more difficult.

The one thing that *was* easier was ignoring the deep pull Korvin and Nyota's runes were exerting upon them. Even the powerful pigment drawing their bodies closer seemed to know to tone it down a bit. Their lives were at stake, and a dead mate could not consummate the bond.

Of course, that didn't mean it was entirely gone. They still both felt a twinge in their nethers whenever their eyes met, but the exertion of the trek and drain of their glycogen stores remaining hyper-vigilant at all times served to keep them putting one foot in front of the other rather than scurrying off into the bushes for a quickie.

They walked in silence for several hours before reaching the gaping chasm Korvin and Nyota had previously traversed. With tired bodies, crossing would be difficult under any circumstances, but with varying degrees of injury slowing a few of their party it could be even more so.

Fortunately, with two Nimenni on hand, things would be a lot better than had it been otherwise.

"You have crafted a rope," Halvax said, appreciating his friend's handiwork. "This will speed the process.

"But we will need a proper harness and belay system to help the weaker and injured ones across."

"On it. You see to your mate. You have spent far too much time apart for the newly bonded."

Korvin nodded his thanks. "It is appreciated, brother."

Halvax took the coil of rope and headed off to fabricate the other parts of their traversing apparatus from what they had on hand along with whatever he could fashion from the vegetation in the area. Fortunately, this part of the planet was lush and strong-fibered plants were plentiful. It would be no time before he had completed his task.

Nyota settled down beside her man and rested her head against his shoulder. His natural heat felt amazing, even after a long and sweaty hike. And speaking of sweat, she was amazed how quickly she became aroused by his natural odor. It was like the pinnacle of pheromonal attraction almost to the point of

229

being distracting. Judging by the way he was looking at her, he felt very much the same.

"How do you fare?" he asked, offering her a sip of his water. "Are you well?"

"All good," she said, drinking deep, then leaning up and giving him a refreshingly wet kiss. The barely dormant length between his legs roused at once, pushing hard against the fabric of his trousers.

"Oops. Sorry about that," she said with a wicked grin.

His hand grazed her left nipple as he reached up to caress her face. Her whole body jerked with electric bliss at the touch.

"Oops, sorry about that," he said, a soft chuckle in his voice but a burning-hot look in his eye.

She looked around at the other survivors. "We *really* need to do something about this."

"We will. When we reach Molok, we will consummate the bond. *Repeatedly*."

Nyota shifted, her legs crossing and uncrossing, applying just the right pressure. "God, I hope so. I *need* you. I can't take much more of this. Is that normal? Like, we're out here fighting for our lives, and all I can think about is riding you until you can't walk straight."

The bulge in his trousers pulsed visibly.

"It-it is normal," he said, his voice hoarse with restrained desire. "The newly bonded do not normally wait to seal their bond, but sometimes there are obstacles to the process."

"Like running for our lives from Raxxians and Dohrags?"

"Something like that."

"Then we need to get back to safety ASA-fucking-P, because I really don't know how much longer I can take this, and I don't think jumping your bones in the middle of the trail would be appreciated."

"Likely not. We will make the best time back we can. And

know this," he said, his long fingers gently caressing the nape of her neck until goosebumps sprung up. "The sentiment is most certainly mutual."

"I-you..."

"Yes," he said, rising to his feet. "I should help Halvax prepare. A little distance for now would likely serve us both well."

With that he reluctantly pulled away and joined his friend in the preparations. It was a good idea, and with the two of them working together a basic harness apparatus was rigged in under an hour.

While quick for what they were doing and with the lack of equipment they were doing it with, it was still far longer than either of them would have liked. Every minute they were not moving forward was an added risk to their safety.

"The injured first," Korvin directed the survivors. "I will cross and receive them. Halvax knows what to do on this side. Follow his instructions and all will be fine."

Korvin didn't wait for a reply, instead turning and leaping into the air above the gorge, swinging across on his hand-braided rope with ease. He landed softly on the far side and pulled the rope to him, then threw the unsecured end back across to his partner.

Halvax quickly tied it tight and slung a makeshift pulley into place. The injured human was already in the harness, which the alien tied into place securely. He gave a nod to Korvin who then pulled him across, his arms and back flexing from the effort, much to Nyota's distraction.

The system worked as intended and the injured man made it to safety soon enough. Halvax then reeled back the harness for the next passenger.

"Would have been so much easier if we did it this way the last time," Nyota mused.

A strange sound hummed in the skies above. The trees were protecting them from being seen by the naked eye, but who knew what sort of scanning equipment was on board the craft.

The two warriors shared a look.

"Next in the harness," Halvax urged the others. "We must move quickly."

No one was about to argue that, each strapping in and crossing in turn. Upon arrival, they would then move down the trail a little bit, creating room for the next person's landing.

The whole process went relatively quickly, but a few hiccups were to be expected, namely, the improvised pulley jamming on a few occasions. Fortunately, a little elbow grease on Korvin's part freed it up and helped the poor passenger dangling over the gorge reach the far side safely.

Nyota was the second to last to cross, a surge of lust flooding her as she reached the safety of the dark soil, sliding blissfully into her lover's arms. He pushed his own feelings aside, quickly unfastening the harness and untying the rope, the end sliding over the edge.

"What about Halvax?" she asked.

"What about him?" he replied as the chunk of wood tied to one end sailed through the air and lodged securely in the crook of a tree branch.

A moment later Halvax soared across, quickly taking down the rope he'd just played Tarzan on and coiling it as they walked. "All accounted for," he said. "A bit spread out though. More than I would like."

Korvin glanced down the trail. He had told them to move ahead a little to make a safe space for the others to land after crossing the gorge, but they seemed to have kept on walking, and with his attention focused on the people dangling over certain death, he had somehow missed that.

"I will get to the front," he said, picking up the Raxxian rifle.

A cry rang out before he could even take the first step.

"Dohrags!" one of the alien survivors shouted.

Korvin and Halvax didn't hesitate, sprinting toward the sound of conflict rather than away from it. In no time they saw the cause of their predicament.

A small clearing, not large enough for a proper ship to set down in, had a small contingent of Dohrags in it. Apparently, their transport was just small enough, and it had dropped down through the branches to surprise their quarry. The injured human was already incapacitated and bound, his inert body being rudely thrown into the craft.

"We have to stop them!" Halvax blurted, firing the Raxxian hand weapon while charging the Dohrag forces.

Korvin would have urged caution in this instance, but the ball was already in play, so he ran after his friend, firing the rifle from a full run, not even slowing to aim.

The Dohrags, though superior in number, had apparently not been expecting that sort of firepower, and when they realized it was Nimenni warriors coming for them, they made a quick decision. Take the one they had already captured and flee. There would be time to come back for the others with more men and firepower.

"They're taking him!" Nyota cried out as the Dohrags piled into the ship and sealed the hatch.

"Korvin, their communications equipment!" Halvax shouted.

For the first time Korvin stopped in his tracks. But he wasn't scared or confused. He was prepared.

In one motion he pulled the Raxxian rifle tight to his shoulder and cranked the weapon's power to full, taking careful aim as the Dohrag ship lifted off, hoping their shielding wasn't too robust. Gently, he squeezed the trigger, letting out half a breath as he did to steady his aim.

He would only get one shot before they were too high up. It had to count.

The ship rocked from the impact, smoke wafting from the damaged section as its course abruptly changed.

"You got it!" Nyota cheered.

Korvin did not look so pleased. The ship was damaged, but it had already cleared the treetops. If his shot flew true, their communications array would hopefully be down and the other Dohrags would be none the wiser for a short while longer, hopefully enough time to effect their escape.

But the ship had moved as he fired, and the blast seemed to have hit a more vital area than he had planned. Worse, it seemed they had not engaged their shielding unit at all. A rookie mistake he now chided them for. His shot had impacted with full force.

He watched the smoke trail grow, the craft lurching and shuddering as it flew past overhead.

"It's going to crash! Everyone, run!" Halvax commanded.

The survivors didn't have to be told twice, all of them following him as fast as they could while he charged off down the path. The trail would have been invisible to most, but he was not most people, and Korvin had left just enough sign of passage for him to be able to backtrack his friend's path.

A small explosion rang out moments later, a flash of orange in the trees on the other side of the gorge. Korvin turned and looked back but only for a second. There would be no survivors.

He slung the rifle and hurried ahead, taking point while Halvax shifted to the rear. His friend might have been a fantastic tracker, but these were his tracks ,and he knew exactly where to lead them.

They ran as hard as their weakest member could maintain for as long as they were able, then ducked under a rocky overhang in a hillside to catch their breath.

"No sign of anyone following," Halvax said, his gaze fixed on the trail and sky behind them.

"I hit the comms array, of that I am certain. It is entirely possible that no warning message was sent," Korvin replied.

Halvax seemed pleased. "If that is the case, they will investigate it as a crash rather than a hostile act. At least, until they discover the human remains among their crew."

Korvin's head sagged a little. He had just killed one of the people they had come to save. One of the humans, no less. He looked at Nyota with pain in his eyes. There was now one less of her kind on this world, and it was at his hand.

She came and sat with him, wrapping his arm in her hands, knowing his thoughts and regrets without his having to say them aloud. "It wasn't your fault."

"I fired the shot. The ship crashed because of my actions."

"But you had no way of knowing that would happen. And if the ship had gotten away, he would have been as good as dead while the Dohrags would also have a pinpoint on our location. Don't beat yourself up over it. You can't control everything in life, and sometimes things don't go the way you want no matter how hard you try."

Korvin's frustration clung to him like sticky sweat on a Louisiana summer. "We have so few resources," he grumbled. "Almost no weapons to speak of. We were prepared for the Raxxians and handled them accordingly. But if the Dohrags come back in numbers, we are woefully unprepared for that sort of adversary."

Nyota slid back and looked him in the eye. "You want to help, and that's noble. But our priority is to get these people to safety."

His demeanor seemed to shift as he met her gaze. His mate needed him. Crushing the Dohrags could wait. "We're close to Molok territory. If the Dohrags haven't sent a commando team out by now, I am confident we can make it to safety before we're discovered. But it may require a bit of creativity."

"What do you mean?"

He turned to Halvax, who was already on his feet. "Like the battle of Pinzlar?"

"You read my mind, brother." Korvin stood tall, commanding the attention of all present. "Listen to me well. We are near safety, but it will not be easy. You are tired, I know, but you must push through your exhaustion and cover ground. Nyota will guide you. Follow her lead. We will rejoin you as soon as we are able."

"You're leaving us?" Steve asked, panic in his eyes.

"You will be safe so long as you do as I say." He turned to Nyota. "Follow our trail. You know how, I've seen it."

Strangely enough, she knew he was right. "Be safe," she said.

"Be stealthy," he replied, kissing her hard, then breaking from her and running the other way, his comrade at his side.

Nyota felt the twinge of his departure tug at her Infala then turned her focus to the task at hand. It was what he would have done.

"You heard the man," she said without a hint of doubt. "Follow me."

The others fell in behind her without complaint or comment, hurrying along in her path.

"Step like this," she instructed, showing them how to pivot their feet on the ground to spread the weight and quiet their steps.

Steve did as she said but seemed a little confused. "How do you know all of this?"

It was too much to try to explain all she'd experienced with Korvin. The trekking, the survival, the bonding of their runes.

"I just do, okay?"

"Okay, okay. Just asking."

As she led the way, his, and everyone else's, doubts faded away. Nyota was *good* at this, and their confidence in her grew with every step. Even the rescued aliens who had no reason to believe a human could thrive in this environment found their doubts assuaged.

"You've done well," a familiar voice said from just up ahead.

Nyota's heart raced faster. "Korvin!"

"Where'd you guys come from?" Steve wondered. "I didn't hear a thing."

"Then we are not losing our touch," Halvax said with a chuckle.

A nervous grin twitched across Steve's lips. "But where were you? You guys, like, vanished back there."

"We were setting a false trail for the Dohrags should they pursue us," Halvax replied. "And a good thing we did."

"It certainly was," Korvin agreed. "The Dohrags had a few men on the ground already. After the crash they are stranded, for now."

"So they're coming after us?" Nyota asked.

"No. At least, not for a while. They took the bait. Bait which led into dense forest. They will have no aerial advantage there and will be forced to proceed on foot to search."

Nyota grinned. "In the wrong direction."

"Exactly, my love."

"Well, then. What now?"

"Now? Now we move as fast as we can that way," he said, pointing off in the distance. "If I am not mistaken, cutting through that marsh will take us in the vicinity of the transit route to Molok."

"Through a marsh? Seriously?" she grumbled half-jokingly.

"To save a day's trek and avoid the Dohrags, yes, I am afraid so. Would you prefer I carry you?"

Halvax rolled his eyes with an exaggerated groan. "If you two are quite through, we have our survival plan to enact."

The lovers took off without another word, leading the way, hand in hand.

It was a difficult trek through the marshy wetlands, but as Korvin had hoped, the result was worth the effort. Mud-streaked and exhausted, they came upon a small caravan of trading transports as the sun began to lower in the sky. Korvin waved them down, and within minutes all the survivors were helped aboard and offered fresh water to drink.

"You say it was Dohrags?" the trader asked.

"Dohrags, yes, but first Raxxians," Korvin replied.

"Krikes! That's bad business. I'll pass word along to my associates to be on their guard."

Korvin seemed pleased at the idea. "A wise move, my friend."

"Thanks to your warning. But you say you are heading to Molok, yes? That's our next stop." The trader looked them up and down, taking in their filthy attire. "I'll drop you in at the trading neighborhood. In your state, you might fare better there."

Korvin sat up a bit taller, an amused gleam in his eye. "Actually, if you would be so kind. Please relay a message to the magistrate."

"The magistrate? You're pulling my leg. *You* know the magistrate?"

"That I do. Tell her Korvin of the Bohdzee returns. And he comes with survivors."

CHAPTER THIRTY-TWO

"You certainly know how to make an entrance, my friend," Halvax said as he took in the throngs of Molok residents lining the causeway, eager to catch a glimpse of the Bohdzee Guard whom their magistrate had befriended. When word spread that a second of his ilk was now joining him, the crowd's numbers inflated even more.

"Wait until we are properly greeted," Korvin replied with a knowing wink. "You will not have eaten so well in years, I would wager."

"A challenge I accept willingly," his friend said with a laugh, reveling in the moment. Normally, they worked in relative secret, and the vast majority of their exploits would never see the light of day. But this? This was something they had jokingly dreamed of but never really thought would happen.

They were being greeted as heroes, and it felt amazing. Rescuing Raxxian captives from those horrid creatures while also fighting off the Dohrags, with whom there was always conflict and certainly no love lost, gave them immediate clout in Molok. With a lengthy history of skirmishes with the Dohrags, that enemy was never far from the citizens' minds.

The Dohrags had eventually been beaten back to their own territory over the course of several violent years and were no longer raiding the fringe neighborhoods of Molok. But even so, they were an ever-present threat outside the city limits. As a result, anyone who put them in their place was sure to be something of a celebrity.

Celebrities, plural, in this case, as the two Nimenni drew the admiring gaze of men and women alike as their trader friend flew them to their meeting with the magistrate.

A full entourage was awaiting them, not only the magistrate's personal guard but also a sizable portion of the councilmembers and ruling elite. It was quite the reception to say the least.

The trader's conveyance came to a stop and lowered to a hover just above the ground. "You weren't kidding," the captain said. "You have friends in high places."

Korvin shook his hand as the others disembarked. "And you will be well compensated for your assistance. I will see to it." He then scrambled down to join the others, walking hand-in-hand with his mate to greet the waiting magistrate.

"So many survivors! This is fantastic, Korvin. Quite the coup, really," the magistrate said, looking over the newcomers.

Her gaze lingered a long moment on Halvax, her expression cool yet interested as she sized up the Nimenni newcomer. He was as one would have expected of his ilk. Strong, chiseled, and with an air of absolute confidence.

He also felt a little flush of excitement. This powerful woman's interest seemed to be more than mere idle curiosity. At least, he was pretty sure, and in these matters his gut instinct was correct more often than not.

Korvin clocked the interaction without a change of expression, but he felt the slight squeeze from Nyota's hand telling him she saw it as well. There was only one thing to do.

"Magistrate, allow me to introduce my dear friend and comrade of many years, Halvax."

"Magistrate," Halvax said, bowing his head respectfully.

The magistrate reached out, her slender fingers grazing his face and lifting his chin up. "Please, stand easy. Another Bohdzee Guard? We are most fortunate to have you with us," she said, extending her hand.

He took it in his much larger one, the heat of his kind running hot today, warming her flesh delightfully. A little twinkle seemed to shine in her eyes, and she held his grip a bit longer than normal.

Halvax felt a strange twinge in his gut, an unfamiliar knot forming in his stomach as his heartbeat quickened a little. From the pulse visible on her neck, the magistrate's had increased as well. She squeezed his hand once then let go, her fingers gently trailing off of his, a slight blush coloring her cheeks.

She seamlessly transitioned to greeting the other survivors with all the grace and warmth one would expect of someone of her position, but Halvax caught the little glance she cast back his way. He looked at his friend, the traces of a restrained grin clear on Korvin's lips. He had seen as well, and clearly had the same impression.

Halvax, for the first time in longer than he could imagine, allowed the possibility of "what if" to enter his mind. It was not something he ever really considered. But perhaps, just this once, life could take an interesting turn.

The magistrate made her way down the line, spending a moment with each and every one of the survivors, graciously welcoming them to her city. She then stepped back and spoke to the group as a whole.

"You have all endured much since your arrival to our world, and I am sorry for the adversity you faced. But here in Molok you are safe. Esteemed guests of our fine city. Now, I am sure you are exhausted from your journey and hungry as well. Please, follow Torpa. You will be examined by our medical team then shown to your private chambers and provided clean attire. When you have bathed and feel ready, you will be shown to the dining hall where a welcoming feast has been prepared."

"Did you say feast?" Halvax asked.

"I did."

"How delightful. And, might you be joining us?"

The magistrate blushed again. "I will."

"Most wonderful. I look forward to seeing you there. And allow me to thank you once more for your hospitality. You have made our arrival in Molok one to remember."

He gave a little wink and followed Torpa for a quick medical examination, hoping he'd played it smooth enough and not gone too far with his flirtation.

He needn't have worried.

The magistrate composed herself quickly, her skin returning to its normal hue with a well-directed bit of self-control reining in her blush response. It had been a long time since someone made her lose her composure like that, and she found she rather liked it.

She turned her attention to Korvin and Nyota, the two standing close by one another, their demeanor quite different from when they had first come to her city.

"You two seem well," she said, a curious tone in her voice.

"We are, Magistrate," Korvin replied with a tiny bow.

"Different, though."

"That we are."

"I cannot quite put my finger on it, but there appears to have been a rather drastic shift in your relationship since we last spoke."

"Thanks to your Skrizzit, in fact," he confirmed, opening his shirt enough to reveal his faintly glowing Infala. Nyota squeezed his hand warmly and did the same, a happy smile plastered to her face.

"Your Infalas? They match?" She stared at Nyota in shock. "But you have only just been marked. And yet they somehow have grown to form the bond?"

Korvin nodded. "They do, and they have, Magistrate."

"But how? No, nevermind that. This is to be celebrated. It is just so highly unusual. Impossible, really. It normally takes *years* for the Infala rune to fully bond to its host, and longer, if ever, to find its mate. To have happened so quickly, I have never heard of this happening in all my days."

"I think the Skrizzit is to thank for that," Nyota chimed in. "It seems somehow our blood and pigment were mixed."

A look of shock, annoyance, elation, and disbelief flashed across the magistrate's face all at once. On the one hand, she was flabbergasted to learn her Skrizzit had been so careless. But on the other, even in rare instances of mixing implements, it had never resulted in an Infala bond. Infection, perhaps, but never this.

But now these two were paired. Mated for life. And even the stoic Bohdzee Guard seemed thrilled for it.

"Congratulations are in order. You have fully bonded as Infala mates. It is cause for celebration."

"Well, about that," Nyota quietly said. "We haven't exactly, well, you know."

"What my mate is trying to say is we have been, uh, busy with other pressing matters."

"Fighting the Raxxians," the magistrate noted. "And rescuing that large group from their clutches."

"Indeed."

"So, there has been no, um *alone* time as of yet?" she asked with a knowing grin.

Korvin's pent-up look answered the question before he even spoke. "That is the situation, yes."

"Well, that changes things," the magistrate said flashing them both a huge grin and a knowing look. "You require lodgings, and at once. Minnix, see to it, will you?"

"Of course, Magistrate."

"Oh, and Minnix?" she added with a gleam in her eye.

"Yes, Magistrate?"

"Do make sure it is well insulated for sound. We want to afford our guests the utmost privacy."

CHAPTER THIRTY-THREE

"It will take only a short time to have your suite ready," Minnix informed the new couple as they were led from the reception area. "The magistrate also requested that I ensure you are both seen to by the medical staff. Your injuries will be tended, and your bodies primed with a nutrient supplement to speed your recovery and aid in your, um, well, whatever other activities you may have in mind."

Nyota was well past blushing at this point. She wanted Korvin, and she wanted him now. But she could wait a half hour if she had to. And with her aching body, she had to admit it would be nice to finally have him when feeling her best.

"Works for me," she said.

"Excellent. Nyota, if you will please come with me. Auskus here will show your mate the way to his examination. You should both be done in no time."

A blue creature with velvety fur covering its skin stepped forward from its post along the wall. It had a long body, almost like a ferret, but it walked tall on two legs and had longer arms and legs than any in the weasel family. Additionally, it seemed to possess a more developed musculature along its torso. As for its gender, that was anyone's guess.

"Please, follow me," Auskus said to the Nimenni in a sing-song voice.

Nyota raised an amused brow at Korvin who couldn't help but chuckle. "Very well, my little friend," he replied. "Lead the way."

"Just up ahead. Only a short walk to the medical compound. Very good facility. Top-notch care."

"It is appreciated." He turned to Nyota. "I will see you shortly."

"Oh yes," she said, her desire clear in her eyes. "Oh yes, you will."

Korvin felt a twinge as he and his love parted, but it was tempered by the knowledge of what was to come. Namely, both of them, and many times at that. It was indeed a short walk, as Auskus had said, and he was just reclining back into the medical attendant's examination chair when he felt a violent tug in his Infala. A moment later an alarm sounded in the complex.

Shirtless and barefoot, Korvin leapt out of the chair and raced outside, his heart pounding. The surge of adrenaline he was feeling, he realized, was not his own. A throng of armed guards were huddled near the adjacent building. Minnix lay on the ground, bleeding but alive.

"Where is she? Where is Nyota?" he demanded, ignoring the aide's injuries.

"Calm down, sir," a guard foolishly said.

Korvin spun on him, rage in his eyes, his runes starting to glow in a frighteningly menacing way. "Calm down?" he seethed. "Where is my mate?"

"It was Dohrags," Minnix said, coughing up a mixture of spittle and blood. "There were five of them, disguised and waiting."

"They do not enter the city. It is simply not done," a guard blurted.

"Normally, no. But they wanted revenge for their fallen friends. One was their leader's son, from what I overheard. They wanted any of the people responsible." Minnix coughed up more blood. "They took her. I tried to stop them, but I was too weak."

"You are not a fighter, Minnix," the guard said. "You did what you could. Now lie still, medical help is coming."

Halvax came running from the building he and the others had been given lodging in. He didn't know what the problem was, but like Korvin, running toward danger rather than away from it was in his blood. He raced to his distressed friend, eyeing the faintly glowing runes with concern.

"What happened, Korvin?"

"They took her. Dohrags took Nyota," he growled, his rage barely contained.

"Oh, shit." Halvax said, then spun toward the guards. "Where did they go?"

"We're sending—"

He grabbed the guard and nearly yanked him off his feet. "This man is one of the Bohdzee Guard, and they have just taken his mate. *Before* they could complete their Infala bonding. Do any of you realize just what that means?"

None could say for certain in the case of a Bohdzee, but it was undoubtedly a very, *very* bad thing. To have someone of his skills and power angry was one thing, but all bets were off when Infala bonding was concerned. Even the most placid sort could get violent if prevented from completing the process. And this one? The very thought sent a chill through them all.

"That way," the guard said. "Five at least, but they likely have backup."

Korvin nearly ripped the poor fellow's hand off when he

snatched the rifle from him and took off running, moving at a full sprint, barefoot and not giving a damn.

"May I?" Halvax asked, quickly relieving another guard of their weapon. "Thank you." He turned to follow his friend.

"We'll send backup!" the guard called after him.

Halvax glanced back over his shoulder. "You'd be better served sending a cleanup team instead," he replied, then sped his pace, trying as best he could to close the gap.

Korvin raced through the streets and alleyways, his runes glowing brighter with every step. This was a city and there were no muddy tracks or bent twigs to guide him. But he had something else on his side. Something the Dohrags had no way to take into consideration when they embarked on their ill-advised revenge.

Korvin had a bond with their prisoner, and that bond was leading him right to them.

Halvax had no such tool at his disposal, but the confused faces of citizens the raging Nimenni left in his wake were enough to steer him in the right direction. He just hoped he'd get there before it was all over.

The Dohrags had moved quickly, the group clearing the way as they hurried to their rendezvous. A small ship was waiting for them in one of the peripheral landing sites. It wasn't a Dohrag craft but rather one they'd captured not long ago, refitting it for their purposes. Today's job was as a makeshift retrieval ship.

No one was loitering outside—that would have drawn far too much attention—but when their five comrades were seen approaching, pulling a sixth person along with them, they popped the hatch and primed the engines.

Everything was going as planned. Their commander would have his revenge and they would be handsomely rewarded for their efforts.

Two blasts hit the guards just as they stepped out of the

hatch, dropping them in rapid succession. The retrieval team hurried their pace, firing blindly behind them, forcing people to scatter for cover before daring to turn to see who was coming after them.

The guard who first saw the man with the glowing runes charging right for them, not swerving with their weapons' fire but rather intensifying his pace, felt his stomach abruptly sink with the horrible realization who, and what, they had chasing them.

"Bohdzee!" he yelled, his panic clear in his voice.

The others didn't even bother looking back. They had no option now but straight ahead, and fast, at that. With the prisoner in their midst their pursuer would not fire at them. At least they hoped not.

"Stop him!" one yelled to the ship's crew.

That seemed to break the momentary panic that had frozen them all in place. Nearly a dozen troops poured out of the ship, weapons blazing. Korvin was unafraid. He was also positioned in such a way that only peripheral attackers might line up a shot on him. The kidnappers were unintentionally blocking him from the others, and he intended to use that to the utmost advantage.

Korvin fired off a volley to the left.

The two Dohrags at that end fell in a heap.

He repeated the same to the right.

Only one was foolish enough to give him a clear shot, but in his state of heightened rage, every sense and reflex was cranked up to eleven. The shot took the man's head clean off, spattering his comrades with gore.

"Stop him!" the others yelled as they drew closer to the ship.

Korvin saw and drew deep from his runes, his legs pumping impossibly fast as he charged ahead. Nyota felt a familiar twinge as he grew close, but something else was present this time.

Something powerful. Something frightening.

Korvin's runes were glowing bright when he reached the five who had taken his woman. He reached out his enormous hand and crushed the nearest one's head like a grape, tossing his body aside like so much refuse. They had reached the ship, but no one could safely fire. Not with him right in their midst.

After the next four bodies fell in rapid succession, they rethought that safety precaution and opened up with their rifles and pistols anyway, consequences be damned.

Rounds struck their attacker, but he paid them no mind, his scorched flesh not slowing his rage-fueled assault. Korvin was a whirling dervish of violence, ripping limbs from bodies and heads from necks, using his knife when he could, his bare hands otherwise.

Halvax burst from a parallel alleyway onto the landing area, only a little shocked at the scene unfolding before him.

"Oh, Korvin," he sighed, then raced to his friend's aid.

Korvin had completely lost his cool and gone full-on berserker. Halvax had only seen this happen once before, and heaven help whoever was the focus of his rage. As dire as the moment was, he couldn't help but admire the precision with which his friend was wielding his power, out of his mind with fury but also brutally technical with his implementation of their secret skills.

This was why the Bohdzee were so feared. Their abilities lay not only in their training and dedication, but also the power they could channel through their special runes. Only a select few could control them. Those foolish enough to receive the runes without proper screening and subsequent training beforehand would typically die in the first weeks.

But those specifically selected for the honor were a different sort, and they soon transformed into nearly unstoppable killing machines.

By the time Halvax reached his friend, all the Dohrags lay dead or dying, all with the most horrible of injuries. Korvin breathed hard, his wild eyes scanning the area for additional threats.

There were none. All lay broken at his feet.

He dropped his knife and snapped Nyota's bindings with ease, sliding the blindfold from her eyes and gag from her mouth.

She looked around in shock at the carnage. Then she saw his hands, dripping with Dohrag blood. More than a dozen dead, she counted. Somehow, against all odds, Korvin had saved her.

"How did you—" she began, just as he slumped to the ground. "Korvin!"

Halvax came running to her side, crouching beside his friend, eyes sharp and ready for any hidden attackers who might have been lying in wait. None came.

"What's wrong with him?" she asked, panic in her voice. "What happened?"

"*You* happened," he replied. "We Bohdzee can tap into power beyond what normal people can. It is usually not an issue; we are trained not to do so. But in the rare instance such as this when one ignores their training and draws too deep it can have a detrimental effect."

"Is he going to die?" she asked, her voice quivering.

Halvax rested a hand gently on her shoulder. "Do not fear. He will recover fully. But for now he will need to rest."

Halvax and Nyota had cleaned much of the blood from Korvin by the time the magistrate's troopers arrived. They were glad to see a cleanup team had been sent with the guards as well.

Korvin slept through his transport to the medical facility where his various injuries were tended to. The medical tech was particularly shocked that the Dohrag weapons had so little of an effect on his body.

"It's a Bohdzee thing," Halvax noted without going into detail how the power they could channel was capable of diminishing the forces of such an attack.

Back in their room some time later, bandaged and clean, Nyota tucked him into his bed and gently kissed his forehead, a fierce pull from between her legs calling her to him despite his injuries. She pulled back, setting the tray of food closer to him for when he woke then forced herself to turn and walk to her own temporary room.

He needed rest, and even injured as they both were, she knew that if he woke and she was beside him, there was still no way they could refrain, despite his condition. She looked back at him, love welling in her heart.

"Soon," she said, then quietly closed the door behind her, leaving her love to rest and recover.

CHAPTER THIRTY-FOUR

Korvin slept for a day straight through. Whatever it was he had tapped into in his fury, he had gone farther than the Bohdzee were supposed to. Much farther, and the strain had taken its toll.

In the aftermath and subsequent clean up, Halvax had explained some of the lesser known, but still acceptable for public discussion, aspects of the Bohdzee, including their ability to operate at a much higher level of power use than normal people.

He told her that it would put a strain on the pigment in their runes, and the results could be rather excessive, but that was why their special runes were inscribed onto their bodies using pigments containing a very specific degree of power, selected specifically for each person.

What no one had ever guessed was how the more powerful pigment the magistrate had so graciously given both he and Nyota would react with his existing markings. It shouldn't have happened, but somehow the symbiotic ink had gradually reached out and connected to his other runes far more intensely than any would have imagined over the days he and Nyota had been searching for their friends.

The result was readily apparent. Korvin pulled deep in his anger, but what he tapped into was far stronger than what he'd been accustomed to. It protected him from mortal wounds, but it also left him utterly spent.

"With a bit of study, this might actually prove to be a boon to the Bohdzee," Halvax told the magistrate over a nice cup of tea. "If you have a little more of that remarkable pigment to spare, of course. I would not want to impose."

The magistrate grinned at her guest, with whom she had been spending an awful lot of time with since the event. "It will not be an imposition at all. Of course, it would require you to stay in Molok a bit longer."

"I think I could manage that without too much trouble," Halvax said with a little wink. "Now, tell me more about this world."

"What would you like to know?"

"*Everything.*"

She laughed warmly. "Quite the request. You do realize, that could take a while."

He grinned back at her. "Good."

Nyota had done her best to leave Korvin to recover, spending her time with his friend and the magistrate as well as the other survivors, but after a day of that she could wait no longer.

She keyed the entry panel to their suite, set to only allow her and the magistrate's most trusted aide access. The room was dimly lit, the windows set to reduce the amount of light they permitted to enter.

He had eaten, she noted, the plates cleaned entirely and piled on their tray. Apparently, he had quite an appetite when he roused, though how long ago that was she was unsure.

She walked to the large bed upon which he lay, fresh

bandages in hand ready to change the dressings of the few injuries the medical staff could not heal outright. Certain things needed to mend a bit on their own before artificial means could be used to speed the process, his charred pigment lines among them.

His lines and runes were mostly unscathed, but a few had taken a beating in the fight and would need to settle down on their own for a few days before being completely healed.

She gently lifted the bandages, checking for any seepage. He was already healing quite quickly. In fact, his skin seemed almost restored, though the flesh beneath it would likely be tender for some time.

A rush of that familiar heat in her belly hit her hard when her fingers grazed his skin, a fine sweat breaking out on her forehead. Motion caught her eye as the sheet covering him quickly raised up, a tent pitched at groin level in an instant. She reached out and gently stroked his erect cock through the fabric with her fingertips, the heat of it radiating into her hand as he pulsed and throbbed under her touch.

She looked up at his face as his eyes slid open. Gone was his exhaustion, replaced with a look of fire and lust. She felt his length strain and harden even more, wanting her on such a visceral level she almost gasped from the pull it had on her Infala.

"I see you're awake," she said, her voice low with desire.

"I am. And you are here with me, as it should be. You and I—"

"I know," she said, leaning in and gently kissing his forehead.

Her nipples grew hard, and her clit twinged with want, but now it was her turn to show some restraint. At least for the moment.

"Come on, we need to clean you up and re-dress those bandages," she said, taking his hand and urging him to his feet.

Korvin stood, the sheet falling away, revealing his naked body, chiseled and firm, his cock standing at attention, pointing at her like a divining rod in search of water. And she was wet all right, but in a very different way.

Nyota shed her clothes slowly, watching his reaction as each piece slid off revealing more of her bare skin. Korvin's lids drooped slightly, his pupils wide with desire. He reached for her.

"Not yet," she said, then activated the shower, setting the water to hot. She took his hand, though she nearly grabbed something else, and led him into the cleansing stream.

The shower system detected his injuries, as she now knew it would, washing him thoroughly with invigorating heat while avoiding the few spots still too damaged for full contact.

She rinsed as well, turning her back to him, her ass dripping with hot water grazing across his erection with cruelly wonderful bliss. She felt him twitch, wanting her so badly, just as she wanted him, but she refrained, continuing the most fantastically agonizing edging for them both.

His hands gently rested on her hips, sliding over her bare skin, rubbing her clean in the heated stream. His right hand slid higher, tracing the line of her hip, moving up her ribs until he was cupping her breast, her nipple gently nestled between his thumb and index finger. He gave a little squeeze, sending bliss shooting through her body.

Nyota felt her knees wobble for a moment. Korvin reacted immediately, his arm tightening around her, pulling her close, his erection now pressed firmly against her ass, his other hand snaking around her body, but this one moving lower.

He slid his fingers over her hips and across her belly before moving down, parting her folds, and coating them in her wetness. Nyota's clit was positively thrumming, straining for his touch. Now it was his turn to tease, his lips locking onto her ear gently as his fingers moved around her swollen bud, so close but not yet touching it.

She was in agonizing ecstasy, every fiber in her body straining for him, wanting him to fill her up. To take her and make her his forever. Korvin was her mate, bonded and inseparable, and his body reacted to her instinctively, throbbing behind her as she slowly moved her ass against him until they could both take no more.

"I must have you," he growled, the rumble of his voice setting her on fire even more than before.

His arms tight around her, Korvin moved his hips back, dipping his cock lower, sliding in between her ass cheeks until it jutted straight in front of him, sliding between her legs, coated in her juices, his own pre-cum mixing with it, making what she'd found to be the most delightful lube imaginable.

She jerked hard, her body nearly out of control with want, pressing herself back on him, trying to force him inside. Korvin refrained, holding back, the tip of his cock just barely pressing into her.

Finally, it was too much.

He pushed forward, squeezing her tight as his ridged manhood slid inside her, the rippling sensation as he penetrated her joined by his talented fingers as they now began rubbing small circles on her clit, their Infalas linked, each of them knowing what the other wanted, feeling what the other felt.

"Mine," she gasped, tightening her squeeze on his cock. "All mine."

He thrust slowly at first, the sensations of fully bonded penetration overwhelming them both. Nyota slammed herself back hard, forcing him deep, taking every inch of him, her pussy clenching hard around him with every stroke.

Korvin groaned with delight, his thrusts slapping against her ass with increasing force. Nyota felt something else. Something beyond his cock and fingers doing their magic. A wonderful sensation was now stimulating her ass as well. She slid one hand back and found the rune on his pelvis was hot to the touch, the lines dancing under her fingertips, spreading blissful sensations into them as well.

So that's how it works, she managed to think before losing herself in the pleasure. Facing each other the rune stimulated her clit, but from behind it worked its magic on the sensitive nerve endings on the other side, the pressure of his cock inside her compounded by his amazing rune.

"I-oh, fuck!" she gasped as her first climax hit, crashing over her like a tidal wave, every muscle in her body tensing as the world flashed white before her eyes. She gushed from deep inside as she clenched him hard, her body reacting as it never had before, her wetness running down his length as he relentlessly pounded into her as she came over and over.

Korvin's hands tightened, and his cock swelled as he joined her in orgasmic bliss, his massive load spurting with incredible force, the sensation of his hot cum filling her up taking Nyota over the edge even further until her body ceased functioning and her vision went black.

She floated in orgasmic wonder, riding weightless in ecstasy for a long time before slowly returning to her body. She was on her back now, she realized. On the bed, it felt like. A moment later she felt something else. Korvin's cock was slowly churning inside her, that remarkable rune now making now her clit sing with joy.

He had her legs up over his forearms, his hands cupping her ass and spreading her wide. She opened her eyes, her vision slowly coming into focus to see him watching his length disappear into her, slowly teasing it back out. The look on his face was one of pure ecstasy, and when he shifted his gaze to her face, it was one of pure love.

He leaned forward, pushing her legs up higher as he latched his lips to hers, kissing her with a deep intensity the likes of which she had never felt in her life. Their tongues danced with one another, her hips bucking as another climax burst from within.

Korvin's mouth slid from hers, kissing the salty tears of joy running down her cheeks before resting at her ear.

"I am yours, and you are mine," he said, his voice thick with emotion. "We are bonded until the end of us."

"I want you with me," Nyota gasped. "Like this, forever."

He thrust harder, his cock swelling with their shared pleasure.

"Yes. Yes!" she groaned as the ball of hot bliss in her belly erupted, spreading across her entire body in a flash.

Her hands clutched at his back, flailing as her head thrashed side to side. Her feet curled tight, her legs trembling uncontrollably as he exploded inside her again, their Infalas linking their orgasms together, compounding them into something greater than either could ever achieve on their own.

Korvin's body went rigid, his legs and arms shaking as he emptied himself into her, as if his very soul was pouring out of him, bonding with hers in an eternal embrace.

The two of them lay there out of their minds and out of their bodies, floating on a cloud of ecstasy, two lovers entwined in body and spirit for the rest of their days.

It was nearly twenty minutes before they regained their senses.

Nyota stared into his beautiful violet eyes and clenched on his semi-erect cock still buried inside her. She grinned wide as it twitched back to life almost immediately.

"More," she moaned, moving her hips.

Korvin responded in kind, happy to oblige all day long until they simply could no longer.

CHAPTER THIRTY-FIVE

Nyota and Korvin spent two days in their suite, living off of room service and sex, more than once both at the same time.

Korvin had said this was only the beginning and that lovemaking between Infala mates only intensified over time. On the third day as they lay together in sweaty bliss, Nyota happily wondered how much more she could take. It was a challenge she would be most thrilled to accept.

Interestingly, the more they indulged in each other, the more she felt her other runes besides her Infala growing in strength. They were sharing *everything*, well beyond mere fluids at this point, it seemed. As a result she was now far stronger than anyone so newly inked.

It was a dynamic they were both rather enjoying.

"Damn, that was hot," Nyota exclaimed as she lay beneath her mate's sizable mass, breathing hard from the wonderful expenditure of energy.

"Indeed, you are proving most innovative in your newfound strength," Korvin said, nuzzling her neck, his weight pressing down upon her in that most delightful way.

He was still hard, as she had learned he was more than

capable of doing even after several rounds, and still deep inside her, precisely where she wanted him to remain—something he had been more than happy to oblige for the past several days.

"You think I'm getting stronger?" she asked, clenching herself around his cock hard enough to make him gasp.

"Yes, and in ways one would not normally expect," he said with a happy groan.

"I guess I picked up a few new tricks from our bonding."

"I guess you did. And I, for one, rather like it."

"Oh, do you now?" she asked with a lustful chuckle, shifting her legs, and leveraging against his hip, flipping him over onto his back.

She remained firmly atop him, not letting that delicious cock escape for even a moment.

"You remembered the defensive move I showed you," he said, a happy grin on his face as she started grinding atop him, pressing her clit into the rune on his pubis, bringing them both a healthy serving of that particularly delightful and novel sort of pleasure.

"I remembered," she said in a husky voice. "And I think I improved on it, don't you?"

Nyota shifted her feet, moving to a low squat over her mate. He was so long and hard inside her it felt like she was impaled in the most wonderful way possible. She lifted up, her lips gripping his shaft, sliding over the engorged ridges until she reached the thick head of his cock before slamming back down, the impact making her clit throb.

Her hands clutched his chest, sliding over the dense muscles, moving to his neck, one hand sliding behind his head, grabbing his hair tight.

Korvin's hips jumped, pushing hard up into the woman riding him, his own hands reaching out, grabbing her breast with one and her neck with the other, squeezing just right.

They had tested each other's limits and pushed them continuously, egging one another on to even higher levels of bliss as their play became ever more vigorous. And they would have a lifetime to improve upon it.

Nyota let out a groan, her fingers pulling his hair hard. He squeezed her nipple in return, sending jolts of heat shooting to her sex as her pace increased. Faster and faster she rode him, pressing his cock against just the right spots, her climax building as she knew it would.

In her old life she could count the number of orgasms she had in an entire relationship, let alone a few days, but this? This was out of this world—literally, as the case may be. She had come so many times and with such intensity that she lost count on the first day, and her body had only grown accustomed to this new paradigm, craving ever more.

"Yes! Yes!" she grunted as she felt the climax ready to burst free.

Korvin cried out, his hands tight on her as his cock twitched and gushed inside her as her pussy locked down on him hard, quivering and pulsing in time with her mate.

The two of them kissed fiercely, lips mashing together hard, their love and lust overwhelming them both until their bodies finally relented and allowed them to think straight again.

Nyota rolled off him, leaning down to suck him clean, reveling in the blended taste of their sex. Korvin's body twitched as she did, sensitive to her lips and tongue teasing his cock.

She slid up his torso and gave him a wet kiss, their tongues entwined as they savored one another's flavors like a starving man given a fine meal.

"So strong," he said, pleased. "I see we might need to reinforce our bed if this continues."

"Gladly," she replied, resting her head on his chest, smelling his musky-sweet sweat.

"But eventually, we will have to leave this room."

A flash of reality crept into her moment of bliss. "I know. I'm just sorry we didn't find your friend."

"We will find him, my love. Halvax has already departed to continue the search with the magistrate's blessing and assistance."

"Which I thought she wasn't going to do. That whole avoiding conflict thing."

"Her position until the Dohrags entered her city. Crossing that line seems to have inspired her to change her stance and take action. Having a Bohdzee in the fray helps as well, naturally. And with Halvax leading them, I have been able to clear my mind and take this time with my mate to properly consummate our bond."

"Oh, man, have you ever. But eventually, I know you're going to want to get back out there. Your general is important."

"Yes, this is a quest I need to be part of. But this thing of ours is my priority now as well."

Nyota considered his words a long moment. "You know, I'm stronger now."

"As you have said—and demonstrated most delightfully. Your runes are tied to mine, we are bound by pigment and blood, and it even seems some of my Bohdzee enhancements are now a part of you as a result, even without your possessing those modified runes."

She sat up and looked at him, serious for the first time in days. "Then teach me. Teach me more and we'll find your general together."

Korvin gazed up at this magnificent woman he now called his own, a feeling of pride and joy welling inside of him. She wanted to learn. To be a part of everything he was. It seemed it would be a wonderful life together indeed.

"You wish to learn?"

"Did I stutter?"

"You never stutter."

"Shut up. You know what I mean."

"Very well, I will teach you," he chuckled. "I look forward to it."

"Yes!" she blurted, bouncing with excitement. "When do we begin?"

Korvin reached out for her, a wicked gleam in his eye. "Soon. But we have a few things yet to do, you and I."

She felt that insatiable fire spark within her yet again at his touch. For now they would frolic, and well at that. And soon they would partake in other physical activities. And then? Then the stars were the limit.

36

BONUS CONTENT

Dearest reader,

If you enjoyed this tale of Nyota and Korvin's adventures, I invite you to come download the free steamy bonus chapter for a little more of their spicy fun.

Get it at KiraQuinnBooks.com

And thank you for rating and reviewing this book. Writing can be a solitary endeavor, and every little bit you can do, especially taking a few seconds to review, really helps keep this author's creative fires burning.
Stay saucy,
~ Kira ~

ABOUT THE AUTHOR

When she's not coming up with the next steamy space adventure, you can find Kira online across the usual social media sites and at kiraquinnbooks.com
Come and say hi!

BOOKS BY KIRA QUINN

Printed in Great Britain
by Amazon

35756945R00155